SECOND STAR

A NEVERLAND TRANSMISSIONS NOVEL

J.M. SULLIVAN

Bleeding Ink
Publishing

SECOND STAR

The Neverland Transmissions Book 1

Copyright © 2018 by J. M. Sullivan

Bleeding Ink Publishing

For information contact:
Bleeding Ink Publishing
253 Bee Caves Cove
Cibolo, TX 78108
www.bleedinginkpublishing.com
info@bleedinginkpublishing.com

Cover design by Desiree DeOrto
Book design by Inkstain Design Studio
Editing by Holly Atkinson
ISBN: 978-1-948583-00-8 (paperback)

First Edition: February 2019

For my children
Never be afraid to grow up.
Life can always be magical if you remember to believe.

"To live will be an awfully big adventure."

—J.M. BARRIE. PETER PAN

CAPTAIN'S JOURNAL [ENCRYPTED]

James Tiberius Hooke

November 4, 2291

It has been five months since we set course to explore the Uncharted Sector. The new jump technology cut our travel time exponentially. Though the tech is still in early stages, I can see it being helpful to the Fleet in the future. It's unfortunate I won't be with them to see its progress.

We have found the Second Star.

I must admit, after searching for eighteen years, I was beginning to lose hope. And then it appeared, nestled behind an asteroid belt on the edge of the Krawk Nebula, hidden in plain sight, more beautiful than I imagined. Eighteen years of searching, and still I could not anticipate the way it took my breath away.

Perhaps my reaction was a mixture of awe and amazement in finding the myth true. After all, the existence of the Star was a discovery I merely stumbled upon during a standard exploratory mission. Who could have guessed that inside the cave of an abandoned planet would be the key to life eternal?

I often wonder what happened to the inhabitants of that planet. It was desolate, with only the faintest traces of life remaining. Maybe they followed the *Star* themselves. *Their abandoned records indicated a certain reverence for the heavenly body.*

But why wouldn't there be? The Star saved them from the darkness. The Star saved them from fear. For what fear can darkness hold if death does not exist?

What mankind has coveted since the time of the Ancients, and soon it will be mine. Soon, there will be no reason to return to the Fleet. I'll have everything I've been searching for.

I will be immortal.

SECOND
STAR

1

PETER BREAKS THROUGH

PETER

Frantic sirens shrilled in Peter's ears as he yanked copper wiring from the underside of the control bay. The door to the command center's hatch dangled open, revealing a tangled web of severed blue, yellow, and white cords. Exposed wires spat angry sparks at his face in protest.

Earsplitting keening from the machinery space alarm over the *Jolly Roger*'s loudspeakers throbbed in his head, confirming his sabotage was working. Just a few more cables and the ship's central navigation system would shut down, taking the steering and autopilot along with it. Hooke would have to do some fancy flying to maneuver out of the bind Peter had put him in. There was no doubt the renowned captain could do it, but it would take all his focus and energy to stabilize the vessel.

Peter would use that to his advantage.

A garbled electronic tone buzzed through the tiny communication implant in Peter's ear. Even though the device was secured against his eardrum, he could barely hear it over the deafening blare of the *Roger*'s alarm.

"You know I won't understand a word of what you're saying until I fix your audio biometrics, Tinc." He tossed an exasperated glance at the nanobot flittering impatiently over his shoulder. The tiny machine responded with another unintelligible message, but the red sparks erupting from her tiny body gave him a good idea of what she was trying to say.

A wry smile danced on Peter's lips. He winked at his Technological Interface Nano-Companion, who he called *Tinc* for short. He had been assigned the nanobot when the Londonierre Brigade had given him his Maintenance Tech orders, per company policy.

Unbeknownst to the Fleet, however, Peter had made some of his own modifications, providing Tinc with much more sophisticated coding than the standard model, along with a rather snarky attitude. It was one of his favorite things about her.

Tinc garbled what Peter was sure was a slew of colorful language before she dove into the box of wires. She disappeared into the tangle of cords for a moment before she flitted back with a thick black cord in tow. She flew in front of Peter's face, her polycarbonate wings tickling his freckled nose like an obnoxious gnat, and jangled at him again. His eyes widened when he saw the cable, but he fell into an easy grin as he severed it with his switchblade.

"Nice catch," he said offhandedly. He swept his hand across his forehead, brushing away the wild auburn strands tickling his eyelashes. "I was wondering when you'd find the cable."

Peter flashed a roguish grin and dropped his knife into the cargo pocket of his jumpsuit. Tinc whirred in his ear, but flew alongside him as he dashed down the hall.

"*Warning: External force field detected,*" a smooth voice crooned over the cacophony of the screeching alarm. Peter slowed to listen to her announcement. "*For your safety, please secure your position in the Residence Hull. Warning ...*"

Peter swore and turned to his bot. "What force field? I thought we were in the clear!"

Tinc hovered in the air, buzzing excitedly. Sparks shot out of her wings, the way they always did when she got worked up, making her look more like a fairy from a children's book than the advanced mechanical device she was.

Peter raked his hands through his hair. "I know it's not your fault" He grimaced. "But this could complicate things." He racked his brain to visualize the map he'd seen in Hooke's quarters earlier. The quadrant they were in was safe, he'd made sure of that. *What external force field was she talking about?*

His eyes widened as he remembered.

"Tinc, what was the territory next to the Krawk Nebula?"

He didn't need the answer. The map in his mind was clear as day. "The Uncharted Sector." He swore again. But the ship shouldn't have been anywhere *near* the borders of the Nebula. The course they had charted went through the middle of the Nebula, not the outskirts. *So, what was the problem?*

"*Warning. External force field detected.*"

"External force field." Peter smacked his forehead as understanding dawned. "The Uncharted Sector is pulling us in!" He dragged his palm down his face in exasperation.

Of all the dumb luck. The ship was being pulled into the gravitational field of an Uncharted Sector and nobody had noticed because he had disabled the ship's navigation system.

"For your safety, please secure your position in the Residence Hull."

"Shyte." He couldn't go to the Residence Hull. Hooke had to know what he had done by now. He'd be keelhauled for sure.

"We're going to have to take control of the ship before Hooke wires more lies back to Control." Who knew what his old friend had already told them. Peter grimaced, wondering if everything James Hooke had done was all for show. After nearly ten years of working with the famous Captain, he hoped not. But when you're nine and someone plucks you out of the disease-ridden gutters of New London to give you a place to eat and sleep, you don't really ask questions.

An impatient buzz from Tinc shot through his ear, pulling Peter from the grayed city streets of his past to the steel vessel of his present. She was going down quick, and she wasn't happy about it.

"I know, Tinc." Peter scowled. "But we severed the wires…" His brain whirred through all the possible outcomes of the scenario he had put himself in. None of them was pleasant. Worst case, death by an explosive inferno of doom; best case, survive the force field catastrophe long enough to be skinned alive for mutiny.

An assault of garbled tones sounded in his ear as Tinc hovered in front of him with sparks of violent red hues cascading from her wings. He had never seen her that upset.

"I know, Tinc. But we don't have a choice. If we don't, the ship will—" His words cut short as the ship lurched, forcing him to brace against the wall to keep from falling over.

"Perfect," Peter muttered after the turbulence subsided. He hated working under pressure. He scanned the corridor and crowed in glee when he located the Personal Interface Panel. Every Brigade ship had its own artificial intelligence cybernetic system installed onboard. Aside from the Navi, it was the tech that controlled most of the ship. There were bound to be parts Peter could repurpose to repair the wiring he'd disabled.

He reached for his switchblade and placed it securely between his teeth. The break in the panel was directly above him, a good five feet overhead. He'd practically have to fly to reach it.

No matter. He'd done worse before.

Gripping the blade in his jaw, Peter dropped back, then ran toward the wall. Before he hit, he jumped and used the curved wall as a springboard to propel himself up. He leaped, extending his arms toward the hydro-piping that ran along every major corridor in the ship.

His hands clasped the cool metal, and with a satisfied smirk, he tugged himself to the roof and settled in. The tight cords of his muscles bunched, pulling his wiry frame into the steel rafter beams.

From his perch, he had perfect access to the paneling. He grated his knife against the rusting screws to pop them loose. The heavy metal piece fell to the side with a loud clang, exposing a ripe crop of wires to harvest. Tinc flitted around his hands as he worked, offering her central lighting system as a freehand flashlight. Her intricate wings lit like a firebug, casting the small space in an ethereal glow. The lighting reflected off the ship's interior and danced on Peter's face.

Peter worked furiously, blocking out all outside distraction. Soon, the grating alarm was nothing more than static in the back of his mind as he combed through the tangled cording. The heat radiating from the humming electronics formed beads of sweat on his brow as he clung to his perch. Carefully, he removed a small black box nestled deep inside the maze of wires and let out a loud whoop. With a quick slash of his blade, the tiny treasure box was freed from its prison. He cradled it to his chest as he dropped to the floor.

"I can't believe we found one," he breathed, observing the pirated piece of machinery. It was a Personal Interface Cross-Electro Positron, often called a pix.E for short. "Most newer models don't use these anymore. The tech got swapped for the Virtual AI Models."

Tinc jangled indignantly, as if the use of advanced cybernetics personally offended her.

"Not many people know how versatile it can be," Peter explained. "Most of *London's finest* didn't have to raid junkyards for parts to use for their training supplies." He gripped the tech. For such a small box, it was surprisingly heavy. If his survival didn't depend on the *Roger's* functionality, he would have been tempted to salvage it for later.

Disappointed at the wasted opportunity, Peter sighed. It didn't matter how great the tech was if he was dead. "Come on Tinc, we don't have much t—"

The lights in the corridor flashed and the machinery alarm was replaced by an even more obnoxious emergency alarm. The vibrations thrummed in his bones as the warning blared. The ship lurched again, more violently than the last time, sending him sprawling. As Peter fought to stand, he realized he *had* felt vibrations, but it wasn't the alarm. It was the shaking of the *Roger* as it was taken hold by the Uncharted Sector's gravity field.

Peter glanced worriedly at Tinc before yanking her from the air and stuffing her into his pocket as he fled for the safety of the maintenance hull.

"It's too late," he whispered. "We're about to go down."

2

PETER

Peter woke up sprawled on the roof of the *Jolly Roger*.

"That wasn't supposed to happen" He pushed himself off the bay light as he scanned the empty hull. Angry sparks in his left ear let him know Tinc was all right, if not put out. He freed her from his pocket and set her on his shoulder as he calculated his next move.

"You shouldn't have pulled all those wires, Tinc. You broke the ship."

Peter laughed at her slew of indignant jangles and reached for his handheld scanner to check for live signals.

"Just what I thought. The ship is dead. Completely bl—wait. No! There's a signal!" Peter peered at the faint blip on the screen as he tried to decipher the map. "And it's coming from…" He groaned and scrubbed his face before muttering, "The signal is coming from the Captain's Quarters."

His revelation set Tinc into a frenzy of jingles and fiery sparks exploding from her mechanical core as she bobbed around Peter's head.

"I know, but we're sitting ducks here. Our best bet is to hijack the escape pod. To do that, we're gonna need power."

Tinc let out an unhappy hum, but she bobbed in agreement before shooting down the corridor of the hull, like a tiny floating orb. Peter hustled to keep up. Outside her dim glow, the rest of the *Roger* was pitch black.

As they ran, Peter noticed the ship had remained mostly intact after the crash. Although the power was out, the *Roger's* frame was sturdy. The only exception was the Security Mainframe. All the *Roger's* access doors were open, granting entry to any room he desired.

Better for him.

Peter heard the muffled shouts of disoriented crew members arguing behind the door. The loudest cries came from the kitchen as Cook's raised voice blustered over the poor crew hands assigned to him.

"Oi! 'Urry up and pick up those pans! Mind where you're stepping! I could 'ave saved that soup if you hadn't buggered it!"

Peter ducked behind the frozen door and peeked in, daring a quick view of the scene. Cook's red face popped out against his stained white jacket as he continued to bark orders at the boys in the kitchen. One sopped spoiled soup with a dingy old towel while the other scrambled to right the pans that toppled in the crash. Peter thought he was seeing double when he looked from the first boy to the second and saw the same face. He was about to hurry on when another loud voice sounded down the hall. He knew the gravelly tone before he saw who it belonged to.

Peter barely ducked out of sight before Skylights, the ship's Artillery

Commander, barged into the kitchen. Standing well over six feet tall, the commander was solid muscle, a fact he liked to emphasize by walking around shirtless. It was technically against Brigade regulations, but in-flight dress code was lax, and it wasn't like there was much the Brigade could do to enforce it from several galaxies away.

"What's this, then?" Skylights yelled over the commotion. He glowered at the others through muddy brown eyes. His face contorted in a disgusted sneer, as if he'd rather be anywhere else.

Cook's eyes flashed. "Me 'ole kitchen's in bloody ruins! *That's* what's this then!" He pushed his girth against Skylights in a challenge. Though he was a good foot shorter than the commander, his kitchen-grown midsection added to his ample bulk.

"That's what these buggers are for." Skylights turned his attention to the twin beside him, and with a swift kick, sent the young man sprawling into the sickly green soup. "Make these bilge rats clean it."

Skylights' diversion worked. Cook cackled and tossed another dirty towel at the twin, who cowered close to the ground to stay out of the way.

"Clean the floor, you!" he barked before turning back to Skylights. "It's what I'm trying to do. Useless lot, these two."

Skylights laughed—a mean sound that matched the angry glint in his eyes. He turned to the other twin, who panicked under the large man's attention. He dropped the pan he'd held with a loud clang. The commander grimaced and strode forward to lift the scraggly teen up from his shirt collar.

"Useless lot is right," he growled. He chucked the boy across the tile to where his brother frantically wiped up soup, cackling as the boy tried to right himself. "Get Jukes and his men. Tell 'em Cap'n wants to see 'em. And be quick about it!" His last statement was unnecessary. The panicked twin scurried out before Skylights finished his first sentence.

Peter watched as the boy barreled out of the room. He waited for him to round the corner, then stuck his arm out to snag him. The twin's scruffy hair flew in his eyes and he let out a terrified squeak before Peter clapped his hand over his mouth. "Be quiet, will you?" he hissed. He dragged the twin to his hiding spot. The boy nodded with wide eyes. Slowly, Peter took his hand away. "You work in the kitchen, yeah?" An idea was forming. If he played his cards right, he might get off the ship alive.

The twin's mouth gaped as he stared, mesmerized at Tinc's erratic orbit around Peter's ears. Another loud shout from Cook rang through the hall and broke the spell, pulling his attention to the kitchen.

"Don't worry about them," Peter snapped, but softened his tone when he saw the haunted gaze in the boy's eyes. "Do they treat you like that all the time?" Aside from his interactions with the Captain, Peter's work in maintenance kept him away from the rest of the crew, and he was left blessedly alone.

The twin lowered his gaze and a wave of anger surged through Peter. The poor kid was probably a Lost Boy—the crew's name for kids from the poor sectors. Kids whose parents had surrendered them to the service of the Fleet to man the shyte jobs none of the trained men wanted. Judging by how scrawny he was and the fact that there were two of him, Peter figured he and his brother were probably consigned recruits. Dropped on a boat and stuck serving the more respected enlisted crewmen as no more than an indentured servant.

Hooke had explained it to him once during one of his first Brigade training sessions after he'd brought him aboard. Said at least that way the kids had a safe place to sleep and something to eat each day. It also made for one less mouth for the parents to feed—or two, in this case. The same thing probably would have happened to Peter if his parents had bothered to keep him that long.

"Look here." Peter drew the boy's attention with a snap of his fingers. "I need you to do something for me. The ship's down—done for. I can get us out of here, but I'm gonna need help. Are there any other crew hands?"

The twin's light eyes widened as he nodded.

"Good," Peter said. "I need you to round up as many of them as you can. Tell them whatever you need to, but make sure they don't snitch, or we're dead. Got that?"

The twin nodded once more before he scurried down the hall. Peter hoped he understood.

"No time to worry now," he muttered. He needed to locate the power source. He was about to dash off when Skylights' voice caught his attention, and he peeked inside. Skylights and Cook had pulled out a large bottle of whiskey and were passing it back and forth as they took turns hurling insults at the remaining twin.

"Looks like Hooke's finally gettin' his uppance," Skylights growled as he took a large swig from the bottle. "Command ain't gonna be happy to find he's lost control of the ship. No surprise if you ask me."

He handed off the whiskey to Cook, who brought the glass to his lips. He took a longer swig before giving Skylights a slow nod.

"Everyone thinks Hooke's summat special," Skylights continued, his gaze trained on the bottle in Cook's hands. "Bamboozled 'em, he has. But he's been acting funny as of late—something ain't right in his eyes no more. I tell you what. If I were Captain, this'd never happened. No sir." Skylights reached for the whiskey. He took another huge gulp before wiping his mouth clean with the back of his hand. "If I was Captain. I like the sound of that."

There was a hum in Peter's ear as Tinc jangled impatiently. A spark shot from her wings and landed on Peter's neck and burned where it hit his skin.

"Not now, Tinc." Peter strained to listen. It seemed he wasn't the *Roger's* only mutineer. The large Italian was still freely drinking the whiskey. At that rate, there wouldn't be any left.

Using their distracted state to his advantage, Peter hurried to the Captain's Quarters. A quick check on his scanner confirmed he was headed in the right direction. The signal, though faint, grew steadily stronger the closer he got to Hooke. Within a few moments, he reached the entry to Hooke's room. Unfortunately, the access panel monitoring the Captain's doors had survived the crash, leaving Hooke's doors secured.

"Shyte!" Peter swore as he pressed against the metal door. Tinc flitted around his shoulders, silently lending her light. He was considering how to dismantle the panel when the door slid open with a soft click, giving him just enough time to scrabble back before Hooke's cybernetic first mate bumped into him.

Every Fleet ship was equipped with an automated hand to assist the Captain. Hooke's model, the Synthetic Maintenance Engineering Emissary, SMEE for short, was top of the line, programmed with all the bells and whistles—not least of all, impeccable etiquette.

"There you are, Pan!" Smee's rose-gold eyes blinked as he primly readjusted his Fleet cap. Tall and slender, with fabricated dusty brown hair and pale cream skin, the first mate was perfectly average. He was designed that way. Aside from the impossible shade of his mechanical eyes, the First Mate's robotic features looked as human as any of the other men on the ship.

"The Captain has requested your presence. He would like for you to run a test on the mainframe." Smee stepped backward and tipped his head, waiting patiently for Peter's reply.

"Yes, sir." Peter nodded. Although he was automated, as First Mate, the AI was still his superior—at least for now. "I'll be right in. But sir?"

"Yes, Pan?" Smee's question reverberated from his voice chamber.

"You might want to hurry to the Main Bay. There's quite a stir going on down there. I heard Cook and Skylights getting into it over food rationing." Peter fabricated the story, hoping Smee would leave him to enter the Captain's Quarters on his own.

It worked. Smee let out an uncanny gentlemanly sigh. "Thank you, Pan. I will see to it before we have a mutiny on our hands." Peter flinched at the term, but the distracted First Mate didn't notice. "Report to the Captain immediately."

"Yes, sir." Peter saluted before hurrying through the open door. His guts twisted as he rushed toward Hooke's room.

He stopped before the Captain's door, an ornate, wooden frame installed per Hooke's request. It seemed strange to Peter, but then, he'd never held much stock in the concept of homes. Someplace warm to sleep was enough for him. Compared to the grimy streets he'd grown up on, the cables and wires of the *Jolly Roger* were like his own personal palace.

A large crash rang against the door, followed by a furious bellow from the Captain.

"Here goes nothing," he muttered. Steeling himself, Peter placed his palm against the door. "Stay close, Tinc," he whispered. "This should be interesting."

3

Peter winced at the loud string of expletives from behind the Captain's door followed by the crash of shattering glass. He hoped it wasn't the expensive Chinese vases the Captain had imported. Hooke loved those things. If he was using them as ammo, it was not a good sign.

"Damn it all, Pan! What has he done to my ship?"

Peter ducked his head as he stepped through the door. The antique vases had indeed been smashed. One lay in pieces on the floor at his feet while the other formed a pile of broken glass on the wall by the Captain's bed. Hooke towered in the middle of the room, storming back and forth as alarms shrieked in the background.

"Captain?"

Hooke whirled around and glared at Peter through storm-blue eyes. They offset his tan skin and onyx hair. Mixed with the fury crackling from his temper, he looked like the embodiment of a raging thunderstorm. His shoulders bunched, turning his strong physique into a tight coil.

"You asked to see me, sir?" Normally, Peter wasn't so formal with the Captain, but the murderous glint in Hooke's eyes urged him to tread lightly.

"What have you done with my ship?" Hooke raged, abandoning the telecommuter. Peter eyed him warily. The machine wasn't far. If he could snag it, Tinc could run a diagnostic on the *Roger*'s power systems without the Captain even realizing it.

"Power grid went down. Whole ship's offline—save your room. I've been trying to pinpoint the glitch, but haven't had any luck. Have you heard from Comms?" Peter breezed calm into his voice, but his whole body tensed. If Hooke reached the Fleet, they would inform him the *Roger*'s breach was internal.

"With this blasted thing?" Hooke swatted the telecommuter away in disgust. "The only thing this infernal hunk of metal has done is spit lightning."

As if to prove his point, a weak whine of feedback screeched from the headset. Peter heard the distant voice of a Comms Tech, but it was so garbled under layers of white noise he'd never understand it.

Good.

Peter extended his hand. "Give it here."

Hooke threw the device at him as if discarding a piece of garbage. Peter flipped the telecommuter in his hands. The tech was fine; the error was a systems failure. But Hooke didn't know that. Peter tapped his scanner against the telecommuter and pretended to run a systems test. Really, he was checking to see from where the *Roger*'s remaining power originated. Hooke must have had some hidden generator. Considering the Captain's intentions, it didn't surprise Peter that he kept secrets—even from him.

"Did you fix it?" Hooke demanded, impatient.

"No," Peter admitted. "It's not the device." He had learned the best way to tell a lie was to weave pieces of truth into it. He wondered if that was how Hooke had been so believable. "Something went wrong in the mainframe. I'll troubleshoot it in the Bay. Problem is, it'll be tough to do without lights."

"Can't you use your gremlin?" Hooke gestured at Tinc. She buzzed in a furious tornado, flinging bright red sparks from her midsection.

Peter's eyes narrowed. "She's a nanobot, Captain, not a Swiss Army Knife."

"I don't care what the damned thing is! I want my ship fixed!" Hooke raged. "Do your job, Pan, or I'll find someone else!"

Peter's temper flared, but he bit his tongue. Mad as Hooke was now, it was nothing compared to how angry he'd be if he found out *Peter* had grounded the *Roger*.

He studied the scanner, willing it to reveal the secrets he needed. The reader flashed—the diagnostic was complete.

"Well?" Hooke demanded. "What have you got?" He stormed to the navigation panel, whose blinking lights warned of multiple systems errors decimating the *Roger*'s infrastructure. "It looks like a bloody Christmas tree!" He pulled levers and buttons to readjust the settings, but his interference only made the alarm shrill louder.

"I'm working on it, Captain. I can only go as fast as the tech'll let me."

"As fast as the tech will let you, or as fast as you feel like?"

"It's all about the tech, Captain."

Peter spoke evenly, but his blood boiled. He had worked hard to prove himself his whole life—on the streets, at the Academy, on the *Roger*—far too hard to have a shady Captain insult his abilities during a tantrum.

"Listen, Pan. The only reason I brought you on my ship is because you assured me you'd keep her running. If I had known you were this useless, I'd have left you in the gutter!"

Red dots danced across Peter's vision.

"Left me?" He motioned to the tech scattered around the room. "And where would you be without all the modifications I added to the ship? I bet the Fleet would love to hear about all those unsanctioned changes. The trackers, the external cloaking device... And I'm sure they'd be especially interested in the transmission scrambler you've been using so much the past few days."

Hooke's jaw clenched. He had struck a nerve. Peter continued, smug.

"Actually, *I'm* rather curious about the scrambler as well. I had it all set so the Fleet couldn't recover your transmissions. I spent *weeks* making sure everything was coded perfectly. Imagine my surprise when I ran a diagnostic and realized all the coding I installed had been changed. Who could have done that, Captain?"

Hooke's only response was to crunch his teeth in frustration.

"No matter," Peter continued. "I cracked the encryption pretty easily. It's less sophisticated than the program I installed, but I guess that wasn't your concern, was it? You just wanted to keep secrets. Too bad I found you out. I wonder what the Fleet would do if they realized that you were planning on going AWOL. Probably wouldn't be too happy. Poor James." Peter pulled a face. "Losing his ship, his crew, and his freedom, all in the same day."

"You wouldn't dare!"

Hooke surged forward to attack, then thought better of it. "I brought you here. If it wasn't for me, you'd still be a flea-infested street urchin begging for scraps. *I* brought you to the Fleet. *I* advocated for you to be enlisted, and *I* am the one who acquisitioned you to the crew. You owe me!" Flecks of spittle sprayed from his lips and his eyes blazed with hatred.

"I don't owe you anything!" Peter blasted, the sting of abandonment ripping open old scars. "My recruitment had nothing to do with the *Roger*, and it damn sure didn't have anything to do with me. You *brought me here* because even as a flea-infested street urchin, you saw what I could do with tech." Peter pressed toward the Captain, brazen in his temper. "You *pulled me from the streets*, as you so graciously put it, because even as some abandoned kid, I could code circles around any other hack in the Fleet."

"Don't pretend you understand anything about Fleet dealings, Pan. The situation at hand is so far ahead of your pay grade, it's laughable."

"I know you were planning to jump ship and leave us all behind. Were you afraid if you brought us, someone would see that you're nothing but a codfish?"

"Some sacrifices must be made for the greater good," Hooke said. "There are things the Fleet doesn't know that would make your skin crawl. Things no ordinary man could withstand."

"Greater good," Peter scoffed. "Like the oath you swore to God and country? I guess that doesn't mean anything to a liar like you." Peter paused as his mouth twisted into a wry grimace. "You're not a soldier, James. You're nothing but a dirty pirate!"

Hooke's eyes flashed. In a blur, he freed his szikra from its sheath and whipped it to Peter's cheek. Electric energy crackled along the conductor beam, setting the tiny hairs on Peter's face alive with static.

"Pirate?" His voice dripped ice. "I'll show you a pirate!" The tip of the szikra pressed against Peter's face, firm enough that he felt the sting of the spark, but with enough restraint for its buzz to leave his flesh unscathed.

Peter refused to be intimidated. "You have no honor!" he yelled. "You were going to leave us to rot!" Speaking the words cut his scars deeper. "Why save me only to change the location that I died?"

"No honor?" The fire in Hooke's gaze betrayed the calm in his voice. His eyes burned as he seethed. The szikra powered down, leaving the length of the razor-sharp conductor pressed against Peter's cheek. "Arm yourself, Pan. A gentleman always keeps good form."

Peter didn't move. Hooke knew he had no formidable weapon. Not that it would have mattered. The decorated Captain always horribly outperformed him when they sparred. Even if Peter had his own szikra, Hooke's superiority handling the weapon and manipulating its energy was unparalleled. The only advantage Peter had was speed.

Behind Hooke, a large dagger bit into a printed map on the desk. If he moved fast, he might keep Hooke on the defensive long enough to make a break for it.

Peter stiffened and sauntered toward the desk. Hooke wouldn't attack until he had a weapon in hand—his imagined honor guaranteed that much, at least. But as soon as Peter gripped the hilt, Hooke's szikra would surge to life.

He would just have to move faster.

Peter moved for the dagger, pausing for half a breath before he ripped it from the desk and whirled to face Hooke. Sure enough, as soon as he touched the cool handle, Hooke charged. Peter dropped back in a low stance, ready to spring when another figure charged Hooke from the side.

With unparalleled speed and grace, Hooke spun and activated the szikra, turning the metal into a deadly beam of electric energy.

"Skylights?" Hooke's demeanor was cool, but a flash of confusion flit across his features. "What's the meaning of this?"

The hulking Artillery Commander sneered at Hooke as he muscled down his own sparking blade. Peter watched, knowing the only advantage Skylights had was sheer force. If the weapons-tech didn't overpower the Captain soon, they would be fighting a losing battle. But the overconfident tech didn't know that. His leer turned into a smug smirk as he brandished his own szikra, his eyes taunting the recovering Captain.

"Not what you were expectin', Cap'n?"

"I can't say it was." Hooke's muscles strained, but he didn't back down. Slim as the Captain was, he held a strength of his own, hidden in wiry muscles. A confident smile crept to his face as Skylights' arms stopped their trajectory. "I didn't think you were that stupid."

In a blur, Hooke skip-stepped back, spinning from Skylights' reach. The tech's burly arms crashed to the ground, swinging through empty air until his szikra slammed against the floor. The conductor smashed into the steel paneling, catching Skylights in a momentary paralysis as the electricity in his blade shorted out.

When the sparks fizzled, the heavy tech stumbled to his knees. With the deadly grace of a shark, Hooke advanced, straightening the banded collar of his Captain's jacket with one hand and gripping the hilt of his still-crackling blade with the other. His face was a blank slate, but Peter saw the fury burning under the surface.

"I wonder what's caused this momentary lapse in judgment," Hooke mused as he closed the distance to Skylights. "You must realize this is terribly poor form, even for an Ammie."

A low snarl escaped Skylights' throat at the rank-slur.

"It's that attitude that's gotten you in this mess, Cap'n." He wiped his mouth with the back of his arm. "You don't got no respect."

"I respect plenty of people, Skylights." Hooke chuckled, a rumbling growl that built from the base of his throat. "You just don't happen to be one of them."

Skylights roared and threw himself at the Captain. He swung his meaty fist wildly, but now, Hooke was fully engaged and easily parried his erratic attacks with controlled and calculated moves of his own.

Peter watched, transfixed, until a spark singed his shoulder. Tearing his eyes from the fight, he followed Tinc's hummed demand to search Hooke's room for the hidden tech. It was more challenging than it ought to be, as the Captain had designed the interior of his quarters to match the gilded door. There was a reason the men called James the "Elegant Captain Hooke."

A small break in the gilding betrayed the device's location beside Hooke's desk. Peter flung open the masked panel. He shoved external wiring aside to reach the treasure buried within. Behind him, the battle raged on, and the sizzling szikri formed a soothing cadence as they crashed against each other.

Peter ignored it. As long as they fought, neither pirate's attention would be on him. Still, he needed to hurry. If he was right, the tech should be —

"There!" Peter crowed. "Got it, Tinc!"

A misstep in the swords' striking rhythm perked Peter's ears. The conductor zapped, filling the room with the sickening smell of burnt skin, followed by the hollow thud of something heavy hitting the ground.

Hooke bellowed in pain.

Peter whirled around and saw the Captain bent over, clutching his wrist. His face was white with shock, making the pallor of his flesh even more striking against the contrast of crimson flowing from where his left hand had been. Skylights towered over him, teeth bared in a gruesome smile as he watched Hooke writhe in pain.

"Bad form, Captain." Skylights tsked. The distress in his voice didn't match the exultation in his eyes.

Hooke fixed Skylights with a menacing glare then released his injured arm with a manic growl. Ignoring the blood seeping from his wrist, he retrieved his discarded weapon and straightened to full height. He teetered on his feet, dizzy, but held his ground as he raised his blade.

"You don't know the mistake you just made."

"Big words from a man who's about to bleed out on the floor," Skylights taunted.

Hooke's eyes filled with cold hatred. "Men of proper breeding never use big words. Only true ones," he said, his voice eerily calm. "You will not walk away from this alive."

Skylights' confident sneer dipped. "Oh, I'll walk, all right. Right off with that fancy jacket of yours."

Hooke said nothing, but the look on his face could have curdled milk. He feigned right and Peter knew the fight was almost over. He had sparred with the Captain on many occasions and recognized his signature kill strike. James used it to bolster his opponent's ego. He allowed his counterpart a small succession of strikes while pretending to tire before he dropped back in a lightning fast dodge. His overzealous opponent would lose balance and their focus. While they tried to regain footing, Hooke would plunge his blade into their chest.

A clumsy attack from Skylights signaled the beginning of the end. Peter watched Hooke "stumble" and hurried to signal Tinc. They had a matter of minutes.

"We gotta go," he said. "After Hooke finishes Skylights, he'll be out for blood. I got the tech. Let's get outta here."

Tinc sparked in agreement and shot down the hall. Peter spared one last glance at the Captain who had saved him so many years ago. Skylights bore down on him with an overconfident sneer. Though Hooke's body language indicated fatigue, the calculating look in his cold blue eyes told a different story entirely. Peter shook his head.

If there was one thing he knew, it was that he had not seen the last of James Tiberius Hooke.

4

eter wasn't a hundred feet down the hall when a pained cry rang out behind him. Skylights was finished. Hooke would be after him soon.

Tinc followed his sharp turn around the corner, emitting a surprised shower of sparks as they skidded into Smee. Unable to stop, Peter clipped the first mate's shoulder, striking bone to solid metal. The impact jarred Smee's body, sending the stiff synth toppling. It would have been comical if Peter hadn't been running for his life.

"What has gotten into you, Pan?" Smee's golden eyes flashed as he fumbled to collect himself. Peter was about to spout off another lie when Hooke bellowed behind him.

"Pan!"

An artificial wrinkle covered Smee's forehead, but before the synth could react, Peter dashed off, flying through the corridor. He barreled past the kitchen door where Cooke lay passed out on the table, his whiskey bottle tipped toward the floor beneath his drooping hand.

Neither of the Twins were in sight; Peter hoped they had found others to join. Behind him, he heard Hooke's shouts, echoed by Smee as they chased after him, screaming, warning of mutiny and murder.

"Shyte!"

Peter picked up the pace. A wave of anger rolled through him as he hurtled down the metal corridor.

Although the mutiny accusations were true, pegging Skylights' death on him was low, even for Hooke. It would also make it harder to escape. But it was a smart move on the Captain's part. Now he'd have the whole crew on his tail, out for blood. It didn't matter whether they loved Skylights or hated him—the Fleet wouldn't stand for killing one of their own. Hooke would have some serious explaining to do if it came out he was the one who had ended Skylights. Even in self-defense, he risked men turning coat. Now, using Peter as an out, Hooke had cleared his own name and given the men one more reason to bring Peter in for punishment.

Peter turned another corridor, hoping to distance himself from the shouts ricocheting through the ship. He hadn't gone two steps when a strong arm grabbed him from behind.

"Gotcha!" The man's rancid breath assaulted Peter's nose as he was spun around to face his captor. It was the addled old deckhand, Noodler. Peter winced and drew his face back. He didn't understand how a man with only one tooth could have such terrible halitosis.

Noodler's bottom lip wrapped around his gums, enlarging his already protruding jaw. He squinted at Peter through cataract-ridden eyes.

"What's this we have, eh?" A wheezy laugh escaped his throat, assaulting Peter's nostrils. Another frenzied shout rang out through the cavernous hallways, carrying the cries of mutiny.

"Mutiny?" Noodler's brows shot up to his scraggly hairline as he wheezed. "We can't have that." He pulled a pocket-knife from his trousers. "Can't have that at all."

He pressed his blade to Peter's jugular. The rust covering the steel made the weapon look even more sinister. At least a sharpened blade would run him through quick and clean. That monstrosity would tear him to pieces.

"It wasn't me," Peter gasped. Noodler pressed the knife harder against his throat. The pressure on his windpipe triggered his reflex to cough, but Peter stifled it, afraid the movement would surprise the notoriously trigger-happy rigger. "It was Skylights—"

"Eh?"

Peter raged at the idiocy of it all. He had managed to get caught by the one crew member who was nearly deaf and blind.

"Sure, that's what you want me to believe. Run you to the Cap'n, I will. He'll clear up this whole mess." Noodler pushed Peter down the hall, strong for such an old man. Compelled by the jagged knife, Peter grudgingly complied, unwilling to risk any sudden jerks to his throat.

A heavy clang reverberated through the hall. Noodler's grip on Peter's arm loosened. The blade fell to the floor at the same time the deckhand did. Peter stood, stunned. He turned and saw another Lost Boy, who couldn't have been older than eleven or twelve. The *Roger* hadn't docked at home base for four years. His parents had given him up young.

His boyish-face was more pronounced by the shock of bright blond hair that fell just in over his dark brown eyes. Paired with his chubby cheeks, the kid looked like he should be finishing Primer School, not working as a lackey on the *Jolly Roger*. An oversized skillet drooped from both hands as he gaped at Noodler's collapsed form.

Peter retrieved the heavy skillet and ruffled the boy's moppy hair. "Nice job kid. You just saved my neck." He rubbed his hand against his throat where the ghost of the rusty blade still tickled. He swallowed. "Literally. What's your name?"

"T-Touto-Toutolo," the boy stammered.

"Huh?"

"M-my n-name is T-Toutolo. R-r-Robbie T-Toutolo," the boy managed through his terrible stutter. Peter wasn't sure if it was shock or a speech impediment.

"What a mouthful." He smirked. "Listen up, Tootles, we gotta get outta here. I'm in a tight spot with the Captain and you won't be much better off after they see what you did to Noodler."

Tootles looked down at the deckhand, who slumped on the floor, out cold. At least he wouldn't have the deckhand's death on his hands.

"Do you think you can keep up with me?"

Tootles nodded.

"Good," Peter said. "We're gonna have to move quick. Do you see my nanobot?"

Tootles' eyes trailed on Tinc as she buzzed angrily around his ear. Peter took that as a yes. "Her name is Tinc. She's going to show us how to get off the ship. You have to follow her *exactly*. Can you do that?"

"Y-yes." His chin set in determination as he answered. Maybe the kid was a fighter.

"Good. Let's go!"

Tinc jetted down the hall, leading them through the dark corridor with the faint light of her trailing spark. Peter grabbed Tootles' hand so he wouldn't lose him, but the little guy kept pace. Peter let go and pulled out his scanner. The map of the ship was still up, but now the diagram grayed out, reflecting the power outage. Peter didn't need it, but the image provided some comfort.

"Take us to the Loading Dock, Tinc!" he ordered, praying the men chasing them were too far to hear. Based off the shouts behind them, he doubted it. They needed to move fast if they wanted to make it off the *Roger* alive.

Tinc led them through the ship at breakneck speeds. They almost lost her after a sharp corner near the cabins, but Tootles caught the spark of her wings and pulled Peter down the right hall. The kid had saved him twice now.

Finally, they made it to the Loading Dock. They burst through the doors into the oversized cargo room. The crash hadn't been kind to the supplies. Sticky mixtures of liquid and broken glass covered the floor, ruined. Peter hurried through the gooey mess to close the heavy doors behind them. He picked up a large broken beam from one of the supply racks and forced it through the door handles to form a quick barricade.

"Peter? Is that you?" a nervous voice whispered from behind a stack of upturned crates. Peter craned his neck and saw the Twins watching him nervously.

"If it wasn't, you'd be dead," Peter snapped. The Twins flinched, but he didn't apologize. They might be young, but they needed to play smart. If they didn't, Hooke would keelhaul all of them. "Did you get the others?"

Their heads bobbed in unison.

"Yeah. Not everyone wanted to come," the first one said.

"But we brought a few," his brother finished.

They ducked behind the crate and Peter heard doubled whispers before three more Lost Boys filed out. Whether accidentally or on purpose, they had lined up tallest to shortest behind the Twins. "This is Slightly, Nibs, and Curly."

"Glad to have you, men," Peter said, voice firm. "Now let's get out of here. Tinc, find the pod—quick."

Tinc dipped in quick agreement before she swooped into the dark.

Suddenly, the metal doors slammed against Peter's makeshift barricade. It made a horrendous sound, but the bar held. Hooke's roar of frustration raged against the other side, followed by a chorus of angry crew members. He had recruited quite the mob.

"TINC!" Peter screamed. He almost yelled again when she flitted around with another round of furious jangles.

"What do you mean?" Peter roared. "That's our only way out!"

Tinc buzzed again, filling the dark room with a burst of orange. She zoomed to the corner and cast a faint glow on the crumpled pod. Based on the fluid seeping from the engine and mixing into the murky puddle on the floor, Peter doubted it would fly again.

"Then what are we going to do?" he yelled.

The main door shuddered again under the crew's doubled efforts against the metal hatch. Behind the heavy panels, Hooke's malicious laughter roared.

Though they tried to remain stoic, Peter saw the panic that covered his newly formed crew's faces. Tootles grabbed Peter's hand and looked at Peter with his big brown eyes.

Peter's heart wrenched. Even if the pod hadn't been wrecked, it was only big enough to fit one person, maybe two. And this wasn't just about him anymore. He ran a quick scan with his handheld, praying for a power source that hadn't been detected earlier. With the pix.E in his pocket, even the tiniest amount of electricity could be amplified.

The scanner blipped, announcing the completed diagnostic. The Loading Dock was dead. Peter swore under his breath. He would have to get creative. He searched the bay for a way to open the cargo door.

"Look for a pulley or a lever of some kind, Tinc," he ordered the nanobot. "It'll be somewhere near the door, probably by the corners. You check the top, I'll look below." He felt the sides of the door, searching for anything that might activate it. Before he could, Tinc was back in his ear, buzzing excitedly.

"You found it? Where?"

Tinc zoomed to the top of the bay and hovered near the upper right corner. Her inner processor cast a dim light, illuminating a tiny switch-frame. She fluttered against it, but her body was too small to move the heavy steel pieces. Peter would have to activate it.

He studied the frame, calculating the vertical he would need to reach the switch. The door was massive, but if he lined it up, the boxes scattered around the room would provide springboards for his feat. He would have to be quick—one misstep and he was done for.

He took in a quick breath and lurched forward, ready to go. The doors behind him shuddered, and he faltered, pausing to see if the barricade would hold. Amazingly, the rod held, but he could see the buckling metal. It wouldn't last much longer.

"Here goes nothing." Peter leaped onto a toppled rectangular box. Three steps and he was across the top, hurtling toward an oversized square crate. Two more and he made it to the next box, using each as a small step in a mountain of cargo. Tinc hurried alongside him, lighting every footfall.

Miraculously, he made it to the top. He used the final box as a ledge to leap toward the switch-frame. This was the tricky part. If he missed, they were as good as dead.

"Think happy thoughts. Think happy thoughts," he muttered through clenched teeth as he stretched his arm toward the lever. His stomach plummeted until his palm brushed the switch. He smashed it down to initiate the override. The whoosh of the atmosphere stabilizer rang in his ears as the door slowly opened.

Panic seized Peter's lungs as he realized too late that their respiratory systems were about to be overtaken by a foreign atmosphere. But there was nothing he could do. The doors had already slid halfway open. He hoped none of the boys' heads imploded from a sudden case of the bends.

He peeked out the door, and the breath he didn't realize he was holding rushed from his lungs. The air was fine. His breath came out short and raspy, but it was filled with oxygen. Peter turned to Tinc and the others, who gaped out the dock in awe.

They were staring at Paradise.

The planet was beautiful, filled with lush plant life that grew in dazzling hues. Flowers sprouted from every bush and tree, peppering the tropical canopy with bursts of the most vivid colors Peter had ever seen, including some he hadn't. He led the boys from the edge of the dock onto sturdy ground. At their feet, a turquoise pool surrounded them with an almost unbelievable sparkling surface. The ship had crashed on the edge of the shoreline, leaving half of the *Roger* propped on the sand while the rest dipped into the crystalline water. If Peter hadn't seen it with his own eyes, he would have said it was impossible.

A fresh round of pounding against the doors behind them interrupted his stupor, followed by the clang of the pole as it finally broke in half. The crews' shouts broke the peace of the night as they flooded the Loading Dock. Hooke raced forward with murder in his eyes. His wounded arm had been haphazardly bandaged to staunch the bloody stump, but even he slowed as he took in the wondrous sight before him.

Peter used the distraction to his advantage. Quick as a flash, he yanked the slingshot tucked in Slightly's pocket and aimed it at the flip-switch. It wouldn't take much to activate the panel.

"Happy thoughts," he breathed and released the shot. It hit dead center. The doors let out a loud, lurching sound and began to close, pulling Hooke from his hypnosis. The Captain surged forward, but it was too late. The dock sealed too quickly for Hooke's men to fit through. Hooke glared at him through the shrinking space between the paneling before letting out one last furious cry.

"This isn't over, Pan!" he raged. "This isn't over!"

Peter raised his hand to his brow in a mock salute, meeting the Captain's glowering sneer until only his winter blue eyes remained visible, and then, nothing.

Relief surged through Peter. They'd made it. Against all odds, he was on solid ground, with Tinc at his side, and a small group of Lost Boys. Hooke was right—it was far from over, but right then, he felt safer than he had since he'd found that blasted transmission.

He had won.

The ragtag group stood on the beach in a moment of silence, the only sound coming from Tinc's snapping mainframe as she flittered and sparked. Nobody spoke. It seemed they hardly breathed until Tootles' little voice broke the quiet.

"W-where do we go, Peter?"

Peter looked out at the breathtaking world in front of him, its untamed appearance given an almost ethereal beauty by the dim green light cast from the stars burning in the sky. Back home, sailors relied on the North Star for direction. They would do the same.

He looked at the sky. There, in the middle of the alien skyline sat a huge star, resting high in the evening light, emanating a bright white sheen while another star hovered near its tail. Unlike its brother, the second star cast a brilliant green, clear light over the planet, like a giant homing beacon. Peter pointed to show the crew.

"There." He squeezed Tootles' clammy hand. Whether to reassure the boy of himself, he wasn't sure, but his decision was made. "Follow the second star to the right, straight on 'til morning."

5

WENDY'S STORY

WENDY

"Sit up straight, darling. You look boorish when you hunch like that. Positively Neanderthal."

Wendy's mother sniffed daintily and adjusted her pearl hand gloves. Her slender nose tilted toward the roof as she considered Wendy's posture with haughty disdain.

"Yes, mother." Wendy stiffened her spine to draw back her shoulders the way her mother liked. When Mrs. Darling quirked an appeased smile, Wendy twisted to gaze out the hovercraft window, mindful to keep her shoulders straight. Through the sleek glass paneling, she saw the ghost of herself thrust into the midst of a gigantic city. The translucent reflection of her long, chestnut curls and rose-pink lips faded under the bright lights of skyscraper advertisements and busy office spaces.

New London. The heart of the empire and proud host to the Londonierre Academy. Wendy's future home. It was strange she would attend so soon; most recruits didn't join the ranks until age thirteen. But her results on the nationwide aptitude test had been high—very high. When the Academy called to offer Wendy early admission, West Brighton had erupted, fueling the socialite gossip fire for weeks, especially since her scores outranked the esteemed army General's own son. General Boyce had been furious, a fact her father gleefully pointed out each time he returned from the Rugby Club. Wendy often wondered if he would have been so keen to send her to the military academy had it not been such a sniffy affair.

"Look ahead, miss," the driver chirped, drawing Wendy from her thoughts. His synthetic eyes flashed in the mirror before fixing back on the skies. "The Londonierre Academy."

Wendy's shoulders straightened, as she looked on with keen interest. The Academy was huge, a beautiful cream building in the middle of a golden city. Surrounded by lush trees, the back boasted a training facility that rivaled even the Brigade's. Nerves fluttered wildly through Wendy's chest as the hover slowed and lowered to park in the designated skylot.

Wendy wriggled in her seat, but her excitement was lost on her parents. Her mother looked out the window with mild curiosity while her father had disappeared into another business deal.

"Oh, settle down, darling," her mother chided. "You look as though you are having fits."

"Yes, Mother." Wendy forced her limbs still, but inside, her heart danced with joy. She followed her parents from their hover to stand beside them as they strutted toward the Academy.

Wendy bobbed along, intrigued by all the different people surrounding the school. Women in suits, men in overalls, children with holey jeans—they all looked so different from the men and women her father attended so dutifully. But most fascinating were the Academy residents. Uniformed teachers and students scattered the civilian ranks, standing tall and proud in their gray Academy dress.

Unfazed by the mass of people, Wendy's parents sliced through the crowd, their faces pinched in superiority as they swaggered toward the busy reception area. Scattered seating filled the room filled with other families saying their goodbyes. Wendy scanned the crying mothers and somber fathers as they hugged their teenage cadets. Her brow dipped in a confused furrow. She hadn't expected tears.

"Come, darling." Her mother's tight command pulled Wendy's attention from a set of fraternal twins embracing. The brother cried, holding his sister tight as she wrapped her newly uniformed arms around his middle. Wendy gave them one passing glance, then hurried after her mother.

"Not much of a welcome," her father grumbled, scanning the hallway with disinterest. "No attendant, or on-site reception." He snorted. "This program better be worth what I'm paying."

"Welcome to the Academy," a booming voice interrupted her father's grousing. Wendy looked up to see a giant man clad in a dark gray Brigadierre uniform. His dark brows pulled together as he watched her father with a stoic glare. "Is there anything I can assist you with?"

"No, thank you." Mr. Darling eyed the other man dubiously. "We are here to admit our daughter. She was recruited for her aptitude results." He pushed Wendy forward like a barricade. "Wendy Moira Angela Darling, from West Brighton."

Commandant Martinez watched her father for a moment before crouching to face Wendy. Though his strict features fixed firmly in place, his brown eyes softened when they fell on her.

"Welcome," he said gruffly. "I hear you scored very well on your aptitude exam. Do you think you can do as well in real life?"

Wendy's head bobbed at the giant man.

Commandant Martinez smiled. "Then let's get you settled, cadet." He led them to the reception desk, where a junior officer stood receiving visitors.

"New recruit," the Commandant announced. "Wendy Darling. Needs her papers."

The cadet's eyes widened as he hurried to sift through the stacks of oversized cadet files. Commandant Martinez turned to Wendy.

"Glad to have you on board, Darling. We expect great things from you." He winked, and with a final curt nod at her father, marched from the room.

"Darling?"

The cadet's voice pulled Wendy's attention from the Commandant's retreating form. She nodded, and he passed her a silver file with her name emblazoned across the top next to a tiny picture of herself.

"This is your accommodations and your class schedule. The academic calendar, school events, and of course, code of conduct are all inside. It is your responsibility to review these documents and return them to the proper Commandant."

Wendy accepted the file. As soon as she ripped the silver packaging, her stomach was overrun by butterflies. She opened the file and peered inside, and saw a small, chrome band. Curious, she pulled it out to examine.

"That's your Nana—er, I mean, your scanband," the cadet explained. "It scans your biometrics throughout the day to ensure you are performing at optimum levels, kinda like your nanny at home. If you need anything, N— *the scanband* will tell you."

He lifted his arm to show Wendy his own band. It was similar to hers, except the smooth chrome was laced with Brigade blue in a sleek design around the face.

"She doubles as a watch, too. Give her a go." He gave her an encouraging smile as he looked from the bracelet to Wendy's wrist. "It might be big, but it's the smallest band we have. Usually, our new recruits aren't so small."

Wendy scrunched her nose at the unwanted reminder. So far, everything she had seen just told her how different she was from the other recruits. She clasped the band in place, dismayed at how it gapped around her petite wrist.

"You'll grow into it." The junior officer smiled. "If not, the Commandants will get you sorted." His eyes flitted over Wendy's shoulder to where a line of new recruits had formed. "Is there anything else I can help you with, Cadet?"

Wendy shook her head and clutched her file to her chest. The junior officer nodded. "Excellent. Dorms are in the north building, right after this hall." He pointed. "Welcome to the Academy." He saluted before he moved his attention to the next family in line.

Wendy twisted to face her parents and saw that they had already begun down the hall. She scurried after them, and caught up in the middle of a large, green courtyard filled with the excited chatter of students as they acclimated to their new home. Over the noise, Wendy's father shouted into his comm, his mustache twitching. Whenever Mr. Darling got agitated, his lips would twist and bunch, which made his mustache look like it was dancing. Sometimes it was a slow waltz, other times it was a lively ballet. Right now, it could have been doing the Salsa.

Her father yelled again and smashed his finger to the comm before stuffing the device into his pocket. His mustache gave one final twitch as he turned to face her mother.

"It's time to go, Mary," he said, giving Wendy a cursory glance. "The Mortensen account has an irregularity. If that blasted assistant of mine did anything—"

"Yes, dear." Mrs. Darling placed her hand on her husband's chest with a demure glance at the people surrounding them. "Of course."

She turned to Wendy.

"Be a good girl, won't you, darling?"

Wendy nodded. Her lip trembled and she bit it back, feeling tears film over her eyes. Her mother smiled.

"That's a good girl." She pressed a hand to Wendy's cheek, and then with another soft smile, hurried after her husband. Mr. Darling was back on the comm, barking orders at his assistant. Wendy raised her hand in a tiny wave, her heart wrenching when they didn't look back.

Wendy hadn't expected tears.

She glanced anxiously around the courtyard at the groups of students already forming friendships. A small buzz ran through her wrist and she looked down at the scanband, surprised. The band gave another soft pulse before the screen scrolled through a series of data.

Wendy M.A. Darling, junior cadet.

Height: 126.2 cm

Weight: 25.1 kg

Heart Rate: 100 bpm — accelerated.

Blood Pressure: 118/75 — elevated.

Recommendation: Deep breathing exercises to lower anxiety.

Wendy closed her eyes and took in a long slow breath from her nose. She let it out slowly, noting with surprise that she actually felt better.

"Thanks, Nana," she whispered, then checked her surroundings, feeling silly until a large red ball sailed past her head and she was tackled from behind.

"Sorry!" a surprised voice sounded behind her as steady hands lifted her from the ground. Startled, Wendy accepted the help and stood to face a boy a few years older than her. He smiled and turned to the small group of kids waiting on the other side of the courtyard.

"That was terrible, Stevens! Next time, maybe aim for her head so you miss it!"

Wendy furrowed her brow as the boy retrieved the ball, then spun to wink at her.

"Don't worry," he whispered. "Stevens is garbage. He'll never get you." He looked at Wendy and cringed when he saw the large grass stain he had rubbed into her dress. "Sorry about that," he said, handing the ball to her. "Wanna crack back?"

Wendy looked from the ball to Stevens to the strange boy in front of her.

Nana buzzed again, but Wendy didn't need the biometric to tell her she was overwhelmed. Tears pricked the corner of her eyes and the boy scratched his head. He looked around, searching the crowd.

"Are you lost or something? Don't worry—your family's probably just saying goodbye and they'll pick you up when your brother or sister is all signed in."

Wendy's temper flared. "I'm not lost, and I don't have a brother or sister," she retorted, standing as tall as she could. "I'm here to attend the Academy same as you. Except *I'm* not going to treat it like a game."

She took the ball and threw it across the courtyard, sending it sailing straight into Stevens' head. He hit the ground, then was pulled up to cheers and laughter from the other kids.

The boy next to Wendy let out a delighted laugh and turned to Wendy, his almond eyes sparkling. "Well, hot damn," he said, scratching his freshly buzzed hair. "You must be that girl—the genius. Wanda or something,"

"My name is Wendy." Wendy sniffed, summoning every ounce of propriety she could. "Wendy Moira Angela Darling. Junior cadet." She tilted her chin defiantly, noting with dismay that she barely reached the boy's shoulder.

He didn't seem to mind. He chuckled and looked at her neatly brushed hair to her newly stained dress.

"Looks like we'll be in the same cadre then," he said, extending his hand. "I'm Elias, but here, they'll probably call me Johns." He jerked his thumb over his shoulder. "Wanna play? We could use a player with a better arm than Stevens." He winked.

Wendy looked back at the group of eager cadets. "No thanks," she said. "I should find my bunk."

Johns nodded and pointed to a tall, windowed building. "Dorms are over there. Your assignments are in your introductory papers. It's a straight shot—you can't miss it."

Wendy smiled. "But could Stevens?"

Johns' brows lifted as he let out a surprised chuckle. "Probably not." He laughed and shot off to rejoin the game. Feeling alone, Wendy eyed her silver file, until Johns' voice cracked over the noise.

"Don't look so worried." He cupped his hand over his mouth. "Stevens is concussed, but you..." He dropped his hands and beamed at her. "You'll be all right, Darling."

He spun on his heel to join the others and slug Stevens on the shoulder. The boys shoved each other amicably then ran down the other edge of the courtyard, narrowly missing the other cadets they weaved around.

Wendy laughed and let out a shaky sigh. She scanned the building that would be her home for at least the next five years. She gripped her file and began walking down Johns' recommended path as a wave of excitement bubbled up to replace her earlier unease.

"Darling," she repeated her new Academy classification, relishing the way it danced off her tongue. "You'll be all right."

6

"Johns, *sit down*," Commandant Sentra barked. It was the fourth day of the new Academy cycle, and for the fourth time, the cadet had just squeaked into class before the final bell. Johns grinned and scanned the room for Wendy, looking for the seat she'd saved him. He gave a jaunty salute to the Commandant, whose lips pursed to hide the trace of a smile. Wendy shook her head. Johns was infuriating, but it was part of his charm. They had been best friends for two years now, and Wendy was still amazed at the seamless way he carried himself through life at the Academy.

"Hey, Darling," Johns whispered, sliding into the bench beside her.

"You know, one day you might try being on time for class," Wendy hissed, focused on the front of the class as Commandant Pearce explained the requirements of leadership in the Brigade.

Johns snorted. "I'm on time every day. Otherwise, I'd be peeling your potatoes for dinner each day." He grinned, and Wendy heard Cadet Pearce giggle behind her. The girl had been inching closer to Wendy each day, following Johns around like a daft bird. Johns was oblivious. Wendy didn't understand teenagers.

She turned to her friend and his grin widened, bright against his tawny skin. Wendy tipped her head, considering. She supposed he was handsome, with his dark hair and skin, and striking pale brown eyes. Johns noticed her studying him and twisted his face into a ridiculous pose.

Maybe not so handsome.

Wendy sighed as another giggle squeaked from behind her.

"Are you going to do anything about that?" Wendy pointed to the offending Cadet. "Her stupid giggling is interfering with my studying."

Johns twisted in his chair to check out Cadet Pearce with interest, setting her off on another round of twitters. He chuckled and turned to Wendy with a smug smile.

"Darling, *nothing* could interfere with your studying." He nudged her, schooling his face into a studious pose when he saw Commandant Sentra's furious gaze.

"Johns, please leave Cadet Darling alone." She sighed. "At least one of you should pass my class."

Wendy covered her mouth to hide her giggle as Commandant Sentra turned to the rest of the class.

"You are here because the Academy saw something in you." She quirked her eyebrow as she glanced at Johns. "For some of you, these things were more obvious than others."

The class laughed, and Johns grinned.

"Believe you can and you're halfway there," Johns quoted with a shrug.

Commandant Sentra laughed and activated the Comm Screen at the front of the class. "If only it were that easy, cadet. Regardless, you are among the country's Elite. You will accomplish things other people can only ever dream of." She paused to let her words sink in as she looked around the class. "And some of you will do more."

Wendy's stomach stirred. Visions of her leading a crew on a daring space rescue danced through her mind. Flying a ship, fighting vicious space aliens, saving the lost princess...

Her daydream was interrupted by Commandant Sentra's sharp voice. "To do this, you must rise through the ranks to prove your capabilities. You must become great." The Comm Screen blipped and a large image of a man appeared in the middle.

He was handsome, standing tall and proud before an antique vessel. It matched the sleek coloring of his vintage Fleet uniform—pitch black pants and boots underneath an elaborate Brigade Blue Captain's coat. The bright blue offset his dark curls and tanned skin, which emphasized his electric eyes even more. He didn't smile, choosing instead to set his jaw tight, making him look mysterious and strong.

Commandant Sentra activated the footage, stirring the Captain's still figure to life.

Wendy's eyes widened as she leaned forward. The Captain was amazing. The way he fought was incredible. Moving forward like flashes of lightning, striking powerfully each time. She studied his frame—lithe muscles explained the agility and speed, while the broad expanse of his chest emphasized the strength within.

The comm screen flashed and Hooke was before the Fleet, giving a rousing speech to an enormous crowd, his dark eyes focused on the camera as he captivated the arena.

The footage clipped again and showed Hooke sitting in the pilot's seat of a vessel with his crew. He smiled, breaking the hard line of his face into a softer expression. The film panned out to show the full ship, with Hooke at the helm, maneuvering the giant vessel in ways that defied physics. After a few more impressive scenes, the film stilled and the screen returned to the Captain's imposing image.

Commandant Sentra returned to the front of the room to address the class.

"Captain James Hooke was one of the most decorated soldiers in the Brigade. His leadership and bravery brought notoriety and acclaim to the fleet. Some would argue that he would have changed the shape of the whole Brigade." The shine in Commandant Sentra's eyes dimmed as her face fell. "Unfortunately, the *Jolly Roger* disappeared, taking Hooke and his potential with it."

"Then is he really that great?" a snide voice asked from the front of the room. "An illustrious expeditionary Captain disappears into the 'verse? Sounds more like a rook."

Wendy tore her eyes from the Captain to the cadet who had spoken. Aidan Boyce sat a few rows from the front, staring at the screen with condescension. After being beaten out in the aptitude exam, he had been admitted in the Fall Cycle last year, and with his father's urging, had been placed in the Alpha cadre. Wendy had to admit, he was smart in his own right, but she wondered how often his accomplishments were dismissed because his father was the General.

As she watched Boyce's superior smirk, she had a hard time feeling bad about it. His light features, golden hair and bright blue eyes didn't match his dingy personality. She had tried to befriend him when he'd first arrived, but his arrogance didn't mesh well with her accomplishments, and he quickly made it clear.

"That is for you to decide, Cadet Boyce." Commandant Sentra's mouth formed a hard line. "The Academy boasts a history of housing some of the most brilliant explorers in history." She quirked her brow at him. "But the path is littered with recruits who couldn't cut it."

The Commandant's sharp warning sliced through the air, permeating the classroom. Boyce hunched in his chair, scowling at the Commandant as she turned to address the cadre.

"My job is to give you all the information you need to beat the knife." Her gaze met Wendy's and her head dipped in a tiny nod. "In your comms, you will see a file I uploaded about Captain Hooke. Your task is to complete a research report about his most effective strategies and contributions to the fleet." Her attention swiveled to Boyce. "I expect to see compelling arguments from each of you."

Wendy retrieved her comm and clicked on the tiny file that had appeared in the upper righthand corner. Dozens of articles and reports pulled up, each with the Captain's name emblazoned across the top. Wendy chose the first one and looked at the image at the start of the report. It was the same photograph from Commandant Sentra's board. Wendy pressed her fingers against the screen, trailing the edge of the Captain's jawline, wondering what secrets he had taken with him to the 'verse. Intrigued, she immersed herself in the lesson, scouring the articles Commandant Sentra provided and then cataloguing a list of her own. She was so enthralled that she completely lost track of time until the bell rang, startling her out of her skin.

"Relax, Darling." Johns laughed. "You're going to give yourself an aneurysm and it's only second period."

Wendy shook her head as she hurried to grab her things. She dropped her Comm in her pocket and hurried out the door, Johns trailing behind her.

The hallway filled with hundreds of cadets milling around as they made their way to their next class. The majority was made up of lower cadres, as their class sizes were the biggest. As training progressed, the student body thinned out, proving Darwin's natural selection by leaving only the best of the recruits.

They walked past the lockers where Boyce leaned against a short brunette, toying with the long waves cascading down her back. Without his normal scowl distorting his features, he was actually quite handsome. The brunette squealed playfully as Boyce tickled her side and Wendy let out a disgruntled sigh as she tried to figure out how they had made the cut. Boyce made sense—his father was the General, and for all his faults, he actually was very intelligent. But the squeaky girl? A scoff escaped her and Boyce turned around, his jaw tightening while the brunette scowled at her over his shoulder. Wendy averted her eyes and continued down the corridor, acutely aware of the difference in the subdued cadet-commanders and the rowdy cadets as she passed through the Academy halls.

Wendy hustled through the crowd, ignoring Johns' flirtatious banter with the older cadets as they made their way to class. At one point, she lost Johns to a pretty red-haired cadet and had to physically pull him down the hall, along with his string of grumbled curses.

Wendy was about to remind him of the profanity regulations when the warning bell sounded, sending her rushing down the hall with Johns scuttling after her. They tore through the corridors, narrowly making it to Commandant Westin's room as the final bell squawked.

Wendy's breath hitched as Johns held the door with a broad smile.

"See, Darling?" He grinned. "I'm never late."

Wendy tried not to laugh, which only succeeded in her letting out an awkward snort.

Eager to return to his desk to wait out the remainder of the period, Commandant Westin had already begun his instructions and gave them a stern glance as they slunk into the empty seats closest to the door. They were continuing a project they had begun yesterday, using coding to repair damaged software. It was difficult, and Wendy's brain wouldn't take to the coding, which meant she was always checking the manual, making the work tedious. About the only good thing she could say about it was that she was better than Johns, who had yet to defrag a single line.

There was a knock at the door and Wendy looked up, thankful for the interruption.

"Excuse me, Commandant."

A pretty Cadet-Commander stood at the door with a male cadet beside her. He was small, close to Wendy's size with light brown hair and dark eyes enlarged by wire-rimmed frames. He watched the cadre as though wishing to hide.

Wendy looked at Johns to ask what he thought of the boy and sighed when she realized he was staring at the blonde Cadet-Commander. She rolled her eyes, then nudged him in the ribs.

"Who is that?" Wendy asked, ignoring the glare she earned.

Johns craned his neck to look at the new cadet, whose pale face matched the tight white skin around his knuckles as he clutched his comm protectively in front of himself.

"Commandant, this is Cadet Michaels. He will be joining this cadre for all of their technical engineering classes." She handed the Commandant a small slip of paper decorated by the Admiral's stamp, then retreated, her mission complete.

Recognition covered Johns' features, and he leaned forward in interest.

"That's one of the new recruits. He's in the cadre under us, but apparently he's some sort of tech-genius," Johns whispered. "Wonder why he's here?"

Commandant Westin scanned the paper and moved his spectacled gaze to Cadet Michaels. The corners of his mouth quirked in the first trace of a smile Wendy had ever seen.

"At ease, Michaels," he said. He scanned the room, and pointed to the open desk next to Boyce before burying his face in his comm, oblivious to the murderous scowl Boyce leveled at the smaller cadet. A wave of sympathy ran through Wendy.

"Commandant Westin?" She raised her hand.

The Commandant pulled his face from his device, confused. Wendy wasn't sure how many recruits had ever addressed him. After providing them with their login, all of Commandant Westin's communication was uploaded directly through their comms. He peered at her, then peeked at his comm to check his roster.

"Yes, Darling?" he asked, his voice scratchy from disuse.

"He can sit here, Commandant." Wendy pointed to the open seat beside her. She looked at Michaels and gave him a warm smile. "I don't mind."

Commandant Westin looked at the seat beside her and shrugged. "Have a seat, Cadet," he barked, then retreated into his device, leaving the rest of the cadre to slog through their coding.

Michaels sank into the chair next to Wendy with a relieved look. He gave her a shy smile, then turned into his computer, the light bouncing a blue shine off his glasses. Wendy glanced at Johns, who quirked his brow in a silent question, but she only shrugged, then sighed as she refocused on the foreign symbols dancing across the screen.

Wendy was just getting through a particularly difficult line of code when a small blue box appeared in the corner of her screen. She looked at it curiously, then glanced at Johns' screen to see if his looked the same. Intricate coding stamped across the display, but there was nothing else. She peered at the tiny box and clicked it open.

The box opened to reveal the image of a rose, cobbled from coding symbols. At the base of the stem was a tiny word, spelled with coding.

Thanks.

Wendy glanced around, confused, and her gaze fell on Michaels. He typed furiously, whirring through line after line of complex coding, but there was an open window in his screen with the same rose. Wendy let out a surprised gasp, and Michaels paused, his hands hovering over the keys as he watched her shyly from the corner of his eye. Wendy looked from the flower to the cadet and smiled. Michaels dipped his head in a tiny nod and returned to the keypad, resuming his furious pace.

Wendy turned to Johns with an incredulous smile. "I might actually pass this class after all."

7

THE HOME UNDER THE GROUND

PETER

"Peter, wake up!" A loud whisper tickled his ear, followed by an agitated jingle. Tootles had enlisted Tinc's help. Peter groaned and peeked open one eye. Light streamed through the treehouse window and onto his face. He threw his arm over his head. His body shook as Tootles pulled on his hammock bed. "Peter!"

"What do you want, Tootles? Can't you see I'm trying to sleep?" Peter twisted to face the wall, his hammock swaying even more. He pulled his tattered space blanket over his face. The temperature-regulating fabric crackled as it settled over his body.

"Peter! You gotta get up! Hooke's up to something!"

Even with his eyes closed, Peter could picture the excited way Tootles bounced around on his toes. If the poor kid got anymore worked up, his stutter would kick in. He sighed and rolled over, removing the blanket to glare at the intruders. Tootles looked sheepish, but Tinc whipped the blanket to the floor. She buzzed around, sparks crackling from her core as she scolded Peter for being lazy.

"All right, all right, I'm up!" Peter scrubbed his face with both hands. "What are you two on about?"

"The pirates. They're up to no good." Tootles blinked, looking up at Peter with wide brown eyes. He stood at attention, clad in his tattered Fleet-issued jumpsuit. He was the only Lost Boy who still wore the full uniform. The other boys had long since traded in their bulky crew suits in favor of cargo shorts and T-shirts, but Tootles kept to protocol, even when he had to patch the holes he wore into them. Truth be told, the kid looked more like a ratty boy scout than a recruit, but none of the others had the heart to break it to him.

"They've been up to no good forever, Tootles. You're gonna have to give me more than that."

Tootles' cheeks tinged the softest shade of pink, but he pressed on. "Well, Curly saw Starkey and Bill Jukes set off one of his trigger-wires on the south side of the jungle. Then a couple hours later, Cecco and Noodler set off another by Skull beach. He thought it was weird."

Peter ran his hands through his hair. He could have still been sleeping. "Curly thinks everything is weird. He'd get rid of our space blankets if we let him. Says the texture freaks him out. What's your point?" He shot a cross look at Tinc. "I thought I installed better logistics programming when I ran that upgrade, Tinc."

Tinc responded with a comment that made Peter glad he'd installed a personal cochlear translator, as well.

"I know, Peter. That's why I asked Slightly and Nibs to run a perimeter check. They said the pirates were searching the island. All of them. They thought it was weird too." Tootles kicked the floor.

That did seem strange, but the pirates had acted strangely before. He scratched his chin, pretending to deliberate. "All right, you've got my attention."

Tootle's brightened. "I've monitored the pirates the past few days. They've been all over, like they're looking for something. They go out a few times a day, all at the same time. Every time they hit a different spot, stay for about an hour, then go back to the *Roger*. Same thing every day."

"And Hooke?"

"Hooke's the only one who hasn't left the ship. Even Smee has gone out a few times. I think they're reporting to him."

"Of course they are. The codfish wouldn't leave the safety of his cabin."

Peter rolled his eyes. How very like his old friend, James. Forcing his men to do the dirty work. They had been watching Hooke since they'd first set up camp. Keeping close tabs provided them with the Captain's intel and kept them safe.

When they had first landed in Neverland—Hooke's assigned name for the seemingly ageless planet—his pirates had scoured the island in a similar way looking for Peter and the boys. When they hadn't found them, things had settled down. The pirates hadn't been this active in years. It was worth looking into.

"And the Stjarnin?" If Hooke was on the move, Neverland's natives would be sure to notice. The mysterious warriors were highly territorial and didn't take kindly to the planet's newest residents. "What have they been up to?"

"They've been quiet. Haven't seen or heard from them much at all."

Peter mulled that over. It wasn't like the locals to leave the pirates to do as they pleased. There was a tenuous balance in the Never, held firmly in place by the three groups very deliberately avoiding each other. Contact always resulted in full-on battles belying the larger war. He had to check it out.

"This had better not be another false alarm, Tootles." He fixed a stern gaze on the boy. For the most part, Tootles was an invaluable part of the team. His work on the *Roger* had trained him well in coding and navigation. Peter had to admit, the kid was impressive. The only problem was, being the youngest of the boys, Tootles was excitable and often let his imagination get carried away with him.

Tootles gulped. "Yes, sir. I m-mean no, sir." His cheeks flamed, but he held his ground. "It's not. The pirates are definitely up to something."

Peter nodded. He thought so too. The only way to find out would be to pay Hooke a visit. A mischievous smile danced on his lips. It had been a while since he had tormented the codfish.

"Round up the boys, Tinc. We've got ourselves a mission."

Tinc jangled excitedly then shot through the tree house, buzzing to get the boys' attention. Within minutes, the Lost Boys assembled in the front room of the tree house. They stood in their self-determined ranks, from shortest to tallest. Tootles, the baby of the crew, started off the line. He stood at attention, hand to brow in the traditional Fleet salute.

Next to Tootles, Curly, their resident worrywart, stood biting his nails, a nervous habit he had acquired during his years on the *Roger*. Only fourteen when he'd "enlisted", Curly had had the misfortune of being assigned to Noodler. It was rumored the old janitor was completely off his rocker, and often took to boxing his assistants 'round the ears. Curly didn't talk about it much, but his brown eyes told the stories he wouldn't; darting back and forth, always watching. He had become the Boys' self-appointed security guard and took it upon himself to rig booby traps around the treehouse to ward off potential intruders. He had done a good job; though they had been here longer than Peter cared to know, no one had ever found their little sanctuary.

Next was Nibs, Peter's weapons expert. He'd never had proper training, but the stocky teen could wield any piece you'd ever need. He'd even figured out how to rig small bombs with materials he found around the island. He called them 'Nibblers.' Peter was glad to have him on his side.

Slightly waited sullenly beside him. Though at nineteen, he was technically the oldest Lost Boy, the Twins were taller than him by a few inches. Peter knew it bothered him to no end. It didn't matter that they were also stuck at the same age and height; whenever they did roll call, he pouted.

Last were the Twins. Peter couldn't tell if they stood in the same order every day, or if they alternated because they looked exactly the same. He didn't even know their real names—they were just the Twins.

Peter looked at his ragtag crew. They were a long shot from London's finest, but they were his. "All right men." He fixed them with a steely gaze. "Today's mission: reconnaissance. The pirates are up to something, and it's up to us to stop them."

The boys listened intently as Peter outlined the plan. Tinc flitted lazily around his shoulder, buzzing off now and then to spark in one of the boys' ears as their attention drifted.

"Any questions?"

"No sir!" the boys cried in unison as they saluted him.

He saluted back. He was proud of his little family, these Lost Boys he had saved from the *Roger*. Without him, they would still be under the phony benevolence of Hooke.

Peter looked at the admiration glowing from Tootle's his chubby face. He wouldn't let Tootles experience the same abandonment he had. His jaw clenched, and he thrust his dagger into the air, ready for a fight.

"Let's go men!" Peter crowed, leading his crew into the wilds of Neverland.

8

Peter knew every inch of the jungle surrounding their treehouse. The beautiful land was so vastly different from the dingy streets of New London, it made the planet seem even more alien. Unlike the murky waterways scattered throughout the acrid city, the water here was the perfect shade of turquoise, immaculately clean and free from pollution. It teemed with wildlife—alien creatures that resembled twisted versions of fish back home. The boys called them fish, although they looked more like underwater birds than the scaly, gilled creatures of Earth.

When they first set camp, Peter had caught a few and cooked them over a makeshift fire. The strange creatures filled the boys' stomachs, but they tasted terrible and gave them the worst stomach cramps imaginable. It hadn't been long until the boys abandoned their fishing poles entirely.

Apart from the unblemished environment, Neverland was oddly similar to Earth. The climate was ideal, warm and temperate during the day followed by cool nights under the eerie green of the Second Star. It worked well for Peter and the boys, who had only escaped the *Jolly Roger* with the clothes on their backs. The first few weeks could have been much harder, but the tropical temperatures remained.

Eventually, Peter had found the old, hollow tree. It was large enough that it provided a good entry into the hideout they had dug underneath its massive trunk. From outside, nobody could tell there was a home base hidden underground. Curly had even used the tangled branches to build a discreet lookout. It had taken almost a year to build to Peter's exact specifications. At least, that's what Peter guessed. Inside the tree trunk, Tootles had scratched a new line for every day that had passed until it became too many lines, and they had given up on it. It seemed like ages ago.

So far, the treehouse had held. The old frame was sturdy and securely hidden in the middle of the jungle. With Curly's added perimeter of traps, nobody came near without the boys' knowledge.

Heavy foliage covered most of the island, and what wasn't covered in trees was golden beaches. The one exception was an inlet settled between the treehouse and where the *Roger* had crashed. It was a huge, shallow pool scattered with large columned rocks where the mermaids sat to sunbathe every day.

If Peter could have gotten to Hooke without passing the mermaids, he would. They lazed in the inlet, preening over their reflections as they brushed their hair, their tails stirring the water below them. The only thing that better held their attention was the trinkets they collected and wore around their necks.

It was what made the inlet so dangerous. If something caught their eye, the mermaids would sing a hypnotic melody as they stalked nearer to collect it. No one could ever guess what they would fancy; it might be a flower, a fancy seashell, or an eye. But once the mermaids desired it, they did whatever they could to possess it.

The first time the boys had met the creatures, they had almost lost Slightly. They had walked to the inlet, drawn by the mermaids' beauty as they laughed and splashed each other in the glinting starlight. When they had noticed their audience, the mermaids shrank behind their rocks before shyly peeking out of the water. Their long, silken hair floated on the surface as the mermaids swam closer, mesmerizing the boys with their lovely smiles. As they had drawn nearer, they'd started singing the most beautiful song Peter ever heard.

He'd watched, transfixed, until a loud splash had pulled his attention to Slightly, who was soaked and slipping over the rocks in the shallows of the inlet. One mermaid had waited in the shallows, beckoning him closer. She was breathtaking, with huge doe eyes and flawless skin. Her hair and neck were adorned with jewelry strung together with beads and shells and…teeth?

Confused, Peter's mind had cleared the haze the mermaids had cast. He'd looked again and instead of the beautiful creature that waited before, a gnarled, skeletal monster reached for Slightly as he hurried toward her. Her teeth bared as he'd drawn nearer, oblivious. Even with his gimp, he'd made it waist deep into the pool before Peter had reached him. He was just about to clasp his hand in hers when Peter had grabbed his jumpsuit collar and pulled. He still remembered the way the mermaid's face had contorted and her song warped into an earsplitting screech as Slightly had slipped from her grasp.

When the gorgeous creature transformed in front of his eyes, Slightly had cried in surprise and backpedaled in terror. With Slightly free, Peter had turned to the other boys, who were all still caught under the mermaids' spell, entranced until Peter barreled past them, his wild splashes jerking them from their reverie. The creatures had snarled as they'd fled, screeching in fury at being deprived their prizes. It had been a close call.

"Quiet men, we're coming up on Mermaid Cove," Peter hissed as they approached the inlet. "Let's not give them a reason to sing." He glanced at Slightly, whose face paled.

Peter led them silently around the cove, hanging along the outskirts of the jungle, using the trees for cover. A loud screech sent a wave of panic through Peter until he realized it was just two mermaids quarreling over a necklace. Peter forced the boys on until they reached the edge of the inlet, only relaxing their breaths once they cleared the beach.

They hurried through the trees, listening to the Neverbirds as they flittered around the canopy above. The trees began to thin, signaling their arrival to the *Jolly Roger*. Peter slowed the boys and pulled out his ancient scanner. It had taken some serious work but he had configured the tech to operate without fritzing every time he turned it on. It wasn't ideal, but some tech was better than none.

"What do you think?" Peter asked the bot on his shoulder. Tinc flitted to read the scan results herself. She hovered over the screen, then swooped back to Peter's shoulder and buzzed impatiently.

Peter made a face. "The transmissions? No. Why would I check those? Hooke hasn't repaired the message board; he wouldn't be able to—" Peter stopped mid-sentence as he realized what Tinc was suggesting. "You don't think he'd have been able to…" He trailed off as he typed the command to analyze radio frequencies emitted from the *Jolly Roger*. "It would have taken a lot of work, but I guess anything's possible…"

Peter cursed under his breath as he waited for the scan to upload. A read that didn't turn any transmissions would come back negative within less than a minute. When diagnostics didn't come rolling across his screen after thirty seconds, he held his breath, wondering if Hooke had really pulled it off.

The scanner blipped and coding crawled across the screen. Hooke had been trying for a while to get a message out. Hundreds of error messages covered the screen. There were so many it took a while to pull up the data Peter was after, but there it was. The last data entry.

Unlike the gibberish that filled the other failed messages, this one was much simpler.

Outgoing Transmission. B-35421-cxd-2118n. Message 00:16:48 Sent // date unknown//

Peter's jaw dropped as he whispered the last words.

"Transmission received."

9

WHEN WENDY GREW UP

WENDY

A smart kick to the side of the head rattled Wendy's sparring helmet. The movement jarred her neck but didn't sway her focus. A few chestnut strands fell in her face and she tossed her head to clear her vision. She just had to hang tough a few more minutes and Johns would tire himself out the same way he always did. He fought hard and fast, spending all his energy in the first few rounds. They were in Round Four.

Johns' wheezing signaled Wendy's attack. Mimicking Hooke's signature feint, she allowed him one last punch, and he took the bait. Anticipating his heavy-handed hook, she dodged easily, dropping to a crouch before springing forward with a high knee to his chest. Her kick sent him staggering back, propelling her into hard offense. She charged, throwing a tight combo punch, clipping his jawbone before whirling to dance around him. With the grace of a prima ballerina, she spun, coiling her arms about his throat. In one deft motion, she had him in a complicated choke he'd never escape.

Johns struggled against her grip on the mat, but Wendy held. Commandant Martinez's boxy hands slapped the padding once, twice, three times, and that was it. She had won.

"That's a wrap. Nice work, Darling," Commandant Martinez boomed across the vaulted gymnasium. His face split in a broad smile as he slapped Wendy on the shoulder and tossed her a clean towel. "You finished him off just in time. The Admiral has requested to see you. I hear she's made her decision about the Brigadierre selection." He wagged his brows knowingly. "Make yourself presentable and report to her office."

Wendy's stomach lurched. It was common knowledge the Admiral would select a new Fleet Captain, but it was rumored to happen later this month. The announcement caught her by surprise. Wendy didn't like surprises.

When she didn't immediately comply, Commandant Martinez laughed. The sound was a big as the man it escaped.

"Pull yourself together, cadet. You're whiter than the sweat-rag I tossed you."

"Yes, sir." She saluted and retreated to the locker room. As she walked away, the Commandant's booming voice echoed across the training room as he returned his attention to her defeated opponent.

"Johns! She works you over every time! When are you going to get it through your thick skull that you need finesse when dealing with the ladies? Give me a circuit!"

Wendy chuckled under her breath. Circuits were awful. She'd have to apologize to Johns later. She hated that he'd gotten stuck running because she'd trounced him again.

In the locker room, Wendy opted out of showering and hurried into her uniform. She had barely worked up a sweat, and she didn't want to keep the Admiral waiting. She glimpsed herself in the small mirror taped to her locker door. Her collar was crooked.

"You can do this," she told herself with a quick tug of her jacket. She pulled her shoulders back authoritatively, but her reflection wasn't buying it. Staring back at her was a worried nineteen-year-old with delicate features and big hazel eyes. She was pretty enough, although she wished her nose didn't look so much like a button. It made her seem younger than she was, which she definitely didn't need. Her long chestnut hair pulled away from her face, slicked back in a braided bun to Academy standards. The pins made her head hurt, but she was used to it. She would have to get used to a lot worse than the discomfort of her uniform if the Admiral selected her.

"Oh, who are you kidding? There's no way they're picking you. You're the youngest of the eligible cadets and just look at you. You don't look like you could hurt a fly."

The face in the mirror scowled. Wendy rubbed her hands over her eyes to chase away the headache forming behind her brows. She was going to be sick.

"You don't actually believe that garbage, do you?"

Wendy was met with a sweaty towel thrown in her face. She whipped it off and glared at the offender. Johns stood before her, already shirtless. He winked at a pretty Lieutenant Cadet and Wendy rolled her eyes. Elias was too confident for his own good. Wendy often considered her sparring victories a public service—it kept him humble.

"That you're finished with your circuit already?" She chucked the towel at him. "No way. You're too slow."

"I've had loads of practice thanks to you. My time's gone down a whole minute." Johns opened the locker next to hers and pulled out his duffel. "But with an arm like that, you're right." He scrunched his face in mock apology. "You probably aren't gonna get it. Tough break."

Wendy paused. She hadn't considered whether basic sport would be included in her assessment.

Johns rolled his eyes. "No, Darling. Stop that." He flopped on the locker bench and sighed in exasperation. "I was kidding. You know what the requirements are. Hell, you practically wrote the application form. There is no hidden qualifier."

"But what if—"

"No. Don't be stupid." He picked up his towel and snapped her calf. "You're over-thinking things again. I swear that big brain of yours does more harm than good sometimes."

"Knock it off!" She snatched for the towel, but Johns raised it out of her reach and aimed at her shoulder.

"Only if you stop psyching yourself out."

Wendy sighed. "Fine. No more psyching. I swear." She raised her last three fingers, tapped them to her temple in the Fleet salute and stepped out of Johns' reach. "Just don't snap me again."

"Don't be such a girl." He laughed. Wendy scowled at him. He knew she hated when he said that. No matter—she'd pummel him tomorrow.

"This girl has kicked your ass every day since we got here," she reminded him, shoving her bag in her locker.

"And that's why you're gonna make Captain." Johns smiled. "Just don't forget the little people like Michaels when you're swept up to the bigwigs. It would break his little Techie heart." He snapped her ankle and laughed as she danced out of the way.

"Leave Michaels alone," she said. "You know you're his hero." She slammed her locker shut and made a face at Johns. He straightened to mock attention and blew a raspberry at her. Wendy rolled her eyes.

Johns laughed. "Yeah, well, you're mine. And me and Michaels will be waiting in your dorm to celebrate your promotion, Captain." Johns clapped her shoulder. "Now hurry up. You know how much you hate it when you're late."

Wendy nodded. He was right. She was already cursing herself for getting caught up in his friendly banter. She pulled on her cover and adjusted it to proudly display her Senior Cadet's badge. Johns gave her one last smile, and after a deep, steadying breath, she hurried out the locker room.

She rushed through the hallways, worriedly checking the time on her way to the Admiral's office. It had been six minutes since Commandant Martinez had excused her. She hoped Admiral Toussant wouldn't notice she'd dawdled. A small pulse thrummed against her veins, and she raised her arm to check her scanband. The tiny screen displayed her biometrics and prompted her to practice deep breathing. Distracted by Nana's digital scolding, Wendy rounded the corner into a solid form.

"Oh! I'm sorry! I didn't see—" She broke off and stifled a groan. Boyce replanted his footing, eyeing her with distaste. He scowled at her, marring his handsome features. Wendy tried not to stare as she studied his immaculate appearance. From his muscular build to his sharply-styled haircut Boyce was the definition of an ideal Academy recruit. Add in his chiseled jawline, and you had a Brigadierre spokesperson who could enlist half of New London with a single smile.

Too bad he never smiled.

"Watch where you're going, Darling. I should be able to walk down the hallway without worrying about getting attacked."

Wendy flushed but held her ground. "Maybe if you sparred better, an accidental bump wouldn't feel like an attack."

Boyce's lip curled. "Cute." He raked his eyes over her. "Like you could be if you put on make-up occasionally. As it stands, you look like a little boy with overgrown hair. Not a good look."

Wendy held his glare as she straightened her uniform. "I don't recall asking *or* caring about your opinion on my appearance. But if it makes you feel better for not being able to keep up, go on." She sidestepped around him to distance herself.

Boyce moved to block her. "You should be thankful someone is paying attention." He straightened to full height. It was the only advantage he had over her. "You're not as great as you think you are. Remember that."

"Funny, I might say the same about you," Wendy retorted. Granted, Boyce *was* attractive. His classic good looks combined with his military physique could easily have found him the starring role of any movie. It was his personality that was repulsive.

"More than you think, Darling. Especially to the powers that be." He pulled his attention from her to straighten the sleeves of his uniform. "I just had a meeting with the Admiral and she admitted she was quite impressed with my ideas."

"Like what? Installing mirrors into the steering bay so you can stare at yourself more often?" She knocked him with her shoulder to push past him. She didn't have time for head games.

It didn't keep him from chasing after her.

"Like how to command a team. Maybe if you're lucky, she'll put you with me. It's not like you'd ever have the guts to lead anyone," he leered. "Sure, you've got fancy footwork and you test well. But when it's time to act?" He wrapped his hands around his neck and gagged. "You'll choke."

Wendy bristled as she rushed off, chased by the echoes of his scathing remark.

"Well, for both our sakes, I hope that's not true," she called behind her. "I don't want to have to deal with you any longer than I have to, and I'm sure you wouldn't want to be shown up in front of your crew every day."

She didn't look back, refusing to let on that his words stung. Then he would never leave her alone. That, and he was an asshole. Wendy couldn't count how many times she'd had to hold Johns back from pummeling him in the Mess Hall. Even Michaels had threatened to reprogram the Senior Cadet's assigned orders after overhearing a few of Boyce's favorite taunts.

Wendy's stomach clenched. Was she strong enough to make captain? She doubted it. Although Johns had been kidding, he was right—Wendy was dismally behind in Sport. Tech wasn't her strongest suit either. She just happened to be lucky enough to have the Gandalf of tech as a best friend. To be a leader, you had to be the best. Wendy was good—she knew that—

but she had a long way to go. She had been waiting for a captain's position to open forever, but now that the opportunity was here, she felt horribly under-qualified.

She was so caught up in her thoughts that she didn't realize she had reached the Admiral's Quarters until one of the officers posted outside stopped her.

"Name?"

Wendy saluted. "Senior Cadet-Commander Wendy Darling. Requesting an audience with Admiral Toussant."

The Officer nodded and stepped out of the doorway. "Darling. Yes. The Admiral is expecting you." He knocked to announce her entrance, then pressed the door open, sending her to the Admiral.

10

"Come in Darling."

Wendy hustled to present herself to her commanding officer.

"Prompt as always." Admiral Toussant appraised her before lowering her eyes to a file on her desk. Wendy's stomach lurched. Her Brigadierre File. Such a small thing to hold such significance. It was unsettling to think her whole future rested inside. And her whole past. After all, if she wasn't awarded the Captaincy, what was the point of being at the Academy? More than a decade of her life wasted.

The Admiral coughed, tearing Wendy's attention from the daunting manila envelope. Wendy looked at her, admiring the smart way she wore her uniform. The crisp white linen was a stark contrast against her dark brown skin and all her decorative pins were placed evenly apart, perfectly spaced and aligned. It was a level of organization Wendy only hoped to achieve. She had to clasp her hands tighter to keep from self-consciously smoothing her own appearance.

"You wanted to see me, Admiral?" Wendy cleared her throat, cursing the shake that took hold of her voice. She needed to show she could command authority. Trembling like a shy schoolgirl wouldn't help her.

If Toussant noticed, she didn't let on. "I did. As you are aware, Captain Oswald is retiring at the end of the month, and we have been looking to fill the vacant position."

Wendy nodded, not trusting her voice to cooperate. A tiny pulse throbbed at her wrist and she clamped her hand over her scanband to keep Nana silent.

"Several Senior Cadets have been placed under consideration. We have long deliberated over the decision. Appointing officers to command my army is *not* something I take lightly. I have read your file several times now, and I have to say, I'm impressed. Your aptitude results set high expectations when you enlisted, but aptitude is not always everything…"

The admiral trailed off as she read a page with a wallet-sized photo of a six-year-old Wendy stapled to the top. Wendy shifted uncomfortably. She'd heard rumors about aptitude burnouts, but had never met one. Part of her had thought they were bogeyman stories the Commandants made up to frighten recruits. It had worked. In her time at the Academy, one of her greatest fears had become receiving dismissal papers. In fact, during times of high stress, she had a recurring nightmare where Boyce handed her a huge pile before cackling evilly and transforming into her mother, who fell on the floor in inconsolable sobs, lamenting her failures. Picturing the image now sent a chill down Wendy's spine.

"In your case, however"—the Admiral leveled a shrewd glance at Wendy— "it seems aptitude has paid off. You have the highest marks of any of our recruits in both Offensive and Defensive Tactics. Your marksmanship with weaponry is commendable, and I've watched you fly on several occasions—the Nebula SimCup tournament was especially thrilling. And all your instructors sing your praises. I was even given a glowing, albeit *unrequested* letter of recommendation by one of your peers."

The Admiral smiled wryly and revealed a loose page from the envelope. From where she stood, Wendy made out Johns' cramped handwriting. Her jaw dropped.

"I apologize, Admiral, I—"

Wendy stuttered over Johns' audacity and made a mental note to thrash him later. Toussant, however, let out a throaty laugh before continuing.

"Don't worry Darling. Senior Cadet Johns made it *quite* clear that you were unaware of his contribution. However, it was one of my deciding factors. Being able to elicit that sort of loyalty from your peers—now *your crew*—is an invaluable skill for a Captain. Your men must trust you implicitly and be willing to put their lives on the line for you. Loyalty is not something that can be bought."

Wendy flushed. The Admiral was right. Loyalty was invaluable in a crew. She was embarrassed she had never thought about it that way. She had been taught her whole life that relationships came secondary to training, beginning with her parents.

Admiral Toussant leveled a steely gray gaze at Wendy. "After much consideration, and several glowing recommendations, I have decided I would like to appoint you, Darling. That is, if you think you can handle it."

Wendy balked, but mercifully, her voice held. "It would be an honor, Admiral. I can think of no greater privilege than to serve the Brigade."

"Wonderful. In that case, consider this your official notification of promotion." Toussant rose to stand beside her desk, tapping her head in the official Brigade Salute. "We will make a formal announcement soon, but effective immediately, you are now Captain Wendy Darling, First Class of the Londonierre Brigade. Congratulations and Godspeed."

Wendy mimicked the action, a silly grin spread across her face contradicting the gut-wrenching twist in her stomach as her mind whirred with a million different thoughts.

"Thank you, Admiral. I'm honored. I will do my best to fulfill my duty to Queen, country, and Brigade."

The Admiral smiled as her head dipped in quick acknowledgment before dropping her hand.

"That's enough formality. We have bigger things to attend to. As I'm sure you are aware, I'm issuing the promotion earlier than intended."

Wendy nodded. "Yes, Admiral. I was under the impression the announcement would be made in two weeks' time."

"Indeed. However, certain events have transpired that have... *accelerated* our course of action." She retrieved a small controller from inside her desk. "We received a strange transmission a little over a week ago. It came in over our communications satellite during a regular news broadcast. It sent the station into quite a fit."

Wendy remembered when that had happened. She had been watching the early report after her morning run when the screen blipped to a cartoon man holding a sign promising the station would return. After a few moments, it had refocused on a red-faced anchorman and the show had continued as normal. She'd thought it strange but hadn't considered it since.

"Of course, once we recovered the recording, we had to verify its authenticity. We've had a specialized tech team working tirelessly to decode the signal. Your cohort Michaels was the one who secured our access." She winked. "I'm not surprised. Excellence usually keeps similar company."

Wendy grinned, thrilled at the unexpected compliment.

The Admiral swiveled her chair to face the large portrait of the Brigade's founding fathers. She clicked a small button on her remote and the picture faded to a black screen. Another click and a fuzzy image of a person edged into focus. After a minute, the picture adjusted—although snowy white flecks continued to flurry across the screen—and Wendy saw that it was, in fact, a man. An attractive man. Wendy squinted, trying to make out his features hidden behind the crackling snow. He was tall—or so she imagined, since his head brushed the top of the screen. He had short dark hair that fell in soft waves, providing a stark contrast to his sharp nose and jawline.

What most caught her attention, however, were his eyes. They were piercing blue, and profoundly sad, as if he bore the weight of the world on his shoulders. She looked closer, a sense of familiarity drawing her in, but before she placed it, the screen spat again, hiding the man behind a sheet of white.

"The recording was corrupted," Admiral Toussant explained. "We were unable to salvage all of it, but we garnered enough. Keep watching."

Wendy returned her attention to the screen. The man was speaking—at least, that's what she assumed. His lips moved, but no audio came through. As he spoke, he raised his hand to scratch his face, and Wendy realized it wasn't a hand, but a poorly manufactured cybernetic appendage. The machinery was old and clunky, and it made the man's every movement awkward.

She wondered how that had happened. If he was part of the Brigade, he wouldn't have been cleared to fly the vessel. Still, she couldn't shake the sense of familiarity. But she didn't know how that was possible. He wasn't from the Academy, and that was the only home she'd known for the past ten years. A loud rasp of static exploded and the video cleared, accompanied by a burst of audio.

"... *we were in the middle of our exploratory voyage through the Krawk Nebula when our ship experienced power failure. We drifted too close to a nearby planet and were pulled into its gravitational field. The* Roger *went down. As luck would have it, the ship retained its structural integrity and is now serving as our home base. Most the crew sustained only minor injuries. Unfortunately, several were lost. We have determined the atmosphere is compatible with our biological composition and thus has been habitable. From what we have seen, the planet is similar in composition to Earth, with both land and water bodies. The crew has been working diligently to accrue all the data we can about the planet, and will continue to do so."*

There was another click as Admiral Toussant paused the message. Wendy gaped at the frozen screen. There was no way the transmission could be real. But as she stared at the man's dark features, from his steel-gray eyes to midnight hair, she realized the dashing figure before her was the same one she'd revered for ages.

Wendy jerked her head back to the Admiral so fast she was surprised she didn't give herself whiplash.

"Admiral, is that—" She flushed, unable to vocalize her thoughts. Though her eyes told her what she was seeing was real, her brain—something she believed much more in—screamed its impossibility.

The Admiral's lips quirked in a knowing half-smile. "Yes, Captain?"

Wendy stalled, her eyes wide. The transmission had been received from the Krawk Nebula, just like the other discrepancies she had reported, and it had been sent by Captain Hooke.

She had been right.

"James Tiberius Hooke," Toussant finished for her, drawing Wendy from her thoughts. She peered at the man now visible behind the electronic snow. "Captain of the *Jolly Roger*, sent to explore the Krawk Nebula in the summer of 2291. Communications with whom were lost in the subsequent fall."

Wendy stepped forward in awe, drawn toward the mysterious Captain. Her eyes raked the screen, recalling all of his accomplishments and adventures. A low buzz pulsed through her fingertips and she blinked, noticing her hand pressed against his lips. Her cheeks blazed, and she whirled to face the Admiral.

"Admiral, that mission launched over a hundred years ago!" Wendy studied the handsome Captain as she struggled to make sense of what she was hearing. "The *Jolly Roger* has been missing for decades! This can't be Captain Hooke. It has to be a hoax."

Toussant's eyes sparkled. "That's what we thought, too. But our tech team validated the transmission. It's legitimate."

Wendy studied the Admiral's stony expression. There was no way Toussant would disclose all her intel in such an informal briefing. There had to be more to the transmission than she was letting on. If Toussant trusted it, there was good reason.

"Is there anything else I need to know, Admiral?" Wendy tried to disguise her eagerness, but the tremor in her voice betrayed her.

The Admiral grinned. With another click of her remote, Hooke resumed his hurried speech.

"So far, the strangest phenomena is how time manifests itself on the planet. The days run longer, as do the nights. I'd estimate we have been here for ten earth years, and yet, I look the same as the day we left. It's as if not a single day has gone by. It is this effect on the aging process that has inspired the name we've assigned the planet. We call it Neverland."

11

THE PIRATE SHIP

PETER

"He got a transmission out." Peter stabbed his hands through his hair. "*How* did he get a transmission out?"

He ignored the boys' confused mumbles as he scanned the records. It wasn't just any transmission. The read said the message was over fifteen minutes long. He could only imagine what lies Hooke had cast to the universe in that time.

Tinc flittered in front of his face, sparking wildly.

"I didn't think it was possible either." He squeezed his palms against his forehead. "But now we know he's done it, we can figure out what the message said. Good thing I checked the transmissions."

Tinc paused midair, then buzzed between his eyes before making a rude gesture and shooting to the tree branch above him.

"Yes, Tinc. I know you helped," he grumbled as he tried to figure out the best way to break in. "Don't be like that."

Tinc's only reply was another series of rude comments. He was glad the boys couldn't understand what she said. If Peter had remembered his mother, he might have been offended.

"What are we going to do, Peter?" Curly asked.

"Tinc and I are gonna sneak onboard and see if we can crack the transmissions log." Peter formed the plan as he spoke. "It'll be tricky, and we'll probably need a diversion…"

"I can help!" Tootles volunteered.

"All right." Peter waved the boys over into a huddle. "Tootles, you and Nibs will come with us. Do you have any Nibblers with you?"

Nibs nodded and pulled back his jacket to show three tiny bombs nestled into the coat's inner lining. "Been wanting to use these beauties for a while." He smiled, patting the nesting weapons.

"Slightly, Curly, I need you two to plant tripwires so if the others come back, we'll know before they're on top of us. Once you're done, find a place to hide and keep a lookout."

Curly gulped and Slightly slapped him on the back.

"Straighten up, Curly, green ain't your color." He nudged Curly in the back before saluting Peter. "You got it, Cap."

"All right then. Twins, you two see if you can track down any of the pirates and figure out what they're up to. Got it?"

The Twins high fived and straightened each other's caps as they snickered, crushing identical strands of sandy-blond hair over the other's ears.

"Between all of us, we should gather some good intel today. If anything happens and you get split up, go back to the fort. This isn't a game. Don't be bringing your mam's with you—"

"Curly." Nibs snickered under his breath. Curly frowned and slugged him in the thigh. Nibs fell forward, cursing as he rubbed the charlie horse in his leg. The others laughed until Peter's fierce look quieted their hoots.

"We'll meet up in a few hours," he said. "Don't get caught."

The boys whooped and ran toward their charges, leaving Peter to grab Tootles by the collar before the younger boy dashed off and left Nibs behind.

"Hold on, dummy." He chuckled at the boy's enthusiasm. "You're gonna get caught before you even get on the ship."

Peter ruffled Tootles' golden hair, reminded of how young he was. With the way he acted and how smart he was, sometimes Peter forgot he had only been twelve when the *Roger* had gone down. Tootles raised his head, revealing his chipper smile.

"Here's the plan." Peter lowered his scanner so Nibs and Tootles could see. "We're gonna sneak in through the loading dock—it looks like that's the easiest access." He pressed his finger against the entry point on the screen. "Then Tinc and I are gonna head through cargo down into the Main Bay. From there, we'll work our way to the Captain's Quarters." He trailed his finger along the path so the boys had a visual.

"With the pirates gone, it should only take a few minutes to get in and find a place to hide." He looked at the two boys. "You guys are going to hang out here until we get in. Once Tinc and I are set, you'll distract the Captain. Set off a couple of Nibblers, start a fire—I don't know. Something that will get both Smee *and* Hooke's attention. If they figure out what we're doing, we'll never find out what the transmission said. Hooke will destroy it."

"Yes, sir."

Peter nodded, proud of the resilience etched into their faces. They might have been volunteered to the Brigade, but they had warrior hearts.

"Give us five minutes, then get to it. We aren't going to have any way to signal you, so pay attention. As soon as you hear someone coming, you run. Find Curly and Slightly and take them too." Peter looked directly at Tootles. "Don't wait for us. Get out and back to the treehouse. Got it?"

Tootles blinked, his brown eyes wide with innocence. The bottom of his lip puckered, but he nodded.

Satisfied, Peter squeezed their shoulders. "All right, you two, make it good. Give 'em hell."

Nibs retrieved a Nibbler from his pocket and held up the tiny device, grinning mischievously. "The codfish won't know what hit him," he said, his tawny eyes brightened, contrasting starkly against his dark skin.

Satisfied, Peter turned to the bot perched on his shoulder. "Well Tinc, looks like it's just me and you."

Tinc jangled breezily, then jetted toward the door. Peter hustled behind, using her processor to light the way. He took it as a good sign when he got to the loading dock and saw it had been left ajar. Hooke's men must be getting fed up with the search.

Peter hurried through, following Tinc to cargo, eager to reach the cover of the ship. He kicked himself as they ran past the supply shelves and saw all the everything the pirates weren't using. Especially the tech. There was so much he could have used that the pirates had left to accumulate dust. He should have told Tootles to sweep the shelves while they waited. Realizing his pace was slowing, Peter scowled and yelled at himself to keep moving. The pirates might come back any second. They needed to get in and out fast.

Peter pressed on, through familiar halls and rooms. As much as it pained him to admit, the *Roger* was the first place that had ever felt like home. It was part of the reason he'd kept her running so smoothly. They spoke the same language. He followed Tinc as she zigzagged past the crew's quarters, the mess, and the mechanics bay. Again, Peter struggled to not duck into his old stomping grounds. Not being able to visit his old tinkerings hurt his heart. His steps slowed, and Tinc was in his face, sparking furiously as she scolded him to hurry up.

"Ok, Tinc. I got it." He threw a longing look at his old bay, then sighed and hurried on. Tinc was right—they needed to make it to the Captain's Quarters before Tootles and Nibs' distraction started. It wouldn't do them any good if the diversion got them caught.

"We won't find cover in the hallway, Tinc. Our best bet is to lie low in the kitchen until Hooke and Smee leave. Hopefully whatever Nibs has planned works."

A large explosion sounded down the halls, sending a jolt through the *Roger*. It wasn't strong enough to knock Peter off his feet, but the hanging pots swayed, and a few of the larger pans fell from the racks. Before they settled, another tremor shuddered through the ship, followed by another.

"Damn it all!" Hooke's shout curdled through the corridor. "Smee! What's the meaning of this?"

His voice grew louder as he tore down the hallway, searching for the source of the offense. Peter had just enough time to duck behind the door before Hooke stormed into the main hallway with his First Mate on his heels.

"I'm not sure, Captain." Smee trailed after Hooke, straightening the Captain's jacket as the furious pirate stormed down the corridor. His joints creaked as he gave chase, making Peter wonder the last time the poor synth had been serviced.

"There better not be anything wrong with my ship, Smee," the Captain growled. "I don't have time to worry about her falling apart. The Shadow is coming, and the natives are organizing. Those damned Starchasers are always interfering—"

Peter strained to hear, but Hooke's words were lost as he stormed down the hall.

"Starchasers? Wonder what that was about," he murmured.

Tinc responded with a quick buzz and shot out from behind the door to Hooke's quarters.

"Yeah, yeah. Add it to the list," Peter muttered, chasing after her. First things first, he knew, but he couldn't shake the cold chill that bloomed in his chest.

Outside the Captain's Quarters, Peter pressed his palm against the access panel, but it beeped angrily at him. Access denied. Peter checked his scanner. If he overrode the coding, he could disable it, but it would leave a print. A simple diagnostic would show it had been hacked, and it wouldn't take long for Hooke to figure out who it was. The natives weren't exactly tech-savvy.

Tinc bobbed around Peter's head, showering him in golden sparks.

"Cut it out, Tinc, I'm thinking," he snapped. Tinc's sparks turned fiery red as she yelled through her static.

"All right, all right, I'm sorry!" He typed in a quick code to initialize the hack. If he had more time, he could have found a cleaner route in, but that wasn't an option.

"Remind me to auto-configure your language coding, Tinc," he muttered as he studied the screen. "You've got a potty mouth."

The bot responded with a very unladylike buzz and rocketed down the hall to make sure Hooke and Smee weren't on their way back.

Peter typed in the last character for the sequence and the panel flashed green before the doors slid open. He beelined to the navigation panel.

Hooke's room hadn't changed much. Maps still sprawled across the Captain's desk, but now they were all hand drawn graphics that showed the layout of Neverland. Peter examined them, surprised at the accuracy of Hooke's charting. If he wanted to, he could have pinpointed the boys' treehouse. He wondered how long the map had taken Hooke to draft. His snooping was cut short when Tinc swooped into the room and landed on his shoulder. Peter turned to the comms board. If a transmission had gone out, any remaining records would be here.

"Talk to me." Peter linked his scanner to the networking. "What's James been up to?"

The machine whirred under Peter's coded instructions. After a moment of processing, a wall of script stacked across the screen, listing all of Hooke's attempted transmissions until reaching the last. Peter selected the details then keyed in another command. The screen pulsed as the device worked to recover the embedded transmission.

"Hold on to your hats..." Peter murmured. If his hack worked, Hooke's message would soon be downloaded onto his handheld.

The screen flickered and Hooke's image pushed through a flurry of static.

"Greetings. My name is Captain James Tiberius Hooke of the Londonierre Expeditionary Fleet. My crew and I were tasked with journeying into the Uncharted Sector to explore unidentified areas in the Krawk Nebula. We launched 23 June, 2291. At approximately 0445 on 7 August, a systems error severely impacted our navigational mainframe as well as several smaller mainframes. Dead in the air, we were pulled into the gravitational field of a nearby planet. The Roger went down..."

Peter pocketed his scanner with a growl. So, that's how Hooke was spinning it. He was surprised he hadn't reported Peter's sabotage. He supposed having to admit the defection of multiple crew members could bring some uncomfortable questions James' way. But that was a problem to deal with later—approaching footsteps warned him Hooke was back.

"...and tell those codfish if they aren't back by then, they'll be keelhauled against the *Roger*."

Peter cut the transmission and stuffed his scanner into his cargos as he searched the room for a place to hide. The only reasonable option was the tall wardrobe across the navigation panel. Peter buried himself behind stacks of Hooke's uniforms. Tinc perched beside him, shining to light his view, revealing the shape of the room through the delicate crosshatching carved into the armoire doors.

"How many jackets can he possibly need?" Peter griped. Tinc buzzed at him to be quiet. He bit a smart retort as he strained to hear the pirates.

"But Captain," the First Mate stammered, betraying the frustration under his prim facade. "You sent them to search for the Shadow. They're all the way out at t—"

"I don't care how far out they are! Fat and lazy, the lot!" Hooke raged. "Besides, the ship could use a good cleaning. The blasted sea-rats have gotten out of hand again. And have them—" He stopped mid-sentence when he reached the gaping doors still operating under Peter's manual override. Peter hadn't bothered to shut them because he'd planned on being gone before the Captain returned. Hooke wouldn't even need a diagnostic to tell him there had been an intruder. Peter had done it for him.

Hooke peered in, his steely eyes scanning the room for signs of a disturbance. Peter wasn't sure if it was the dim lighting in the room or the shadows cast by the heavy coats in the armoire, but the pirate looked older than he remembered. His shoulders and face were sunken in, but he stormed around the room with the same dangerous determination that had earned him his rank a lifetime ago. His mechanized limb flexed absently as he walked—the tech's way of ensuring the gears didn't seize—a passable prosthetic, but the fixture was awkward and bulky, a poor replacement for the Captain's own hand.

Peter mentally berated himself as he watched Hooke's good arm whip to stop Smee from walking farther into the open room.

"Looks like the rats have found their way into my ship." Hooke's szikra sang as he ripped the conductor from its sheath. "Scurrying around where they don't belong."

"But Captain, it is highly improbable that the sea-rats could reach this far without water." Smee's mechanical eyes flashed as he scanned the room for evidence of an infestation.

Hooke shot Smee a withering glare before his mechanical fingers pressed to his brow with a rusty creak.

"Never mind that! Check the navigation panel!" The bite in the Captain's tone snapped Smee to attention and the slender synth hurried to the oversized panel. Behind him, Hooke ventured into the room, scanning the area warily. His eyes fell on the wardrobe, and he grinned wickedly as he stalked toward it, a cat bearing down on a trapped mouse. Peter held his breath.

"Captain!" Smee's outburst pulled Hooke's attention from the wardrobe. Peter let out an inaudible sigh of relief.

"What is it, Smee?"

Peter gritted his teeth. Nearsighted though he was, there was no way the First Mate wouldn't notice the reading on the screen.

"Someone has been in your transmissions." Smee's golden eyes illuminated to peer through the reports Peter retrieved. "It seems they were trying to access the recordings." His brow dipped, giving him a very human appearance as he followed the electronic bread crumbs Peter had stupidly left behind.

"Captain…" He peered at Hooke under his dusty brows. "It appears they got it."

"What?" Hooke stormed to where Smee hovered, pointing out the reading on the screen.

"Here." He tapped the screen, sending a spark of static from his metallic finger into the antiquated machine. "It looks like they were trying to download our records."

Hooke's brow furrowed as he read the report himself. His prosthetic hand scraped the glass as it followed the text, setting Peter's skin crawling.

"Download completed." He rapped his faux appendage against the screen in frustration, then paused. "But wait, look at this." The screen clanked as Hooke punched the final message with his finger. "The download just finished. That scan can't be more than five minutes old." He stormed back over to the dresser. "Which means they're still here."

12

Hooke wrapped his metal appendage around the wardrobe's handle. Watching through the crosshatching, Peter studied the bunching wrinkles surrounding the Captain's face as he reached for his dagger. He raised it above his shoulder, straining to move silently against the hanging clothes. Hooke pulled on the handle and Peter bunched his muscles, preparing his body to attack.

"Here mousey," Hooke crooned. "Come out, come out wherever you are."

He flung the door wide and raised his szikra, poised to strike. The conductor flashed, sending a live current crackling to life. As soon as the light hit the wardrobe's interior, Tinc careened into his face, blinding him with her sparking ambush. Hooke cried in surprise as red-hot embers burned his skin. Seizing his chance, Peter barreled out of the wardrobe. Smee lunged for him, but a forceful shove sent the rusty pirate stumbling over his own feet.

He grabbed the Captain's desk to steady himself as he fell, drawing Peter's attention to the maps sitting on top. In a brazen move, Peter reached over the first mate and snatched Hooke's chart off the desk.

His jerky motion knocked over an ornate pillar that looked like an altar sitting beside the desk. Hooke stiffened as it clattered against the ground, filling the room with a hollow, haunting ring. The unnatural sound sent chills through Peter's spine, but he hurried on, stuffing the stolen chart into his gray jumpsuit as he bolted into the corridors of the *Jolly Roger*. Tinc was at his side, buzzing in his ear.

"Nice job Tinc," he panted. "You saved my neck back there!"

Tinc jangled back at him, then put on a burst of speed to guide him through the darkened halls. They hurried along, with the angry shouts of Hooke and Smee closing in on them from behind.

"We're almost out," he shouted when the nanobot stopped to wait for him. "Go, I'll catch you!" He was about to drop to the beach when a vise-like grip clamped his shoulder.

"And where do ye think yer going, boy?"

Noodler hurried to where Peter hung in Cecco's grip. The wizened man laughed through his toothless grin. Peter jerked his arm, but the pirate held tight. Wicked laughter surrounded him as the rest of the crew circled, trapping him in their ranks.

"Been causing trouble for the Cap'n ye have." Noodler's cough shot saliva into Peter's face. "Wonder how he'll reward us for bringing ye in."

The pirates' laughter grew more sinister as they tightened their barricade.

Peter whirled around, searching for a plan. He had been in plenty of situations like this before. On the sketchy streets of New London, tight scrapes were a daily occurrence—between pinching food, picking pockets, and dodging the cops, you learned to be quick on your feet. But surrounded by a dozen brandished weapons, he had to admit, even he was feeling claustrophobic.

"Listen fellas." Peter's brain whirred to wheedle himself out of the mess.

He was robbed of his smart remark when a small brown ball rolled past the circle of men, landing between his feet. Streaming wisps of smoke escaped from a tiny seam as it rocked in bobbed along the sand. The wisps merged and bloomed until smoke poured out, sending the little ball spinning with the force of the steam. It spun faster and faster, emitting a loud whistle through the smoke. The pirates gaped at the tiny device, openmouthed. Leaving Peter with Cecco, Noodler leaned forward to examine the agitated toy. He shrieked in rage when a loud pop shot a stream of sparks from the Nibbler and covered his face with flecks of fire.

"Get it off, get it off!" he roared, smacking the embers from his nose. The pirates scattered, scurrying away from the contraption. The smoke plumed into a black cloud surrounding them, adding to the confusion, but Cecco held tight. Peter struggled, but the pirate outweighed him, trapping him until a dull thud sounded and Cecco's grip loosened as the pirate staggered back, disoriented.

"C'mon, Peter!"

Tootles rushed through the smoke. He held a shovel in one hand, and tugged Peter's now free hands with the other. He was breathing heavily.

"Hurry, before they see us!"

"Remind me never to get on your bad side, Tootles." Peter laughed as he ruffled the boy's golden hair. "I don't think my head could take it."

Tootles flushed, but pulled Peter's hand again to urge him forward. The chaos he and Nibs had created wouldn't last.

They shot into the jungle, pushing through the brush and hanging branches as the murderous shouts of angry pirates chased after them. Tootles led the way until they met Nibs and Tinc hiding behind a fallen tree.

"Down here, Peter!" Tootles pulled back an overgrown bush, revealing a neatly concealed hideaway hole. Peter slid into the break in the ancient trunk.

They huddled together, fighting to catch their breath. The shouts of the pirates drew closer, and Peter's chest tightened as he held his breath. His lungs screamed in protest at the sudden deprivation of oxygen, but he ignored it as the pirates' boots thundered over their tree.

"Hooke's gonna be furious if he finds out we lost 'em," Bill Jukes' high tenor echoed through the cavernous trunk. Gruff voices murmured in agreement.

"Wait." Noodler's rasp halted the footsteps above them. Peter grimaced and reached for his dagger. Beside him, Tinc wound herself into a tizzy, and held his hand to stop her. They hadn't been found yet. "Hold on."

Noodler dropped from top of the tree and crept to a large boulder in front of them. He ran his hands along the stone, then whirled around to his comrades, pale.

"Stjarnin," he whispered, right before an arrow pierced Bill Jukes' heart.

The other pirates stumbled backward, retreating to the safety of the *Roger*. Furious war cries chased after them, followed by the sound of arrows thumping into the surrounding trees.

A whimper escaped Tootles' throat. Even Nibs' smirk disappeared, darkening his confident features.

"Don't move," Peter mouthed.

The noise around them died down until the jungle was still. Peter's heart slowed, but he held the boys back. They sat in silence for several moments more, listening and waiting. When nothing happened, Peter signaled to move. He went first, cursing his size as the bark groaned and snapped when he squeezed through. He froze, waiting to see if the noise had drawn any attention. When nothing happened, he waved Tootles through.

A loud crack echoed through the clearing as a branch snapped and a heavy net dropped, trapping them against the ground. As soon as they were caught, victorious whoops echoed from the canopy above them.

Peter struggled against the cording, but it was too strong. The fibers were heavy and sharp, and the more he fought, the tighter the bands wrapped around his body. If he kept it up, he wouldn't be able to move at all. He swore, and dropped his cheek to the ground, feeling the cool earth against his face. He saw Tinc buzzing furiously around the log, screaming at Nibs to attack.

"No," he hissed. "Stand down." She responded with a vulgar suggestion for where Peter should go, and he clenched his teeth. Now was not the time for sassy nanobots. "Get the boys. Tell them what happened."

Tinc's wings fluttered sadly as the Stjarnin surrounded Peter, but she obediently let Nibs scoop her up. It was the last thing Peter saw before everything went dark.

13

COME AWAY, COME AWAY

PETER

Admiral Toussant paused the transmission. Wendy used the silence to process the debriefing. Hooke and his crew, proclaimed lost in space and assumed dead one hundred years ago, were alive and well, albeit, stranded on an unknown planet.

Neverland, he had called it. But the Captain only thought he'd lost ten years. How would he react, she wondered, if he found out it was more?

"What does this mean, Admiral?"

"This means, Darling, we now have an emergency rescue and retrieval mission. One *you* will be placed in charge of."

Wendy's eyes rounded as a million questions ran wild through her mind, but she forced her face into a neutral expression.

"Admiral?"

The Admiral chuckled. "You must be wondering why the Fleet decided to send such a green crew." She studied Wendy's reaction before continuing. "There was quite a debate about whether or not you would be the correct choice, but there was one factor in particular that benefited you."

Admiral Toussant moved to Wendy's file. She flipped the pages until she found what she was looking for, and revealed a collated, bound report emblazoned with Wendy's name.

"Some time back, a brilliant cadet submitted a report suggesting there might be Fleet activity hidden in the Krawk Nebula. Back then, her advice was disregarded." She pierced Wendy with her onyx gaze. "I don't like making the same mistakes twice."

Wendy's jaw dropped, but she quickly fixed it.

"Thank you, Admiral. It's a great honor."

Toussant gave her a warm smile before returning to business. "I understand it is a rather large task. However, given your history, I am confident in your ability to complete the mission." She returned Wendy's report and dropped to her seat, clasping her hands over her desk.

"Hooke's transmission provided additional details on the planet they have landed on. It seems they have run into some trouble. This is information you will need going into your mission. Are you ready to proceed?"

Wendy hesitated. She felt slightly overwhelmed, but to be a good Captain, she needed to handle anything thrown at her. If she couldn't take the stress of a simple debriefing, there was no way she would stand the pressure weighting a rescue mission.

"Yes, Admiral." She spoke her resolve into the world. "Please, continue."

The gleam in Toussant's eyes sparked again. She pressed her device once more, and Hooke's frozen body jumped back to life.

"From what we have seen, Neverland runs parallel to Earth's life systems. The atmosphere is stable enough to support ocean, plant, and animal life. It has two light sources, the brightest being the Second Star. It shines constantly, casting the night in the faintest green.

"Already, we have come in contact with several alien life forms. They vary in stages of intelligence, the majority display animalistic tendencies. There is one exception; a group of aliens bearing humanoid resemblance. Unfortunately, we have been unable to learn much about these people, as all interactions have been extremely hostile. We must be ever vigilant as they are thoroughly displeased by our presence here.

"My men have persevered, but we ache for home. I myself find it difficult to find the enthusiasm to carry on in this fashion. I pray this transmission finds those sympathetic to our cause. For Queen and country, signing off, and Godspeed."

There was a soft blip and the transmission faded to black, leaving the image of Hooke burned in Wendy's mind. Her heart wrenched as she thought of the pain Hooke—and his crew—must have endured these passing years. And with no one to even be thinking of them! Moisture brushed her cheeks as she blinked, surprised to find tears collected in her eyes. She forced a cough to avert her gaze from the Admiral's watchful stare.

"That is all the information as we have to date. We will launch as soon as possible. The ship and crew—*your* ship and crew—have already been selected. Once assignments are issued, you will have twenty-four hours to prepare for launch. Do you understand?"

Wendy nodded. It wasn't much time, but she didn't have many people to notify. Her parents would need to be informed, but a simple comm would suffice. She would miss Johns and Michaels more than either of them. "Yes, Admiral."

"Excellent. I knew we could count on you." Toussant extended her hand. Wendy gripped it firmly and gave a quick shake. "Of course, we are interested in gaining as much intel as possible on this *Neverland,* but that is not your priority. You will be accompanied by a specialist whose mission will be research acquisition. I expect you to assist him when possible, but, above all else, this is a rescue. And a rather significant one at that. Bring our boys home."

Wendy left the Admiral's office in a rush of adrenaline. She was given her new uniform—a dark black pantsuit in stark contrast to her heather gray Commander's suit—and instructed to meet Admiral Toussant in the Command Room promptly at 13:00. From there, her formal promotion would be recorded and broadcast over the Academy Comms System. There was not time to organize a full event, but Wendy was grateful. Now she wouldn't have to suffer through the pomp and circumstance. A video broadcast would be just fine.

After the ceremony was filmed, Wendy was instructed to remain in the Command Room to meet with her crew for their first official debriefing. At precisely 14:00, she stood at the head of the long mahogany conference table. The dark, banded collar of her captain's jacket was tight against her neck, but otherwise, the tightly tailored suit was comfortable.

Clasped behind her back, her hands twisted together as she bounced on her heels, full of nervous energy. Her crew would arrive in fifteen minutes. Admiral Toussant had informed her it would be a skeleton crew, comprised of only the best Academy recruits, but she had not disclosed their identities.

So Wendy waited, scanning the roster of Senior Cadets, weighing their strengths and weaknesses to place them in advance. She knew who she hoped to be on her team.

Johns and Michaels would be ideal. As much as Wendy harassed Johns, he was a skilled fighter and excellent at keeping his head under pressure. He would be a great asset for the reconnaissance portion of the mission. And Michaels was a tech wizard. If anything were to go wrong on the ship, he was the one she wanted to fix it.

She doubted she would be so lucky. The Admiral admitted she knew Wendy was close with both cadets. It was unlikely she would risk her newly appointed captain playing favorites. Not that she would, but Wendy understood being above reproach. Her thoughts continued to swirl as she waited and watched the clock. Finally, it was time.

Wendy smoothed her sleek bun for the thirtieth time and shook out the last of her nerves before re-clasping her hands behind her back and arranging her face in a stoic expression. Best to not show too much emotion. Emotions made people weak. As captain, it was her job to be strong.

The doors slid open, and Admiral Toussant walked in, followed by five familiar cadets, each wearing sharp new commander's gear. Their uniforms were similar to Wendy's, but the coloring was lighter, stone gray with Brigadierre blue banding. They didn't make eye contact until they surrounded the table, each beside an empty chair.

Wendy fought to keep her carefully crafted expression. She had to give it to the Admiral—she had assembled a solid crew. To her left stood a tall girl named Marisa DeLaCruz. Though she was a strong fighter, her true strength was her brain. She was extremely clever and had trained as a Medic, progressing so quickly that she had been permitted to attend Medical School in Cambridge until she'd graduated with her doctorate the previous spring; the youngest cadet to hold such a high title in the history of the Academy.

Beside her stood another girl Wendy recognized from Navigations class. Her name was Dawes—Arielle Dawes—and she was a flight specialist. She was also gorgeous. Her long red hair rested over her shoulder, falling in an intricate fishtail braid. Amazingly, her uniform accentuated her figure. Wendy had never been so lucky. But pretty as she was, Arielle was kind and an unparalleled pilot. Though Boyce had been team captain, it was Dawes who had won the Nebula Tournament. Wendy was glad she would be the one flying beside her.

Wendy moved down the line to where Boyce stood with a very ugly glower on his face. She had to bite her lip to keep from smiling smugly as she remembered his words from earlier that morning. Though she wasn't particularly excited to have to deal with his garbage bag of a personality, even she had to admit Boyce was a good soldier who knew protocol to a T. He was also skilled in diplomacy when he wasn't acting like a complete tool. She understood the value Admiral Toussant saw in him. She issued a polite nod to show she meant no ill will, and continued to her next crew member.

No amount of lip-biting could hide Wendy's smile when she turned to the Commander beside Boyce. Michaels stood at attention, blue eyes bright behind his glasses. His dark wavy hair was smartly styled, and paired with his fitted jacket, he finally looked more like a soldier than a refined hacker.

He flashed a quick thumbs up from where his hand sat at ease. Wendy vaguely wondered if he had doctored the list somehow, but with only five cadets selected, the Admiral would have caught the switch. Not that she would have put it past him. Assuming he was just a computer geek, people often underestimated Michaels and left him to his own devices. Really, he was quite sneaky, and used their ignorance to his advantage.

But happy as she was to see Michaels, nothing could compare to Johns' beaming grin as he saluted her, proud as any brother could ever be. He smiled so big, his cheekbones pressed into the corners of his eyes, crinkling them so he almost squinted. It looked like he was fighting with everything in himself to keep from crossing the room. Wendy smiled back, first at Johns, and then the others.

"At ease, men." She indicated for her team to sit. "We have a lot to talk about."

14

"Darling! I knew you'd get it!" Johns ambushed Wendy outside the sliding doors and scooped her in a hug. He twirled her around so fast he left her dizzy.

Beside them, Michaels initiated a slow clap—an inside joke the three of them shared. She was touched they had waited to meet her.

"You were right," Wendy ceded once her feet were planted back on the ground. She still felt shaky, but was convinced it was more from the day's events than Johns' whirlwind of love.

"Damn right I was right!" Johns and Michaels slapped palms. "I love it when she says those three words." He nudged Wendy in the ribs. "And how about you got promoted to Captain just to lead the coolest mission ever. Good on you!" He ruffled her hair again, and this time Wendy left it for a whole minute before her compulsion to straighten it won out. She was in a very good mood.

Wendy smiled. "Thanks for believing in me. I wouldn't have been able to do it without you—seriously." She remembered the letter Johns had sent the Admiral and gave him a stern look. "A heads up on your recommendation letter would have been nice, though."

Johns burst into a fit of laughter. "She showed you that? Ah man! I told her you'd kill me if you found out I sent it to her." He tapped his chin, feigning pensive. "Huh, an admiral unable to keep state secrets. I wonder how the Fleet's lasted so long…"

Wendy bumped his elbow, forcing him to smack his face. "An unsolicited letter from a Cadet-Commander is highly unlikely to be classified as a state secret, you moron." She flung her arms around them. "Let's get out of here before Johns says something dumb enough to get thrown into solitary confinement." She gave him a pointed look. "*Again.* Besides, I'm starving and someone promised me a celebratory dinner."

"Technically as his supervisor, they'd come after you first," Michaels interjected, his nose buried in his comm. "Then it would be your responsibility to deal with the matter." He typed furiously in code. It looked alien to Wendy. She didn't even know comms could do that, but then Michaels had always worked tech magic.

Wendy groaned. "Well, in that case, let's move faster. It's a big base, and Johns has a lot of stupid."

"Hey!" Johns protested.

Wendy laughed and led them down the hall. "Oh, come on, you know I love you."

"*Sure*, now we've gotten you promoted to Captain. This morning it was all about making me run circuits," Johns muttered good-naturedly.

Wendy rolled her eyes and released her brothers. As Captain, public displays of affection with crew members were probably frowned upon. But that was fine—she was content to walk through the halls, enjoying their unspoken camaraderie.

"How do you survive like this, Darling?" Johns yelled from Wendy's kitchenette as he ransacked her cabinets for snacks.

"It's called nutrition, Johns. You should try it," Wendy muttered, knowing he would still hear her. The Cadet-Commander's rooms were a step up from the standard dorms, but were still designed for efficiency, not comfort.

Each dorm had an identical floorplan—a small kitchenette that contained one tall stand-up cupboard, a sink, and a half-fridge keep a few perishables. Squeezed in, a rectangular table sat against the wall with two chairs, in case of visitors. The Academy was thoughtful that way.

There were two doors in the kitchenette. One led to the bathroom sitting adjacent to it—standard with a shower, toilet, sink, and towel rack—and the other led to the living quarters. The living quarters contained a small desk and bookshelf for the cadets' studies and a rather nice futon that doubled as a convertible bed. A mounted comm screen acted as a personal information center for each cadet. It looped Academy news and schedule updates, but each cadet could use it to access their own personal account for updates on their rankings and health information.

Some cadets liked to decorate their dorms with posters and trinkets from home. While it wasn't technically allowed, it was overlooked as long as the dorms weren't damaged. Wendy's room didn't have any of that. Just standard accommodations. She didn't spend enough time there to bother making it homey. When she was there, she was sleeping or studying. Because of this, her kitchenette was also dismally stocked, as Johns liked to announce whenever he came over.

Wendy just didn't see the point. Breakfast and lunch were provided by the Academy, so she was only responsible for her nighttime meal. Usually, she grilled chicken and boiled a bit of rice to go along with it. It wasn't a culinary treat by any means, but it worked.

"Seriously, Darling. I'm gonna starve." Johns moaned. "I need food."

"Why don't you and Michaels run to the commissary?" Wendy suggested. She handed Johns her golden bitCard. "Take this and get what you want. Just try not to buy out the whole shop."

Johns snatched the bitCard from Wendy's fingers. "Thanks, Mom." He grabbed Michaels by the collar to pull his nose from his comm. "Come on Michaels, you're looking sharp in those Commander threads." He nudged Michaels in the ribs, but his bulk sent the smaller boy off balance. "Maybe if we tell the clerk you're going on a top-secret rescue, you'll score a date."

Michaels gave Johns a withering glare before returning to his code.

"Or not." Johns shrugged and turned to Wendy. "Why don't you come too, Darling? You're the woman of the hour. Hell, they'd probably give you everything free."

Wendy doubted that, and she had no desire to test the theory. "No, you two go. I should notify my parents. They'll be thrilled their investment has paid off." Hard as she tried, she couldn't stifle a grimace at the thought of her mother's reaction.

"Why do you do that to yourself?" Michaels unburied his gaze from his comm, catching Wendy off guard.

"What?"

"Torment yourself over what your parents think? You're basically the dream child, but you bend over backwards trying to meet some impossible standard. Your parents should be proud of you. You can't be perfect. If that's what they want, then maybe they should enroll in the Academy."

Wendy shifted uncomfortably as she tried to figure out how to respond. She never talked about her parents with Michaels or Johns. The only time she mentioned them was when she couldn't politely avoid it.

"They'll never let me live it down if one of their friends hears about the promotion before they do." She sighed, realizing Boyce had probably already notified his father.

Michaels blinked behind his glasses, then returned to his comm. Wendy studied him quietly, noticing the way his fingers flew over the small screen. Johns broke the awkward silence with a change of topic.

"Is there anything you want us to get you while we're out? Water, chocolate, a life?" Johns absently tugged the edges of his Commander's suit, accentuating the perfect fit of its tailoring. He grinned at her as though he knew the dark uniform made him even more devastatingly handsome. There was no way they would survive his ego now. "Seriously. You could be spitting killer game tonight, Darling. Why am I the only one who sees the incredible opportunity in front of us?"

"Probably because you're the biggest manwhore in the Academy," Wendy jabbed, remembering the countless times she had been the mediator between several of his lost love interests. And by mediator, she meant Johns would hide while Wendy covered for him until the poor girl got the hint.

"Darling for the win." Johns faux-staggered to the door. "I can see when I'm not wanted." He sniffled dramatically. "Come on Michaels, let's get out of here. We'll be back when Darling decides to *appreciate* us."

Wendy silenced him with an expertly tossed pillow. It crashed into his face, cutting his sentence off with a loud *thwomp*. "Go get your food. Hunger makes you more stupid than normal."

Johns laughed and pushed Michaels out the door. "We'll be back in a few. Don't miss me too much!"

"Whatever." Wendy chuckled as she lifted her comm off the desk.

It would be at least thirty minutes before they returned, if they didn't get distracted by the other cadets. If she finished her call quickly, she could read up on Hooke's file.

Wendy pulled open the drawer and removed the dossier the Admiral had given her. James Tiberius Hooke. Captain of the *Jolly Roger* until it had disappeared off the face of the universe. Still alive and fighting for his crew. She was determined to bring them home; to save him. Maybe then she could get his haunting blue eyes out of her mind.

Get a hold of yourself, Darling. He's part of the mission.

She shook her head to clear her thoughts. She needed her wits about her to escape her call unscathed. Absently, she wondered if the other cadets had the same anxiety when calling their families. She supposed not. It couldn't be normal to prefer the solace of the Academy over the place she should call home. Either way, it didn't matter.

She sighed, then pressed the button that connected to her parents' home port. There was a small low tone as the devices connected, then Wendy's mother appeared.

15

Wendy had to admit, her mother was beautiful; dainty in a way that Wendy's days in the Academy would never let her be. But she did share the same rich chestnut hair and hazel-green eyes, which were, begrudgingly, two of her best features. Her nose was her father's—so was the heart shape of her face. Both her parents were handsome, like money found money in their relationship, the same rang true for pretty. The combination worked in Wendy's favor. Though she was far from a supermodel, she was pretty in her own right. Not that it mattered. Captain's uniforms didn't require makeup.

"Wendy, darling!" her mother simpered. Wendy heard the tinkle of fine china and soft harp music playing in the background of the airy room she was in. Her mother must be hosting one of her weekly tea parties with her heinous group of well-to-do friends. Boyce's mother was probably there.

Wendy groaned. She didn't need an audience.

"Hello, Mother." She forced her voice a pitch higher than usual in an attempt to keep it pleasant, the way her mother liked. "Is this a bad time? I can comm you later."

"Don't be silly, darling!" It was too late. Her mother's response was too loud, she was projecting. She was already part of a show. Wendy could imagine the conversations that would start after the comm ended.

Oh yes, that was my daughter—the Captain—*calling me from the Academy. See how much we love each other? Yes, we are the perfect family. Enjoy your tea, please, while admiring us.*

Blech.

There was an awkward pause before her mother continued.

"What do you need dear?" Her tone remained light, but her eyes tightened, scolding her.

What do you want? Don't embarrass me in front of my friends!

"Oh! Yes," Wendy cleared her throat. "Is Father there? I would like to tell you together, if possible."

The harp music was overpowered by the whispers and sighs of her unseen audience. No doubt intrigued by what could be so important *both* parents were needed. Probably all imagining the latest scandal. Shared with scathing tones, scandals were exactly what those women thrived on, a reprieve from their plastic lives. Her mother's face clenched to freeze her smile in place.

"Is everything all right, dear?"

It had better be, because if you admit we are less than perfect in front of these women, I will never forgive you.

"Yes. Everything is fine." Wendy struggled to keep the frustration from her voice. She must play her part. Obedient daughter, Academy prodigy, walking, talking doll. "I have news both of you will be eager to hear."

Her mother's brow quirked, the only hint she showed any true interest in what Wendy would share. "I'm sorry, darling, he's at the Rugby Club with the other Board Members. He left about an hour ago and won't be back until about eight." Her voice kept the same airy tone.

See how fancy we are? My husband is a member of the Rugby Club, the most exclusive in West Brighton, and my daughter is calling from the Academy. Have I mentioned the charity scholarship we funded them last year?

"I see. I would like to tell you both at the same time. It is rather important—"

It was the wrong thing to say. The women in the background tutted like chickens, voices raised in speculation. This was turning into quite the show.

"Don't be silly, dear!" Mrs. Darling spoke through her perma-smile.

My friends will pester me to death if you don't spill right now. You should have known better than to call during tea time.

"I'll tell your father when he comes home. We don't want to bother him at the Club."

You aren't important enough to comm while he's smoking with his friends.

Wendy rubbed the headache forming between her brows.

"Of course." She shook her head, brushing off her annoyance. "You will be pleased to know, this afternoon, I was selected to be the newest Captain First Class of the Londonierre Brigade Expeditionary Fleet." She included the full title; her mother's elite friends would eat it up.

Her mother's face brightened to its first genuine smile since she'd answered the comm.

"Oh Wendy, darling! That *is* wonderful news!" She paused, her forehead creasing with the tiniest wrinkle as she considered. "But dear, wasn't a formal ceremony announced? Your father and I would have so loved to attend."

Why were we robbed of the opportunity to show off our daughter, the Captain? Think of how many people we could have impressed!

"It was all rather sudden, or I'm sure the Admiral would have followed traditional protocol." Wendy's voice came out sharper than she intended. Posturing was tiring. "That was the other reason I wanted to speak to Father."

"Oh?"

Tell me now!

"Yes. My promotion came with an assignment. Effective immediately, I'll be leading a small crew on an expeditionary voyage. We depart in twenty-four hours." It was actually less, but Wendy didn't delude herself into thinking her parents would care to visit before she left.

Mrs. Darling's jaw dropped. Behind her, the women at the tea table burst into titters. They sounded like a hive of bees buzzing around a juicy dollop of honey. Wendy was sure this would be big enough news to fodder their gossip fire for at least a week. Maybe more, if her mother played her cards right. *Probably more,* Wendy thought. She knew her mother well.

"So soon, darling! How do they ever expect your father and I to make it down to the Academy in time to give you a proper goodbye? Don't they realize that people schedule appointments months in advance?"

How dare they impose on my social calendar?

"The mission was unscheduled until recently," Wendy floundered to answer her mother's question without giving away too much information. One slip and the whole of West Brighton's upper class would know about the mission to Neverland. "It's nothing major. Just a routine expedition." That might have been a lie, but it was less likely to get Wendy extradited from the Fleet.

"Oh Wendy, this is just all so exciting," her mother breathed. Her eyes flitted to the table clucking with gossip. "I want to hear all about it."

And so do my friends.

"There isn't much to tell." Wendy shifted uncomfortably. The conversation had already lasted longer than she wanted it to. "I'm sure the Admiral will provide leave when I return to compensate. I'm sorry I'll miss your birthday."

"My birthday isn't for another three months, darling. It will be that long?"

"I'm sorry Mother, but that information is classified. Military personnel only."

Mrs. Darling changed tactics. Her voice kept its girlish pitch, but now there was a slight whine threaded through her words. "Certainly they can't expect you to keep your whereabouts from your mother. You are my heart. I'm supposed to know everything about you."

How dare you refuse me in front of my friends? I don't care what the Admiral says.

"I don't think the Fleet sees it that way." Wendy forced a smile over her impatience. "Heart or not, I believe once you enlisted me, my loyalty switched to them."

Mrs. Darling's smile remained, but her pretty eyes sparked. "Well, let's hope you never have a daughter of your own, so she won't be deprived of your love and affections as I so cruelly have been." She gave a theatrical sniff and wiped an imaginary tear at the corner of her eye. Her audience tutted in sympathy.

How could she have such an ungrateful daughter? Shame.

Wendy's gut clenched. She knew her mother was playing her, but guilt wrapped her conscience in a gridlock. She would not reveal the secrets she had been entrusted with—it went against all her training. Still, familiar nausea set in the pit of her stomach.

You're a bad daughter. You aren't good enough. You do not deserve the life you have.

Another loud sniffle drew her attention back to her mother. The pinch in Mrs. Darling's lips betrayed the realization that she didn't have Wendy's full attention, and she was not pleased.

"Since we have nothing else to discuss dear, I really should get back to my guests. I've been quite rude in keeping my attention away from them for so long. I thought speaking with my only daughter—my heart—would be worth it." She looked off screen, refusing to make eye contact with Wendy, and sniffed once more for good measure.

Can't you see how you've hurt me?

Wendy took in a steadying breath. "Of course, Mother. I apologize for taking you from your friends. Please send them my warmest regards."

At this, Mrs. Darling turned toward her friends and beamed.

See how polite my Wendy can be when she isn't acting a complete ingrate?

Wendy waited until she returned her attention to continue. "Please have Father comm if he would like to speak with me directly."

"I'm sure he'll be too busy, dear. You know how his work keeps him."

Don't be stupid—your father doesn't have time for you.

Wendy took in a sharp breath. That stung more than she had anticipated.

"Of course. Please send Father my regards. I'll contact you when I return."

"Yes, darling. Do hurry home, we will miss you so." Sniffle.

See how much I care?

"I will, Mother."

The comm blipped off before the words left Wendy's mouth. She felt as empty as the blank screen in the wall. Talking to her mother always turned her into a nervous wreck. She never second-guessed herself as much as when Mrs. Darling's attention was on her. A single tear traced down her cheek as she dropped to the couch, exhausted.

The door to her dorm opened, and she turned to hide her face.

"Hope you like pork rinds. It's all th—" John's laughter died as he stepped into her dorm. "What's wrong?"

"Nothing." Wendy wiped her cheek to clear the traitorous stain. She reached for the bags weighing down Johns' arms. "What'd you bring me?"

"Oh no you don't." Johns lifted the bags out of reach. "What happened, Darling?"

"Nothing!"

Wendy jumped to grab the bags, but couldn't grab them without bumping into Michaels. He watched her with concern, his blue eyes boring into her. She wondered if his laser focus came from all the hours he spent submerged in tech. Realizing the two weren't going to drop it, she let out an exasperated huff.

"I just had a conversation with She-Who-Will-Not-Be-Named." She tried to conjure one of her mother's plastic smiles to her own face. "I just couldn't hide the tears of joy that came from surviving comm unscathed." She forced a toothy smile, hoping to convince them to drop it.

Johns seemed skeptical, but slowly lowered his arms. "And what lovely things did She-demort have to say this time?"

"Oh, the usual. Parties, clubs, busy, busy, busy." Wendy waved her hand but heard the bitterness coloring her tone. Johns rolled his eyes and stormed to the kitchen.

"I don't get why you even bother talking to her. It just upsets you." He banged around, pulling out the few bowls and serving plates she owned for his jumbled feast.

"Because she's my mother," Wendy said. She turned to Michaels for backup, but he studied her in silence. It was amazing how she felt more psychoanalyzed by the tech-guy than she ever hadid any Academy counselor. She smoothed her hair and gave him a small, but genuine smile. He blinked and dropped his gaze to his comm.

"You know, after birth, baby sharks swim away from their mothers so they don't eat them alive. Maybe you should take a page from their book," Johns called from the kitchenette.

Wendy rolled her eyes. "My mother's not a shark," she muttered as her comm vibrated. She pulled up the message. It was from Michaels.

Are you really ok?

Her shoulders sagged, but she nodded. She didn't kid herself into thinking Michaels wasn't aware of everything that went on around him, even with his nose buried in his tech.

I'm fine. Just had to take out some garbage before our trip.

She typed a winking face to end the comm. While it wasn't the most captain-ly message, she figured Michaels wouldn't judge. He lifted his eyes and smiled at her before quickly gluing them back to his screen.

"Could've fooled me," Johns muttered. He walked through the door of the kitchenette, his arms loaded with plates of chips and sandwiches as he balanced a small tray of cookies on his chest. Wendy helped free his hands. "Seriously, Darling, the Fleet should use her as a trainer in psycho-torture methods. We'd never have to worry about terrorism again."

Wendy rolled her eyes. "She's not that bad," she argued, but couldn't hold back the laugh that escaped from her throat.

"Right, just like World War III was a figment of our country's imagination." Johns opened a can of soda and downed it in one gulp. Wendy made a face, but stopped when her comm buzzed and she read Michaels' new message.

She didn't know how, but somehow he had turned the text into a cartoon image of a shark chomping on a smaller fish. The next message showed the same shark holding its belly like it had a stomach-ache. The final one displayed the smaller fish flexing its fins to show its fish muscles while it stood proudly over the word VICTORY typed in bold letters.

"Really, Michaels?" She held up the message for Johns. "You're both ridiculous. I hope you know that."

Johns took her comm to squint at the picture. He laughed and clapped Michaels' hand.

"That's just because we have to save you from yourself, Darling. You're the only person in the whole Fleet who doesn't realize how awesome you are."

"Boyce doesn't seem to have any problems failing to realize my brilliance," Wendy argued.

"Oh, Boyce realizes," Michaels murmured.

"What?"

"Trust me Darling, *everyone* can see you're special. You just need to catch on." Johns threw his arm around her shoulder. "For as much as you've got going for you, you can be really slow on the uptake."

Wendy rolled her eyes, but dropped her head onto his shoulder. As big of a pest as he could be, he always had a way of making her feel better. "All right. I'll try to get on your level."

"That's all I ask. Michaels, put that thing away and let's eat! This is supposed to be a party!"

Johns snatched Michaels' comm and pocketed it out of Michaels' reach. Michaels frowned, but helped himself to a sandwich and a cola while Johns cracked a can for Wendy, then raised his in mock salute.

"To Wendy Darling, the best damn Captain the Fleet will ever have!"

They all tapped their sodas, and took a sip. Wendy smiled. It would be an interesting journey, but with her brothers at her side, she was confident she could handle anything that got thrown her way.

16

Wendy woke the morning of departure with a mixture of dread and excitement battling in her stomach. She stared at the ceiling, listening to her breaths as she thought about the events of the past day and a half. Could it only have been yesterday that she had been stressed about a promotion? Now here she was, hours from leaving Earth to venture to virtually unknown planets.

Her mind spun as her brain ran away with her. Wendy followed the trail of thoughts until Nana chimed at her wrist, announcing her elevated stress levels. She closed her eyes to slow her thoughts, a trick her Academy counselor had taught her. Once the flood stilled, she opened her eyes again. She blinked the remaining sleep from her lashes and pushed herself from the bed.

Wendy stretched, working the kinks that had wormed into her neck.

She blamed the stiff futon—she hoped the sleeping accommodations would be kinder on the *Fede Fiducia*, but she doubted it.

The *Fede Fiducia*. A wave of glee ran through her as she thought of the ship. *Her* ship. She loved everything about the little vessel, including its name—*Faith and Trust*. She was seriously considering making it her personal life motto. Maybe then she wouldn't worry so much.

A blinking light on the low corner of her comms screen caught her attention. She groaned and pressed her hand against the notification icon. She had missed a comm from her mother. Her lip curled as she stared at the screen. She would listen to the message—she had to. But first, a shower. And coffee.

The icon blinked again, and Nana sent another gentle pulse into her skin. Maybe a morning run.

"Ugh."

She clicked on some violin music. She needed calm in her life. Hopefully, a hot shower and the Moonlight Sonata would help. A few minutes later, Wendy was towel-drying her sopping hair. The scalding water soothed the aches in her back and she was feeling more prepared to tackle the day—and her mother's message. She clicked the icon and the message opened, bringing an enlarged image of her mother sitting at her vanity to cover her screen.

"Hello darling. Your father and I wanted to wish you well, even though there's no way we could make it to see you. Your father sends his regards—he went for his morning swim to fit in his workout before the garden party. You know how Dr. Abbott gets on him about his cholesterol."

Her mother blathered on, expertly applying her lipstick as she chattered about her social calendar, a skill Wendy could never hope to have. Wendy watched as her mother finished her mask, alternating her gaze between the mirror and her comm, noticeably more comfortable speaking to her reflection than her daughter. Her hands flitted around her face, tucking stray hairs and clasping dangling pearl earrings. After a moment, she remembered Wendy and turned back to the camera, but not before giving herself one final approving look in the mirror.

"The other women at the club were so impressed when I told them about your promotion. Aidan's mother is beside herself with envy." Mrs. Darling's gossip was interrupted by a dainty chuckle. *"The General was so upset he broke a golf club."* She looked at the screen in a scandalized gasp, then beamed. *"Of course, we never doubted you for a minute, darling. But really, I must dash. The ladies are coming by before the event."*

At the mention of her upcoming social outing, Mrs. Darling returned her attention to the mirror for one last check of her makeup. She brushed her cheeks, then smiled before realizing she was still leaving a message for her daughter.

"Anyhow, do be careful, my darling. It would just break my heart to ribbons if something should happen to you. I don't know how I'd bear it. Goodbye, darling." She brought her hand to her mouth then pulled it away, pursing her ruby red lips in an exaggerated pucker before the comm switched off, leaving Wendy to the silence of her room.

Wendy stared at the blank screen, wondering if her mother would even notice when she was gone. She was certain her father wouldn't. She dropped to the couch in a huff, and her comm screen flashed again, scrolling a message across the bottom to inform her that the Admiral was requesting a connection.

"Crap!"

Wendy frantically searched for her clothes, realizing she was still wrapped in a towel. Grabbing them from the couch, she threw them on then hurried to click the accept button. She gathered her damp hair in a low bun while the comm connected and slicked it back just in time to look presentable for the Admiral.

"Darling." The Admiral's voice was as crisp as her perfectly pressed jacket. "The flight leaves in 0500 hours. You are to report to the loading dock immediately. As Captain, it is your responsibility to run the pre-launch scan and security check. But you know that." A pleased smile played on the Admiral's lips.

Wendy nodded.

"Yes, Admiral. I'll report immediately. I shouldn't take longer than ten minutes."

"Excellent." The Admiral raised her hand to salute Wendy. Wendy mimicked her action as a sign of respect. "I can't stress enough what this mission might mean for the Fleet—and your future." Toussant eyed her shrewdly. "A successful retrieval of a decorated Captain from an otherwise unknown planet would bring notoriety and accolades to the Brigade—and of course, the crew responsible."

Wendy nodded. It had occurred to her on more than one occasion that a successful outcome would secure her position in the Fleet indefinitely. She was also aware that a poor outcome could have quite the opposite effect. Her jaw clenched as she fought a grimace at the thought.

"I'm glad you understand the significance." Toussant cleared her throat. "And Darling?"

"Yes, Admiral." Wendy fought to keep her voice steady.

"I realize this is your first mission." The Admiral dropped her gaze to her desk. She re-stacked the set of papers waiting in the middle before she continued. "It is great responsibility you have been assigned, with little time to prepare. There are others, lesser men, who would not be able to cope with such enormity. I trust you will prevail."

Wendy arrived at the loading dock of the *Fede Fiducia* eight minutes and fifteen seconds after she disconnected with the Admiral. Donned in her fresh duty-gear, she strolled through the hangar, admiring her smart navy jacket. The dark fabric fit her frame perfectly, with the long Captain's coat ending just above her hips. A trail of silver double-breasted buttons trekked from the base of the jacket to fan toward the stiff, banded collar circling her neck. Paired with her sleek leather pants and heeled boots, her uniform was more beautiful than her mother's finest dress.

Her heels clicked against the paved floor until she reached the *Fiducia*. She was beautiful; all sleek angles in a compact design that was built to maximize speed and occupancy. Wendy circled the vessel, staring at it lovingly. This would be her baby for the next six months, at least. Although travel technologies had advanced since the last attempt to explore the newly named 'Neverland Sector', it was still going to be a lengthy expedition.

"Hey Wendy, need a hand?"

Michaels quirked a tight-lipped smile. His Commander dress had been replaced with a standard navy tech-suit emblazoned with the insignia of his ranks. He held his duffle in one hand and his comm in the other as he examined the ship.

"*Fede Fiducia.* Has a nice ring to it," he said. "They weren't kidding about it being small, were they?"

"It's bigger on the inside," Wendy argued. "I'll show you. Follow me."

She led Michaels through the cargo hatch and down the storage hall to the main bay. Since it was where the crew would spend most their time, it was central to most of the ship. Wendy showed him through each door—first to the crew's sleeping quarters, then to the sanitation center where they would use the bathroom and shower. From there, they moved to the rec room, the dining area, and finally, the navigations room, where she would be for most of the journey. Last but not least, she guided him to the underbelly of the vessel to the ship's mainframe, where all the tech and engineering activities would take place. Michaels' expression lit like a Christmas tree as he walked through the wiring and paneling. His giddy smile made it hard for Wendy to keep a straight face.

"Definitely bigger on the inside," Michaels agreed, the sappy grin plastered his cheeks in place. His fingers curled like he was itching to get his hands on the tech. Wendy glanced at her watch. Only twenty minutes until the rest of the crew was scheduled to show up. She wanted to make sure she was settled before anyone else arrived.

"Will you be all right in here?"

"Uh huh." Michaels murmured, too busy fawning over the ship to spare her a second glance.

Wendy laughed and tapped him on the shoulder. "I'm gonna go to Navs. Call if you need anything."

"Yep," he agreed, his nose buried in the maintenance screen. She made a mental note to check at least once a day to make sure he left the room. Behind her, she heard him tinkering away. She smiled and headed to familiarize herself with the front of the ship.

The rest of the crew showed up within the hour, announced by Johns' excited voice echoing through the *Fiducia's* halls. Wendy stretched and hopped out of her Captain's chair to meet them. She was greeted by three smiling faces, and Boyce. His jaw clenched, pulling his face into a mask of cool fury as he waited for her report. Wendy wondered if he knew his father had broken a golf club, too.

She pushed the thought from her mind and returned the others' smiles, appreciating the way they presented themselves. They matched each other perfectly, looking clean and pressed in streamlined kohl flight suits with matching coats and boots. Only DeLaCruz wore a variation, with Brigade blue wrapping around her chest and sleeves to offset the black material.

They looked like a real Brigade unit.

"Welcome." She saluted her crew. They hurried to return her greeting.

"Captain," they echoed.

"At ease." She pointed to the door that led to the crew's sleeping quarters. "You can drop off your bags there—those are the dorms. That room is the

gym. There's the bathrooms, and the dining hall. Navigation is up front"—
she pointed to the room she had come from— "and maintenance is below
you. Michaels is already down below, making himself comfortable." She gave
them time to process the information. "Settle in and familiarize yourself
with your respective stations. Meet back in fifteen to prep for launch."

Wendy stood at attention as the crew dispersed. Boyce, Dawes, and
DeLaCruz hurried to comply with her instructions. Only Johns lingered.
Once the others had gone, he clapped his hand on her shoulder.

"You ready for this, Darling?" He shook his arm to rock her back and
forth, his body crackling with excited energy.

"Ready as I'll ever be." She smiled. "I'm glad you're here. Michaels too."

"Yeah, too bad about Boyce though." Johns sucked in his breath and
made a pained face. Wendy laughed.

"I imagine his pride is more hurt than anything," she said. "Besides, I
doubt he'll be able to pull much with you and Michaels so close by."

"He'd have to be really dumb to try," Johns agreed, then picked up
his duffle. "It would be far too easy to purge him from the garbage chute."
He winked, and Wendy laughed while he tossed a curious glance over his
shoulder. "But I'm gonna go. I saw DeLaCruz giving me the side eye earlier,
I'm gonna go say hi." He waggled his eyebrows.

Wendy rolled her eyes. "It's against protocol to fraternize on assignment,"
she reminded him.

"Who said anything about fraternizing? I'm just getting to know my fellow
crew members. Don't worry—you'll always be my number one, Darling."

"Because *that* was my main concern," she muttered, with a shake of her head. "Just don't do anything stupid, Johns. *I'm* the one who has to deal with the fallout."

"You got it, boss." Johns saluted with a roguish smile, then hurried to the crew's quarters. "Hey, DeLaCruz! You'll never guess what I heard!"

Wendy let out a small laugh as she massaged her temples. Sometimes she had a hard time believing he was her best friend. How did the saying go? Opposites attract? She had no idea how it worked.

She was heading back to Navigations when a throat cleared behind her. She turned and was surprised to see Boyce standing at attention, clad in his tight duty-gear. The sleek uniform accentuated his broad shoulders and the dark fabric offset his fair features, except the decorative Brigade banding, which nearly matched his piercing blue eyes.

"Captain." It sounded as though the word was painful for him to speak. He cleared his throat, then slowly raised his eyes to hers.

"Boyce?"

He shuffled uncomfortably, then extended his hand. "Congratulations." His jaw clenched as he waited for her to take his hand.

Wendy clamped her mouth shut and dumbly accepted Boyce's extended hand.

"Thank you." She coughed to clear the shock from her voice, searching for a compliment. "I'm glad to have a soldier of your caliber on board."

Boyce's bright eyes trailed to her grip, and with a jolt Wendy realized that her disbelief had caused her to shake his hand a touch too long. Embarrassed, she released his hand and stepped back. A wry smile played on Boyce's face as he straightened his shoulders and excused himself to the crew's quarters.

In shock, Wendy retreated to Navigations. *You shouldn't be surprised. You said he was a good soldier. Good soldiers follow orders.*

And good Captains saw past personal conflict. It was time to put her past with Boyce behind her. She chased Boyce from her thoughts and walked to the Flight Panel. Dawes had turned on the radio and made herself comfortable. Reggae music played in the background as she studied the command panels. She hummed under her breath until Wendy approached, then silenced the music.

"Captain, I apologize, I—" She tossed her head to sweep her long, fire-red bangs from her face.

Wendy raised her hand to stop her. "At ease, Dawes. I enjoy music while I fly, too. Granted, instrumental piano is generally my go to…" She ended with a shrug and extended her hand. "I look forward to flying with you."

Dawes beamed. "The pleasure is mine, Captain." She spoke so fast her words came out as one. "Everyone knew you were going to get the promotion, but I was shocked to be selected! Thank you, by the way, if you had anything to do with that."

"I didn't." Wendy stated. Dawes face fell, and she realized how blunt she had been. She rushed to correct her misstep. "Not that I wouldn't have. The Admiral had already made the selections. She chose the cadets who performed best in their assigned tasks. You're one hell of a pilot," she added with a smile.

Dawes' face brightened. "Top of the class," she said.

"That's exactly what I need." Wendy turned her attention to the screen in front of her. It was almost time. Admiral Toussant would be expecting their final call.

As if reading her thoughts, the rest of the crew filed in. Dawes joined her teammates, facing the comm screen. Wendy glanced at her watch. Fifteen minutes exactly. Perfect. She initialized the comm to the Admiral. It was time.

"Good afternoon, Admiral. On behalf of my crew, I would like to express our gratitude for the opportunity to serve the Fleet on this mission."

"At ease, soldiers," Toussant commanded. "The gratitude is mine, and the rest of the Fleet's. You are about to embark on a crucial journey. Your bravery will not only bring home some of London's finest, but will also bring discovery on behalf of the Homeland, which is the foundation of the Expeditionary Fleet. Hold steadfast and true. The eyes of the world are watching."

She saluted the team, and the comm ended. Silence reverberated around the room as the crew awaited instruction. Her stomach twisted. From this point on, she was responsible for the lives of the five people standing in front of her.

"Your mission begins now. Look to the soldiers beside you. For the remainder of this journey, they are your family. An extension of you. If trouble befalls one, it befalls us all." Her eyes narrowed at Boyce's scrunched face. "This is more than an assignment. Remember your mission, remember your country, but mostly, remember your family. The people whose lives entwine with yours. It is a heavy burden, but I am confident each of you is more than capable."

The crew responded in unison, drawing their hands to salute, yelling, "Captain!"

"At ease." Wendy smiled. "Secure your positions. It's time to launch."

The team cheered and hurried into place. They filed out to the passenger seats in the Main Bay. Only Dawes remained at attention, waiting for Wendy. Wendy nodded for her to take the helm. Silent, they sat, taking in the enormity of their task.

Dawes was the first to break the silence. "On your mark, Captain."

Wendy looked at Dawes. She allowed one final pang of panic to flood her chest before she suppressed it. There was no more time for uncertainty.

"Initialize the countdown sequence," she spoke into the microphone, casting the announcement to Mission Control and the rest of her crew. She heard Johns' whoop of excitement from the passengers' compartment and bit back a smile, focusing on the panel in front of her. Switches snapped loudly as Dawes flipped them in place.

"Prepare for launch."

Suddenly, Wendy was a little girl in her room, playing Captain. She sat in a cardboard box decorated with colored paper and markers. *Captain Wendy Darling, reporting for duty!* The memory faded, and she was in the present again, snug in her Captain's chair, strapped in and at the helm.

"Ready in three... two ... one ..."

The ship's engine rumbled, preparing to shoot into the unknown. Wendy's hands were clammy and her suit stifled her with its weight. The roar of the ship was deafening. She would remember this forever.

The little girl was back, this time in Wendy's lap. She looked up with bright eyes and smiled before she spoke in time with Wendy.

"*Blastoff.*"

17

THE SHADOW

PETER

Tootles' terrified voice was the first thing Peter heard when he awoke. "Where are they taking us, Peter?"

"I'm not sure." Peter answered. He tried to sound reassuring, but his chest filled with cold dread. Hooke and his pirates were one thing—the Stjarnin were something else entirely. "Probably back to their camp, out by the Skull."

Tootles' response was a frightened whimper.

Peter didn't blame him. The Skull was a huge cavern that rose from the ocean surrounding Neverland. It earned its name from its macabre shape—a screaming skull swallowing the sea. Though the rock emerged a good five hundred meters from the beach, the whole area felt off, like an invisible force field suffocated the land. Peter's throat tightened as he thought of it—the eerie silence, abandoned beach, and the dark, heavy fog that writhed around the base of the Skull.

Their nets jostled as their captors carried them up Krawk Mountain, pulling Peter from his thoughts. He stared up at the figure carrying him. From afar, the natives could pass as people, but up close, it was easy to see that their faces were wrong, like they weren't actual faces. They were moss-green slates with gaping eyes black as pitch. Underneath, where their nose and mouths should be, rested a set of three horizontal lines resembling the gills of a shark. Peter wasn't sure if they were used to breathe, eat, or communicate.

The rest of their bodies were closer to human, but they were stretched and distorted, like giant trees. Fern-colored skin wrapped taut across strong muscles, marred by the white scars that riddled their skin—slashed lines etched into their backs, arms, and chests.

They didn't wear any clothes, save a wrap that covered their hips to their calves. Decorative bands circled the biceps of some and the ankles of others. Only one wore both. They matched the band woven around his head and down through the ends of his long clay brown hair.

"That's the chief," Tootles said.

"How do you know?" Peter demanded, his eyes flashing at the certainty in the boy's voice.

Tootles' ears turned pink. "I, um…" He paused. "I've picked up some of their language."

"What?"

Peter's roar surprised the natives, who tightened their grip on the net and prodded him with their spears. The cording constricted around Peter's neck, forcing him to cough against the pressure. A few warriors pressed the tips of their spears further into his flesh, like they expected a fight. He clenched his jaw and dropped his gaze, indicating he wasn't going to give them any trouble.

The Stjarnin lowered their weapons and pushed forward, continuing their climb up the mountain. The net clung to Peter, and the rough cording rubbed his flesh, burning it. He brooded sullenly until his curiosity got the better of him. He turned to Tootles, letting out a choked cough as the cord tugged against his windpipe.

"What do you mean you've picked up their language?"

Tootles waited a few steps before he whispered, "Well, I—sort of—learned how to understand some things they say."

Peter groaned. "Yes, Tootles, I get that," he hissed, feeling the cord burn with each syllable. "What I'd like to know is *how*."

"Right." Tootles gulped. "Y-you know how I s-set up the scanner in the treehouse?"

Peter tried nodding instead of talking. It didn't help. The cording scraped against his Adam's apple, rubbing it even rawer.

"Well, I s-set up another receiver at the b-base of K-k-krawk Mountain." He fumbled over his worsening stutter. "You know that—that's how we've been able to get m-m-most of the intel we have now."

"Uh-huh."

"T-the visual was helpful, b-but n-not being able to understand the audio... f-f-frustrated me. I knew I was missing important information. S-so I started listening—really listening. A-at first, I was only able to pick out a f-few things, like numbers, the names of animals—b-basic terms."

Tootles let out a frightened squeak as one of the warriors turned his terrifying gaze on him. He lowered his eyes until the soldier, satisfied, looked away and continued walking. Before he could resume his story, they were met by another cluster of natives who stood guard before a large wall.

The warriors crossed their arms to tap their opposite shoulders before raising their hands in some sort of formal wave. The natives guarding the wall did the same, then lowered their weapons. The chief stepped forward and said something to the guards as he led the troop past. To Peter, it sounded like a jumble of sounds, but Tootles nodded.

"Did you understand that?"

Tootles bit his lip. "I-it was a greeting. An homage to the Second Star."

Peter was fascinated. He remembered Hooke's reference to the "Starchasers" and wondered how much the pirates really knew about the locals. "Why didn't you tell us you could understand them, Tootles? Don't you think that might have been useful?"

"I-I didn't want to get your hopes up," Tootles confessed. "I'm still learning."

Peter wanted to say more, but the warriors closed in again. The path had reached another bend, and the group had to fall in line to fit through the narrow pass. Peter made a mental note of his surroundings. With the standing guard and the rocky terrain, it would be difficult, if not impossible, for Tinc and the other boys to get to them. He would have to figure a way out of this himself.

They turned one last sharp bend, and the path opened to a large clearing. The edges were surrounded by clusters of tiny huts. The largest cluster sat in the middle of the outer circle, with one central shelter surrounded by nine smaller ones. Each structure looked as though it housed only two, maybe three people at the most, but with the number of huts built, Peter estimated a population of about two hundred, maybe more.

The warriors marched them to the center of the clearing where a giant fire pit smoldered over dimly lit charcoal. The residents of the huts peeked out at the commotion. Women and children, Peter guessed, based on their sizes.

The children were easy to distinguish—they looked like miniature versions of the adults, with chubby arms and legs instead of the muscular build of the elders. Peter presumed the majority of the onlookers were female, as their coverings cloaked the whole of their torsos to the napes of their necks. Everything else was difficult to discern. Their hair was the same waist-length earthen shade, and their facial features were almost identical. A few bounced babies on their hips as they glared at the intruders before hurrying back into their homes.

Peter and Tootles allowed themselves to be paraded through the center of the village. They didn't stop until they were directly in front of a large fire pit, pressed against a stone wall encircling raised pyres. A hush fell over the camp when the warrior wearing the elaborate bands jumped onto the ledge of the fire. He raised his hands into the air and tossed his head to let out a victory cry. The others followed suit, stopping only when the leader dropped his arms. The encampment hushed as he addressed them in their foreign tongue.

"He's s-saying something about fortune." Tootle's brow furrowed as he listened. "That the... god? ... is pleased..." He trailed off, his face twisted in frustration.

"What god?" Peter whispered.

"I don't know," Tootles admitted. "He keeps saying the same word—*Itzala*—over and over again. I-I think it may be that."

Peter watched the warrior as he spoke to the others. The longer he talked, the more excited he seemed, and the others responded, working into a tizzy.

Suddenly, a gravelly voice rang across the clearing and they were dumped unceremoniously to the ground. The clan fell silent. The warrior whirled around, whipping his hair as he spun.

A wizened elder emerged from the large cluster of huts, moving slowly, but with authority. He had as many bands as the speaker, colorful circlets that decorated his arms and ankles, and his hair was woven with intricate patterns of bright fabric threaded through. A matching chest piece rested on his shoulders. Shaped like a ribcage, its design was a cross between protective gear and ceremonial garb.

Though his hair was just as long as the others', it had lost its deep hue and was a soft beige instead of dark sandstone. His eyes filmed over, giving them a milky tinge. Peter was certain he was blind. He approached slowly, plagued by a stiffness that came with age but didn't detract from his presence. Instead, it made him appear even more venerable, a suspicion that was confirmed when the decorated warrior dropped to the ground and knelt in front of him. His men followed until all bowed before the elder.

The old one raised his hands and let out a harsh cry. Immediately, the others stood, eyes trained on his ancient form. He stepped toward the young leader and placed his hand on his shoulder as he spoke. It was hard to tell, but based on the way his brow furrowed, he seemed upset.

"I was wrong," Tootles hissed. "*That's* the chief. But he's old. *Really* old. He guides the village in spiritual matters. The one he's talking to is the prince—his son. He will take over when his father dies. It sounds like they don't quite agree with each other. He says he's…disappointed?" He turned his head as he listened, focusing on their words. "He wants to know why he's brought strangers to their home."

Peter didn't respond. He watched the Stjarnin intently, reading their unspoken communication: body language, side glances from the other warriors, worried looks on faces. The prince was speaking. He was agitated, but instead of inciting the crowd, he was defensive. A child explaining himself.

"There's that word again." Tootles growled, exasperated. "*Itzala*. I'm not sure, but it sounds like they're talking about…darkness? Night, maybe?"

"Or a shadow." Peter barely felt the words on his lips. A chill seized his body as a creeping fog rolled over his body, threatening to smother him. Through the haze, he heard the faintest whisper.

"Come… come to me."

"Shadow?"

Tootles considered, oblivious to Peter's fear. "That would fit. It's weird, though. It sounds like they're talking about a person—not a thing."

The prince yelled again, gesturing wildly as he argued with his father. He pointed first at his captives, then the fire behind them before sweeping his arm around the village and back to the chief. His raised voice made the foreign sounds seem even more confusing and dangerous.

"He's saying something about killing—about a sacrifice. To give to *Itzala*…" Tootles' cheeks paled. "Peter, I think he's talking about us."

Peter couldn't respond. His brain filled with darkness, haunted by the unseen voice. Each word it spoke sent searing pain through Peter's mind.

"You. Can't. Escape."

He gripped his head, pressing against his skull to keep it from bursting into a million pieces.

The chief spoke again. His voice barely rose above a whisper, but the village was silent. He stood still, without the wild gestures his son used, but his words conveyed every bit as much power. Peter tried to focus, but the haze filling his thoughts isolated him in his mind.

"You are mine."

"A god. *Itzala* is their god, Peter. They worship it. They—hold on," Tootles listened to the Chief. His voice had risen, and there was a slight tremor in it as he addressed his people. He was no longer speaking only to the prince.

"Hold on. The chief is telling them no." Tootles leaned forward. "He's saying to trust the Star."

Peter knew he should respond, but he couldn't. He was battling an unseen demon, drowning in an imaginary pool surrounded in ice. His arms and legs were heavy, weighed down by the ever-thickening fog in his mind. Soon, he wouldn't be able to fight. He would drown.

In another world, the Stjarnin continued to argue. Tootles took advantage of the distraction to speak more freely. "I still don't know what *Itzala* is, but it—it sounds like they're afraid of it."

Peter understood why. Though the fog threatened to suffocate him, he refused to sink under the pressure. He knew now what the invisible demon taunting him was. It was Itzala—*the Shadow*. The same evil that clung to Skull Rock and infected the beach. What it was—demon or god, ghost or alien—didn't matter. It was powerful.

And old. As it continued to pour its energy into Peter, he realized it was older than anything that had ever been on the planet. Or in the galaxy. He saw from the eyes of the Shadow, like it had borrowed his body. The years it had been here were mere seconds to the demon, a small pause in an immortal life, where it outlasted all others it encountered. The only weakness Peter sensed in the creature came from deep within, a hunger that threatened to consume it.

The Shadow was ravenous.

"I will use you to escape this prison. You are mine now…"

Tootles turned to Peter, noticing his silent struggle. He grabbed him by the arm, worried. Peter felt his grip, but it was distant, like his body had gone numb.

"Peter? Are you all right?" When he didn't respond, Tootles panicked. He shook Peter's arm. "Peter, what's wrong?"

Peter ignored him. What had once been just pain had turned into a constant throbbing ache. He wished his head would explode to ease the pressure building inside his skull. If he was dead, the Shadow would have no use for him. He doubled over, curling into himself to fend off the evil surrounding him. Only Tootles' sharp cry kept him in the present as the brave boy shouted, stopping the Ancient's argument cold. They stared at him as if surprised he dared interrupt. But Tootles wasn't paying attention—he grabbed Peter and rocked him by the shoulders, Peter's only lifeline from his cocoon of agony.

The prince issued an angry command, before grabbing Tootles by the collar and pulling the boy to his face. His eyes narrowed to slits, and he hissed through his mouth-gills before throwing the small boy backward, sending him skidding across the ground.

From the dirt, Tootles let out a strange sound. The warrior gasped and shrank back, watching him in a mixture of fear and amazement. Tootles shook, but he took in a deep breath and slowly stood in front of Peter, his little body shielding his captain. Behind, Peter shuddered as he was wracked with pain.

"You can't fight me…"

None of the clan moved until the chief stepped forward. The soldiers parted to make a path, but their weapons remained trained on the tiny creature that tried to speak their tongue. The chief's clouded eyes bored into Tootles as he demanded an explanation. Peter knew the situation was precarious, but he was helpless. His thrashing had turned to full body spasms, and he writhed in pain as the Shadow encompassed him.

"The Stjarnin know my power. My all-encompassing reach. They have fed me these many years. They are mine. I have grown stronger from the blood of their people. I have learned more than you can imagine. There are secrets in the blood…"

Peter's fists beat the ground in defiance as he struggled to steel his will. The Shadow seemed amused by his attempt to stave him off. An eerie laughter echoed through the fog before it whispered again.

"They could not fight me. You will not either."

Blood red light flashed in Peter's vision, shorting out his senses with searing pain. Only the unending agony of his body being torn to a million pieces remained. It was too much. Unbidden, an earsplitting shriek ripped from his throat. The sheer savagery of the sound brought everyone in the campsite to a complete standstill.

For the first time, the *Stjarnin* looked at Peter, who lay broken on the ground. Their eyes widened at his ashen face and sweat-drenched clothes, and they backed away, hiding behind their weapons. They looked at him as though he was a disease that could infect them all with a single touch. Tootles dropped to his knees, checking to make sure he was okay.

"Peter!" Worry etched his face, and he turned to the Stjarnin. "Help him! Please!"

Peter forced his eyes open. From the thick haze of the fog, he saw Tootles standing guard in front of him, the little golden boy staring down a hostile village. The Shadow was watching too, considering the peons of its universe with amusement.

"You have to—"

Tootles' voice broke. He balled his fists through his hair in frustration. For the first time, the chief looked at him with compassion, as if he knew something Tootles could never fathom.

"Itzala."

Tootles groaned as tears coursed down his cheeks. "What is the Shadow?" he screamed.

The chief's reply was brief. "*Irent'za.*"

Peter knew what it meant. The Shadow translated for him as it laughed at his misery.

"Death."

The chief gave the prince a quick hand signal. The young warrior raised his bow and aimed it, training his arrow directly on Peter's heart. An angry screech echoed in Peter's ears as the Shadow stared down the shaft of the weapon.

"Not this time," it whispered.

A whooshing sound filled Peter's head as the fog cleared, like someone opened a bay door in space and the pressure sucked out all the contents of his ship. At the same time, a wave of black power shot through his body and out into the village, sending the natives tumbling, terrified, to the ground.

"Not this time, but soon."

The Shadow's voice boomed once more before it disappeared. As it fled, the wind whipped around Peter, lifting him to his feet. His body screamed in pain as his mind tried to reclaim his senses. Broken as he was, he knew unless they ran now, they would never escape the Stjarnin alive.

Though it felt like he was dragging his legs through quicksand, Peter rushed to pull Tootles to his feet. The young boy followed, hurrying alongside him. Peter stumbled and Tootles leaned into him, providing his shoulder for support as they fled. They ran until they reached the end of the camp where the mountain met the ocean. Skidding to a stop, they stared at the sheer cliff face, warily eyeing the sharp, craggy rocks beckoning them from below.

Gripping Tootles' hand, Peter launched off the ledge, praying they missed the rocks below. Tootles' terrified scream rode above the wind as they fell into the ocean. The weightlessness of the fall reminded Peter of the *Roger*'s anti-gravity and he was hit by a strange wave of homesickness before his legs broke the surface and he was swallowed by the sea.

Underwater, Peter clutched Tootles and kicked until they broke through the crashing surf. They spluttered out, gasping for air and fighting to stay afloat.

"There—over there!" Peter pointed to the shore. "Swim, Tootles. We've almost made it!"

He swam, fighting the current as Skull Rock drew him in.

"Soon…"

The Shadow's echo rushed over his body, paralyzing him with fear. He dipped under the surface but clutched Tootles closer and kicked, pushing to the beach.

Safely on shore, Peter collapsed, listening to the faint hum of Tootles' ragged breaths mingling with the crashing waves. Cold waves washed over them, stinging their skin with salty tears before scurrying back to the safety of the tide. Like a fish out of water, Peter's breathing came in jagged rasps. His body ached with every gasp, fractured by the Shadow's unseen attacks. Remembering the pain, Peter shuddered and crossed the beach to where Tootles lay, staring at the stars in shock.

"Come on." He shook the boy's shoulder. He wished he could give him more time to recover, but that was no longer a luxury they had. For the first time in years, Peter felt the clock ticking against him. "We've gotta warn the others. They need to know what we're up against."

18

THE FLIGHT

WENDY

The first few weeks of the flight were uneventful. Once the crew launched from the earth's atmosphere, they continued along until they were far enough from Earth's gravitational field to jump into hyperdrive. The simulated map Hooke's transmission provided estimated coordinates to help them plot their HyperShot. They had enough power for two jumps—one to the Neverland Sector, and one for the return home.

Wendy had discussed the HyperShot at length with the Admiral. While most of the mission was wrapped in uncertainty, the HyperShot was arguably the largest gamble they had to take. Though reports from the *Jolly Roger* had been received regularly before contact was lost, the transmission gaps left the Fleet with a blank space that might extend a couple hundred thousand miles.

Wendy's charting helped to narrow the margin, providing a rough marker for the planet, but the flares were unpredictable, making them less than accurate. There were other unknowns to take into account as well—asteroids, moons, microplanets, and a host of astral bodies to navigate around. Wendy's HyperShot coordinates were basically a crap shoot. The odds weren't comforting, but as Captain, she had to decide.

"Dawes, how long until we set course?" Wendy checked the status of the *Fiducia* for the millionth time.

Dawes tapped a sequence into the panel then leaned to read the report. "We have to enter the coordinates within thirty minutes, Captain." She gave Wendy a warm smile. "Have you figured out which points you're going to use?"

Wendy's stomach flipped. "Not yet." She sighed. "I have it narrowed down, I just need to choose."

"Yes, Captain."

Dawes turned her attention to the screen and dialed up the volume on the radio. She bobbed her head in time with the music, sending her red curls bouncing along to Bob Marley's famous "Don't Worry Be Happy" as it played in the background. Dawes had a thing for reggae, she said it reminded her of a simpler time, but Wendy didn't mind. The relaxed chords helped mellow her out. Come to think of it, Dawes had been playing a lot more reggae recently. Wendy wondered if it was intentional.

She looked at the map. They were rapidly approaching HyperShot range. It seemed such a small choice: Point A or Point B. Except one of the points could mean disaster. Or maybe none.

Or maybe both.

Wendy groaned. She and the Admiral had taken in recommendations of the Fleet's best navigators and statisticians to narrow the coordinates' options. Through extensive charting and mind-numbing mathematical calculations, the team had provided ten viable coordinate sets. From there, the Admiral assisted Wendy in further whittling those to three.

Wendy remembered asking the Admiral why she hadn't directed her on which points to use. The Admiral had studied her for a moment, then answered.

"One of the best things an exceptional Captain has going for them is their ability to intuit decisions. A true Captain will know when to compromise or when to fight. When to hold or when to run. It is the small decisions that make you great, Darling. Remember that."

Wendy had no idea what that meant, but she was painfully aware that the Admiral hadn't included *when to choose the right coordinates* in her speech. She pinched the bridge of her nose. How would she decide, knowing her choice might kill the people she was charged to protect?

She pulled Hooke's file from its compartment. She kept it at her station to refer to as necessary. Not that she needed to. She had the whole file memorized. She ran her thumb over the small photo as she studied Hooke's face.

Like always, her gaze pulled to his thunder-blue eyes. They held her captive every time she looked at the photo. His stare was so intense, she wondered how it would feel to be held in it.

"Should I leave you two alone?" Johns clapped his hands on Wendy's shoulder's sending her out of her skin. He laughed and spun her chair to face him then tossed her a dehydrated sandwich. "You didn't come down for lunch, so we thought we'd bring you some."

Wendy eyed it warily. The thought of food sent her stomach flip-flopping in uneasy circles.

"Thanks." She forced a weak smile. With her free hand, she closed the file. Johns already thought she was obsessed; he didn't need any more ammo. "But I'm not hungry." She passed the sandwich back. "You eat it."

Johns' brow furrowed, but he took the sandwich. "You sure?"

Wendy nodded. "I'll meet you for dinner. I promise." She smiled again. She must have done better this time because Johns' worried look disappeared. He stuffed a huge bite in his mouth, unfazed by the brittle dehydrated bread.

"You're miffing out," he mumbled.

"I'm sure." She laughed. "Now get out of here. Go check on Michaels or something. I got stuff to do."

"Aye, aye Captain." Johns snapped his heels and saluted her with crossed eyes. Wendy shook her head and chucked a pen at his torso.

"Make sure she doesn't drool over Hooke too much, Dawes." Johns laughed as he ran out. "She has to return that file when we get back. We don't want the Admiral asking questions!"

Wendy groaned. All the levity Johns brought in disappeared and her headache returned.

"Why don't you tell him what's stressing you out?" Dawes asked, her dark eyes fixed on the screen in front of her.

Wendy lifted her face from her hands. Because they worked so closely, she and Dawes had had several conversations, but they had all been casual. Arielle's journey into deeper territory caught her off guard.

"You don't have to answer that." Dawes flushed and hurried to apologize.

"Forgive me, Captain."

"It's not that." Wendy paused. "I just… don't want to worry them. It's my decision to make."

Dawes nodded, but twisted her bottom lip. "I think they're already worried."

"Am I that obvious?"

"No," Dawes elaborated. "No. I don't mean they're worried about the HyperShot. I meant—I think they're worried about *you.*"

Wendy considered Dawes' words. Hooke's file rested in front of her. Her fingers itched to pull open the cover once more, but she fought the urge. She wondered what Hooke would have her choose. He would know better than anyone. She closed her eyes and tried to channel the correct answer. Nothing. Perhaps her intuition was broken.

Frustrated, she flipped the file to the navigation report at the back. She read it for the thousandth time, obsessing over every mark, searching for a clue.

What happened to you? Where can I find you?

Dawes cleared her throat. "Captain?"

"Yes, Dawes."

"We're approaching HyperShot range. I need the coordinates."

Wendy's heart beat against her ribcage. Her vision blurred, merging all the stars but one. Only one mark remained, brighter than the others. Wendy peered closer, realizing it was the slightest shade of green.

"Captain?"

Wendy shook her head to clear her thoughts, then looked at the coordinates. Three choices, none obviously better than the others. She glanced at the star, then read the coordinates closest to the strange light.

"There." She pointed out the star on the screen. Dawes leaned forward and clicked the coordinates.

"HyperShot sequence initiated."

Wendy drooped back in her seat and secured her safety harness. With her free hand, she pressed the comm at her shoulder.

"Attention, everyone." She cringed as her voice resonated over the ship's loudspeakers. "Report to the main bay. Locate and secure your safety harnesses. HyperShot sequence engaged."

For a moment, she considered saying something to express her heartfelt thanks to the crew, but she thought that might set the wrong tone. She didn't want to panic anyone.

She was nervous enough for all of them.

Wendy leaned against the headrest with her eyes closed to center herself. Though she fought to keep a cool exterior, inside, her heart raced and she couldn't hold a solid thought for longer than a few seconds before it was replaced by another. She needed to keep it together.

She looked at Dawes, who focused on her navigations screen.

"Dawes?"

"Yes, Captain."

"Godspeed."

"Likewise, Captain."

Wendy glanced at the screen. Thirty seconds until HyperShot. Twenty... ten. She leaned back once more, preparing for a sudden burst of speed. Hooke's picture danced in her mind, illuminating Wendy's thoughts with his piercing gaze.

There was a roaring whoosh and Wendy was thrust against her chair. Her teeth and ears ached, as if her sinuses were going to explode. Then, the *Fiducia* stopped. The pressure that Wendy was sure would destroy her disappeared. She peeked her eyes open. Nothing had changed. She hadn't expected it to, but the sameness made it seem anticlimactic somehow.

Everything was calm.

Wendy glanced around the cabin. Dawes looked at her and smiled. *Everything was calm.* They had made it. She let out a small, excited cry, then tapped her hand against her comm.

"Attention," she chirped into the mic, so pleased she didn't even care how relieved her voice sounded. "HyperShot is complete. We are now—"

A huge crash sounded beneath them and the *Fiducia* lurched sideways. Lights flashed and alarms blared, submerging Wendy in a deafening red cavern as she read reports flashing on the navigation panel. The readings didn't say what happened, only that whatever it was had severely damaged her ship. Her worst fears were confirmed as the *Fiducia* shuddered. She fumbled for her comm.

"We've been struck by an unidentified flying object." The Command Center's report flashed obnoxiously across the screen. Wendy read it into the mic. "Navigational systems have been compromised, and we've lost a substantial amount of power." She paused to read the remainder of the report and crossed herself when she realized what was happening. "Remain secured in position."

Her voice broke before her last words.

"We're going down."

19

Wendy watched in horror as the *Fiducia* flashed angry warning signals. "Dawes, report. What's going on?"

"Nothing good, Captain," Dawes said, her eyes flashing in fear. "Whatever hit us took out our main power supply. Everything is running on our secondary generator. It wouldn't be a problem, but the HyperShot used so much energy the *Fiducia's* auto-generators didn't have enough time to resupply. The ship was already trying to compensate for lack of power, and now we're scraping the dredges of our barrels for energy. If we don't figure out something quick, we're done!"

"Keep your head, Dawes," Wendy admonished. She slapped her scanband as a tiny tremor buzzed into her pulse to silence its upcoming biometrics read. Nana's proclamation of elevated stress levels would not help her feigned confidence. "Run a scan for other hazards. We can't afford to get hit again."

Arielle nodded, her head bobbing with the turbulence. "Nothing in the immediate vicinity," she reported. "Must have been a rogue asteroid."

"Fantastic," Wendy muttered as she initiated the link to Mission Control. "Expand your range to see if there are any viable landing options. At the rate we're deteriorating, the *Fiducia* has maybe five hundred thousand kilometers, if we're lucky."

Dawes' hands flew across the paneling, issuing commands. It hypnotized Wendy until a static voice sounded in her headset as Mission Control connected.

"Mission Control, this is Captain Wendy Darling of the *Fede Fiducia*," she rushed through the identification protocol. "We are on a search and rescue mission authorized by Admiral Renee Toussant. We completed our HyperShot from coordinates 987.63.902.12 to coordinates 105.698.548.36. The jump was successful, but upon landing, we were struck by an unidentified object. Our ship has been compromised. We are working to stabilize."

The man on the other end of the transmission tried to interrupt her, but she hurried through her speech. She didn't know how much power comms required, but they needed to save all the energy they could—she would not deplete their reserves on a phone call.

"All crew members are secured and accounted for. We are charting a course for the nearest land body we can find. We will initiate contact once security is no longer compromised," she finished, then ended the comm. She would be under fire for that, but it was a problem for later.

Another crackle of static crisped her ear, and she pressed her hand to the earpiece. She must not have been allowed to disengage. She needed them to hang up. Her voice was stern as she continued. "I said we would initiate—"

"Wendy, it's me!" Michaels yelled over the static.

"Michaels? What are you doing? How did you get into my link—where are you? You should be locked in with the others!"

"I hacked the comm. Stayed in the mainframe during the jump. I was about to do a systems check when everything went haywire. What's going on?"

Wendy recapped the events from the jump. "We know the power has been compromised. What about the actual engineering? Is there any damage in the mainframe?"

"Not that I can see," Michaels' voice was faint. Wendy pushed tight against the earpiece. Alarms screamed over the line as he continued. "...but I can't see much. The lighting is down, and the only visual I get is when the emergency flares flash. It's not convenient, but I'm pretty sure it wasn't designed to help people continue working. Hold on—"

Michaels paused, and Wendy winced as her ear was assaulted by the noise echoing in the bay.

"You there?"

"Still here. What do you see?"

"I ran a diagnostic. The ship was hit in the back, where the loading dock is. The damage is extensive. The main generator went down, and it looks like the impact compromised the atmosphere stabilizer too. If it's not repaired soon, we're going to have much bigger problems than losing power."

"Bigger problems. Wonderful." Wendy rubbed her eyes. "What are those, exactly?"

"If the stabilizer goes, so does the ship's oxygen. We'll have enough air to last four, maybe five hours before it runs out. We'll suffocate to death before we can even worry about using the last of the power."

Wendy's heart dropped.

"You mentioned repair. Can we do that?"

"It's possible, but not easy. From what I can tell, when the generator fritzed, it caused a surge that fried the stabilizer's circuit board. The wiring's wrecked. But if I can rewire the mainframe, it might patch the bum wiring in the stabilizer. It wouldn't be a permanent fix, but it would buy us some time."

"How much?"

"If we're lucky, a few months, if not, it might be a few days. But…" He hesitated. "There's something else."

"What is it, Michaels?"

"Working with live wires is tricky, and the gases in the stabilizer can be…*testy* at best. There's a good chance the machine will explode."

Wendy grimaced, not liking her options. "Do it." She sighed. "We'll have to—"

"Captain!" Dawes burst into the conversation, her pale face cast in red from the damaged navigation panel. "Sorry to interrupt, but the scan found something!"

Wendy sagged with relief. "What is it?"

"You can't tell from our position, but there's a small landform about three hundred thousand kilometers behind us. It's not very big—probably a microplanet—but it's large enough that we should be able to ground there."

"What else do you know?"

"Not much." Dawes admitted. "Although, it looks—" She paused as she studied the reading. "Captain, it looks like it matches the description for Neverland." Her eyes rounded in disbelief. "The planet is composed mostly of water, save a few scattered islands. We're nearest the largest island, though it's not a substantial land mass."

"Get us there."

"I'll do my best. The Navi went down. We'll have to manually steer. It'll be a challenge though— the planet's water to land ratio means we have a lot higher chance of hitting the water."

"Did you hear that, Michaels?"

"I think so. If you can get the ship on the right trajectory, I may be able to reset the Navi long enough to enter a new route for landing. It won't be one hundred percent, but it will keep the *Fiducia* land-bound."

"What about the stabilizer?"

"I'll patch the Navi first. It's an easier fix, and if it will get us grounded sooner, it takes priority. Once we're en route, I'll see to the other mechanics."

"You're amazing, Michaels," Wendy gushed. "Dawes. Turn us around. Let me know when we're in place. Michaels is going to override the Navi so we can land this thing. We may survive this yet."

"On it."

Dawes' fingers flew across the keyboard, a blur as she coaxed the floundering *Fiducia* to comply with her requests. A smile crossed her face.

"Got it. There she is, Captain. Neverland." She pointed at the tiny planet on the screen. It seemed so peaceful compared to the turbulence jarring the *Fiducia*. Two large stars lit the planet, revealing an astral body swathed in clouds and covered by beautiful turquoise seas. It looked like a picture from a children's book.

"It's beautiful," Wendy whispered. "Do you see it, Michaels?"

"Screen's down. Can't see anything. I'll have to wait till we land," Michaels crackled. "Are we on course?"

"Yes. We have a visual. If you can get her Navi online, Dawes can do the rest," Wendy said. Dawes nodded to confirm.

"Give me a second. Tell Dawes her panel may act a little weird, but not to touch anything. It's me working the override. I'll let you know when it's fixed." Michaels' voice was replaced by the cacophony of noise filling the bay. Wendy relayed his message and watched the panel anxiously as she waited to hear back from him.

Though it seemed like an eternity, Michaels' estimate was correct. It only took a few minutes before he crackled in over the static.

"That should do it. Navi is back online. It won't be a smooth ride, but Dawes can enter the coordinates for trajectory. But that's on you. Mechanics can only do so much. I'm going to go see what I can do to patch the stabilizer."

"Got it. Thanks, Michaels. Keep me posted."

"Will do," Michaels promised, already lost in his new puzzle.

Wendy turned to her navigator. "What are our options?" She peered at the tiny planet in front of her.

"With our maps down, we won't get the best reading. But you can see the land mass I was talking about right…there." She pointed to a green blob in the middle of the turquoise sea. "Our best bet is to aim there."

Wendy nodded. "Then that's what we'll do. Enter it in."

"Yes, Captain, but—"

Wendy winced. She didn't think she could handle any more catastrophes.

"Without a scaled map, pinpointing the proper coordinates is guesswork, at best."

"So what you're saying is you could enter a landing point that drowns us."

"In not so many words, yes."

Wendy put on her brave face. "Well, then it's a good thing you graduated top of the class, Dawes."

Arielle's cheeks flushed. "Yes, Captain." She turned her attention back to the paneling in front of her to plot the course of the ship. Wendy watched with furrowed brows. Her head was going to explode. The ship was still screaming for help, the incessant alarms drowned her thoughts in the noise.

"Got it!" Dawes exclaimed. She looked at Wendy victoriously. "Now we just have to ride it out. It won't be comfortable, but if Michaels can get the stabilizer up, we won't have to worry until the *Fiducia* is grounded."

"Good to hear. Keep up the good work." Wendy radioed her tech. "I hope you've got good news for me, Michaels."

Heavy static was followed by a brief hesitation. "Uh, well, I'm wired into the stabilizer. It's a wreck, but not a lost cause…" His voice trailed off as he fiddled with the wiring and muttered through the problem. "The switchboard is fine, there's no damage there…it looks clean, except—wait. There's your problem."

"What?" Wendy demanded. "What's the problem?"

"The flux capacitor is severed," Michaels said in disbelief. Realizing his tech-splaining, he translated. "It disperses fuel and electricity to the rest of the ship. I'm surprised the stabilizer's held this long without it. We've been very lucky."

Wendy came up with a few *different* words, but she didn't argue. "Can you fix it?

"I think so…" Wendy had seen Michaels at work enough that she could picture his forehead crease as he studied the stabilizer. "If I—no, that won't work. But if I …" He paused. "Got it!" The triumph in his voice faded. "Wait, No!" Michaels screamed as a loud boom rocked the ship and the transmission cut out.

"Michaels?" Wendy prayed the comm was still live. "Michaels, can you hear me?"

There was no response except the renewed screams of the *Fiducia* as she cried in pain.

"What happened?" Dawes yelled as she tried to calm the turbulent ship.

"I don't know." Wendy unbuckled the straps across her chest. "But I'm going to find out."

"Wait—you can't do that! The ship is in Panic Mode! Protocol states—"

"I don't give a damn what protocol states," Wendy snapped, surprised at the passion in her voice. Normally she was the one who cited protocol in situations like this. She fought to even her tone. "I have to check on Michaels. I need you to take care of the ship. Can you do that?"

Dawes' eyes were wide. She gulped, then bobbed her head in understanding. "Y-yes. I mean. Yes, Captain."

"Good. Keep us stable. I'll be back soon as I can." Then she was off, out of her harness, bolting through the doors to check on her brother.

"Darling!" Boyce rushed to stand in front of her, his arms crossed in stern disapproval. "What happened?"

"Get back to your harness, Boyce!" Wendy yelled, waving him off as she shot toward the maintenance bay. She didn't have time for him or his ego. "That's an order!"

"If you're going to kill us all, I have a right to know about it," Boyce snarked, but his smug smile was interrupted by another rocking tremor of the *Fiducia*. He stumbled sideways, grasping the metal handrail to stabilize himself.

"Seriously, Darling," he snapped, his eyes wide. "What is this?"

Wendy was about to yell back, when she realized that he could be useful.

"The ship's been damaged. Michaels was working to fix it, but we've lost communication. I need to see what I can do to help. Dawes is up front, but right now she's riding solo." She paused, warring with her pride, but her concern for Michaels won out.

"Report to Navs. Assist Dawes in any way you can. I will return shortly to relieve you of your duty."

Boyce's eyes narrowed before another shudder sent them rocking. "Of all the st—"

"Aidan," Wendy said, startling him with the use of his first name. "I need you to help me."

Boyce's face drew a hard line as he considered her. His slick hair was disheveled from the turbulence, and cascaded in front of his eyes as he stared. Finally, he gave a terse nod before turning down the hall, fighting to keep his footing under the swaying boat.

Wendy watched him with relief then returned her manic dash to Michaels. She flew down the stairwell, descending to the maintenance room. The farther she went, the hotter it got, until it was almost unbearable. Reaching the door, she slammed her palm against the operating panel once more, this time jerking her hand back as the burning metal sizzled her skin. The door didn't budge.

"No!" Wendy screamed. She tried again, pressing her other hand to the panel, only succeeding in burning herself again. She let out a cry of anger and frustration as she stared at the obstacle between her and Michaels.

She was startled by the heavy sound of footsteps on the steel stairs behind her. "Darling! Boyce said you shot down here like a bat out of hell! What's going on?"

Wendy ignored him. She slammed her shoulder against the door to force it open. When it didn't work, she tried again. Then again. She didn't stop until Johns grabbed her wrist and whirled her to face him.

"Darling!"

"It's Michaels," Wendy cried. "There was an explosion in the maintenance room and he's trapped in there!" Her words tumbled out in a mess, but she didn't care. She tried to pull away to resume her attack on the door, but Johns' grip held tight.

"Darling, stop. You'll dislocate your shoulder. That's palladium glass. It's too strong."

"Then what do we do?" she screamed.

"We need to jack it open somehow—get it off its tracks, so we can push it in."

Johns searched the hall for something to use. He stopped in front of the large emergency case that had a metal ax nestled inside. Johns wrapped his hand in his sleeve and punched through the case to free the tool. He pulled it through the shattered pieces, then hurried to the door.

He wedged the head at the base of the frame and pulled. The palladium groaned in protest, but the door held. Johns tightened his grip and squared to the frame to try again. The door let out one final whine, then caved under the pressure. It fell, leaving enough space to squeeze through. Smoke billowed out, filling the hall with a toxic cloud. Wendy buried her face in the crook of her arm to ward off smoke inhalation. Her eyes were left uncovered, and they burned as she dashed into the room.

Inside, the bay was even hotter than the hall. Waves of heat radiated against her body, and Wendy raised her arms to cover her face, bringing Nana's biometric read into her line of sight. Ignoring the scanband's warning against contaminated oxygen, Wendy dove to the ground and crawled along the floor, shrinking away from the smoke. Even though most of it had risen toward the roof, the room was an inferno. Nowhere was safe.

"We've gotta find him!" she yelled, but she doubted Johns heard her over the frantic siren. Her face burned, but she pressed forward, searching for Michaels in the darkened room. "Michaels!" She hacked as smoke billowed into her lungs. She raised her hand to shield her mouth, then tried again. "Michaels!"

Pressure on her ankle startled her, and she whirled around to see Johns tugging her leg, trying to pull her from the room. He shook his head, claiming it was a lost cause. Refusing to believe it, Wendy crawled away, out of Johns' reach. Nana sent another harsh pulse into her wrist, this time accompanying it with a scolding chime.

"Alert. Oxygen levels: low. High probability of detrimental smoke inhalation.

Seek clean source of air immediately."

"Shut up, Nana!" Wendy yelled. Nana rarely voiced her concerns about Wendy's health. Wendy rarely gave her reason to. But now, there were more important things at risk. "Michaels!" she cried. The tears streaming down her face were no longer only from the smoke. "Answer me!"

There was a loud hacking cough, and she plunged toward it. Swallowed in smoke, she thought she heard a soft call, but couldn't tell over the noisy alarm. Wendy strained her ears, her head throbbing as she was assaulted by noise, but then she caught it. A cry. Weak, but there.

"Wendy…"

"Michaels!" She shimmied across the room until she bumped into something firm but soft. She patted its form. When it lurched forward after another cough, she knew she'd found him.

"Michaels! Hold on!"

Wendy pulled him toward her, surprised by his weight. Small as he was, the kid was solid. She struggled to drag him back, then doubled over in a bout of coughs when another roll of smoke snuck into her lungs. She was dizzy and weak, but she refused to give up. Holding her breath, she yanked his arms feebly. This time he hardly moved. She slammed her palms against the ground in frustration, then tried again. He didn't budge.

"Damn it!" She shook Michaels' body. "Michaels! Wake up!" Tears coursed down her cheeks as she hit his back, trying to wake him. She was about to scream again when Johns grabbed her by the shoulders.

"Darling, you idiot!" His rough shake snapped her from her hysterics. "You could have gotten yourself killed!" He coughed, barking out deadly smoke.

"Johns, I—" Wendy's mind was fuzzy. She couldn't form the right words, so she patted the body in front of her. "Michaels…"

Johns pushed past Wendy and looped his arms under Michael's shoulders. "You lead, I'll follow. Get us out of here."

Wendy felt sluggish but nodded. She pressed her belly to the ground and scuttled across the floor like a lizard. Her eyes and lungs burned, but she pushed on, guiding Johns to safety. She had to stop several times to hack black smoke from her lungs, but she didn't quit. Clumsy, she fumbled through, feeling the heat sear her skin. She stumbled as she tried to squeeze herself through the door, desperate to break free from the inferno.

Finally, they made it, gasping for air.

Wendy's first clean breath was like cool gulps of water streaming down her throat. Though her throat burned where the toxins had rubbed it raw, the fresh air was life. Beside her, Johns knelt over Michaels, checking his pulse. Ignoring Nana's advisory, Wendy rushed to his side.

"Is he okay?"

"He's still alive, if that's what you're asking." Johns listened to his chest. "But—"

Before Johns finished, the ship shuddered and lurched sideways. The force flung the three of them across the room. Wendy yelped as her head struck the wall. The world spun, and Wendy couldn't tell if it was the ship or the trauma to her head. In front of her, she saw a dark figure running toward her, holding something long and thin in its hands.

"We're going down!" the figure yelled in her ear.

Something wrapped around her waist, tightening its grip before the ship rocked again. It sent her into sensory overload. The screaming sirens, her burning lungs, the dizziness washing over her, and now vertigo were too much. She fought to pull herself up, but the darkness was too strong. It crashed over her like a flooding river, and with one last gasp of air, she went under.

20

THE PLANET COME TRUE

PETER

Peter heard the ship's arrival long before he saw it. Tangled in the branches of the treehouse with Tinc flitting lazily around his head, he sat playing the wooden panpipe Nibs had made from parts of the hollowed-tree, unwinding the mess of thoughts in his mind with its soothing notes.

He had been up there a lot recently. Since his run-in with the Shadow, the *Stjarnin* had been more anxious and were no longer content to leave the boys be. Peter had seen at least a dozen search parties since they had escaped, and he knew who they were looking for.

Frustrated, he blew a sharp breath, bringing a grating squawk from the tiny instrument. Peter winced and gave the flute a dirty look when the peaceful morning silence shattered with a dull roar that shook the whole treehouse.

Peter brought his hand to his brow to shield his eyes and search the sky.

"What the hell was that, Tinc?"

A loud crack sounded through the sky and Peter swerved to see a large metal contraption hurtling through the atmosphere. It gained momentum as it fell, filling the sky with a keening whistle that needled his ears. He continued to watch as it shot toward the island until it fell behind the canopy and hit the ground with a colossal crash. Wondering where it hit, he scanned the horizon until he saw a huge cloud of smoke billowing from the north. By Skull Beach.

"Shyte."

Peter grabbed one of the hanging vines Curly collected and slid to the ground. His feet hit the earth and he took off at a sprint. He needed to get there before the Stjarnin.

He tore through the jungle, ignoring the leaves that whipped his face in retribution. As he neared the beach, the heavy greenery thinned, providing a clear view of the smoke filling the air. Something was burning. Though he was still too far to see what it was, based on the size of the unfurling cloud, he guessed it was big.

Nearing the beach, the grass turned to heavy sand under his feet as he rushed toward the billowing smoke. When he reached the top of the dune, he lurched to a stop, surprised by the sleek, high-tech vessel grounded in front of him.

A spaceship. An actual, working spaceship.

Peter crowed with glee. It was just what they needed. He would get the boys and—

His joy sobered with a sudden, rational thought. The ship was on fire.

Functional ships didn't catch fire.

"No…" He sprinted down the dune toward the ship. Its nose embedded in the sand, but Peter could still tell it was wrecked. It emitted a faint, repeating whine, like an alarm clock with a fading battery. He walked to the other side and noticed the blackened metal underneath the escaping smoke. Like the nose, it sank into the shoreline, covered in muddy sand. Each time a new wave rolled in, steam sizzled as the water slunk through the cracks of the ship. There had been a fire, but the ocean had taken care of it.

An annoyed jangle in his ear reminded him he was not alone.

"Of course I know it's a ship, Tinc. What I don't know is where it came from."

Peter searched the vessel for any identifiable marks. There was a series of numbers underneath the words *Fede Fiducia*, but they were unfamiliar to him.

"Do you know what this means?" Peter asked, unable to conceal his excitement. "We can use this ship to get out of here!"

Another irritated hum killed his buzz.

"Obviously, it's not in good shape. But that doesn't mean—"

A muffled boom sounded from deep inside the ship. The vessel creaked, and what was left of the pathetic alarm faded into the still air. Peter dropped to his knees, his spirit deflated. It was cruel. An escape route that fell into his lap, only to disintegrate in front of his eyes.

"No!" Peter pounded his fists against the ground. He tore his hands through his hair as he tried to regather his wits. Maybe he could salvage it.

He had to if he wanted to save them.

WENDY

Wendy woke tangled in a pile on the floor of the *Fiducia*. The lights were out, leaving the room pitch black, save a tiny ray of light streaming through the corner of the room.

Disoriented, she reached for Johns and Michaels. She smacked the limb crushing her torso and heard Johns groan in protest.

"Johns!" she whispered. He didn't respond. "Johns!"

She shook him again. When he still didn't answer, she pushed him off her. He let out a muffled *oomph* as his body rolled onto the floor. Now free from Johns' heavy pin, Wendy pulled herself across the floor until she bumped into Michael's unmoving body. She leaned in to listen for a heartbeat. It was there, but faint. She needed DeLaCruz.

Wendy pushed to her feet, and the world spun so dangerously that she almost keeled over before she righted herself. On shaky legs, she stumbled toward the door. Like the mainframe, the main bay was also dim without power. Her footsteps echoed against the metal floor. She hadn't gotten far when she heard DeLaCruz shout.

"Hello? Who's there? Johns, is that you?"

"It's me," Wendy said as she hurried over to her side.

"Oh, Captain. Thank goodness." DeLaCruz's relief was tangible. "Something smashed into my harness lock—it's jammed. I'm stuck." There was a loud rustle as she struggled against the straps to prove her point.

Wendy retrieved the blade from her leg sheath and sliced the straps. She waited until the medic righted herself, then issued a string of commands.

"Johns and Michaels are still in the mainframe. They're both unconscious. Michaels is in bad shape. Attend to them, then find Boyce and Dawes and evacuate the ship." She wished she could stay to help, but she had more pressing matters to attend to. "The maintenance bay caught fire after the explosion," she explained, in a hurry. "I'm going topside to see if I can extinguish it. If not, the ship's as good as lost."

DeLaCruz's eyes widened. "On it, Captain," she promised as she rushed toward the Maintenance Bay. "Take care of yourself."

Wendy didn't wait to respond. With DeLaCruz delegated to the crew, she could focus on the *Fiducia*. She rushed through the storage hall to the loading dock. The force of the crash had crumpled the end of the ship. It jarred the door, leaving a gap between the ship and the frame wide enough for Wendy to slip through.

Standing in the frame, she could tell the *Fiducia* had nosedived into the planet. Her tail end jutted skyward, exposed to the atmosphere, leaving a good eight-foot gap between where Wendy stood and the sand beneath her.

Wendy dropped to the ground and her knees buckled. Warm sand scratched her outstretched palms when she bent to catch her balance. Light reflected from the pale crystals, blinding her sensitive eyes. Tears pricked at their corners, and she raised her hand as a visor. It helped a little, and she cracked her eyes wider to take in her surroundings.

If it hadn't been for the crumpled ship in the middle of the beach, Wendy might have thought she was standing in the middle of a postcard photo. The turquoise water crashed to the shore in calm waves before sneaking back into the safety of the sea. The beach went on for miles, undisturbed. In the distance, the calls of tropical creatures carried on the wind over the large dune resting not far from where she stood. From the ridge, she would have a decent vantage point. She was about to shuffle her way over when she heard an angry curse.

Wendy whirled around, but only saw the *Fiducia*. She paused, wondering if she had hit her head harder than she thought. Her question was answered by a loud yell ending in a frustrated groan. Wendy pressed against the *Fiducia* to conceal herself before following the ship's curves toward the sound until she saw a patch of bright red hair.

She shrank back, ducking so the thing on the other side of the ship wouldn't discover her. It seemed more human than animal, but on the unfamiliar planet, she couldn't be sure.

She peeked closer and saw it was a young man, close to her age. He wore a beat-up cargo suit similar to the Fleet mechanics', but the cut was different—dated, somehow. His messy red hair stuck out at different angles, in need of a good trim. His build was smaller than Johns, but he wasn't slight like Michaels, either. Muscles coiled tight on his frame, sleek like a panther. He wasn't large, but it was obvious he was strong. Wendy watched in surprise as a small creature—a bird maybe—flitted around his shoulder, sparking green as it buzzed in his ear.

"Of course moping isn't going to fix it, but unless you have any better ideas…" He trailed off as a string of jangles escaped the tiny box.

"Well, that was just rude," he said, but a small smile quirked the corners of his lips. It softened the harsh angles of his face, highlighting a small scar that cut a vertical line down the crest of his cheek. Wendy paused as a sense of familiarity washed over her. She studied his rugged features, appreciating the shape of his face from the strong line of his chin to the almond curve in his eyes as she tried to place the feeling. She leaned closer, holding her breath.

"Alert: Elevated carbon dioxide levels detected."

Nana's cool chime echoed into the air, wafting over the soft sizzle of steam. Wendy jerked her wrist, wondering how the voice setting had activated. She slapped her hand over the tiny speaker to dull the sound, but it was too late. The boy started and whirled around, casting a nervous glance over his shoulder toward Nana's betraying announcement, piercing her with his emerald gaze.

PETER

In a flash, Peter was on his feet, dagger gripped in his palm. His face contorted in a warning snarl, but it vanished when his eyes fell on a battered, but striking girl. What caught him most off guard were her enormous eyes. The way the sunlight hit them made them jump from honeyed brown to a deep green. She was tall for a girl—tall and slender in a fitted black flying suit. His eyes followed the shape of her uniform to where the soft curve of her neck was framed by soft curls that had escaped their binding. He caught her gaze, and his pulse quickened, making him more vulnerable than he had felt in a long time.

"Who are you? Why are you here?" he demanded, reacting brazenly to the unwanted sensation. The girl continued studying him, her gaze transforming from wary to shrewd. Her eyes flashed and she straightened her posture, raising her chin to command authority.

"Captain Wendy Darling of the Londonierre Brigade." Her eyes glinted with pride as she held his gaze. She stepped closer to him, asserting dominance with her stance. "We were sent on a mission to locate and recover the crew led by Captain James Hooke."

Peter's eyes widened. Hooke's transmission had made it home. He schooled his face. He didn't want to display any weakness. This *Wendy* might be pretty, but she wasn't going to make him stupid.

"We've been here for ages," Peter said, observing the way the Captain's eyes took in every tiny detail. "Why now?"

Wendy's breath hitched as a thought struck her. "You were on the *Roger*," she said. "You're one of the men Hooke saved."

"Pan." Peter's face scrunched in distaste. "Peter Pan. And just for the record, that's not quite what happened."

Wendy's brow furrowed, but she continued, commanding authority.

"Very well, Pan. I need you take me to your Captain. I am under direct orders of the Expeditionary Fleet to retrieve Hooke and the rest of your crew."

"And how do you plan to do that?" Peter smacked the side of the *Fiducia*. "You busted your ship. Bang up flying."

Wendy bristled. "This coming from a man who has been stranded on an island for a hundred years?" She snapped, piercing him with her hypnotic gaze. "Where's *your* ship? Or have you done a *bang up* job with yours too?" She threw his words back, but Peter hadn't heard them, his mind had latched onto her previous statement.

"A hundred *years*?" He strode to stand before her. "We've been here for one hundred years?" He tried to steady his voice, but Wendy must have caught the volatile edge lacing his throat. She took a small step forward, locking him in her gaze.

"Per today's calendar, it is May 16, 2393," she answered delicately. "The *Jolly Roger* launched 2291. If I'm not mistaken, that's one hundred years. One hundred and two, I guess, if you want to be exact."

Peter brushed his hair back, head reeling. He wasn't sure if he was more upset that it had been one hundred years since they had crashed on Neverland, or if in less than five minutes some girl had stormed in and turned his world upside down.

"I'll wire Mission Control and drop our location so they know where to find us." Wendy tapped her device a few times, before letting out a small growl.

"It won't work."

Peter leaned over to peek at her device. Her screen had blanked out, leaving nothing but a large white square. She turned to glare at him. His stomach flip-flopped uncomfortably when she caught his gaze. From this close, he saw the small collection of freckles that speckled her nose. Her eyes widened at his stare, and she glanced away, leaving Peter to admire the small flush creeping up her neck.

"Why not?" She dropped her attention back to her handheld and smacked it a few times before dropping it into her pocket with an angry huff.

"Tech doesn't work right out here," Peter said. "One of the many wonders of Neverland." He barked a laugh as he remembered the months he worked to get his beloved electronics to behave. "It's the atmosphere or something. It's probably why your ship blinked—you got too close and it fritzed."

Wendy eyed him skeptically. She motioned toward his pocket. "What about your tech? I saw you using it earlier. Or your bug—thing." She pointed at Tinc.

Peter was glad only he heard the slew of curses Tinc slung at Wendy. He didn't think she would take kindly to the analogy the nanobot made to a certain member of the animal kingdom.

"Her name is Tinc." He tilted his head to where the bot settled on his shoulder. "She's not a bug—she's a bot." He laughed as Tinc's angry buzzes translated in his earpiece. "And she's not all that fond of you either."

Wendy's cheeks tinged pink, but she tapped her foot, waiting for him to finish his explanation.

"Not much works out here." He pointed at the device around her wrist. "Older tech works a little better, but not much. I don't even know how Hooke managed to get a transmission out." He ceded, then gave her a quizzical look. "Did he tell *you* how he did it?"

"You don't know?"

"The Captain and I aren't exactly on speaking terms right now." Peter scoffed. She was in for quite a surprise when she realized Hooke's real modus operandi. His eyes twinkled as he thought about how fun it would be to drop that bomb. For the time being, he decided to play along. "But I'd love to find out."

WENDY

Wendy eyed the mechanic carefully. He was taller than her, but not by much. Fiery red hair offset his bright green eyes and pale skin. A soft scrub of stubble covered his chin, matching the disheveled state of his hair. If he was part of the Brigade, he was severely out of dress compliance. She had to admit, his responses to her questions about Hooke intrigued her almost as much as his devil-may-care attitude, but those were questions better saved for later.

"First, I need to help my crew."

She hurried to the loading dock, scolding herself for letting him distract her. She stuttered to a stop when she saw the height she'd have to jump to get back in. Earlier, she had estimated it was around an eight feet drop, but from the ground, she realized it was at least ten. She scanned the vessel, looking for a foothold.

"What are you waiting for?" Peter was beside her, holding her gaze.

Wendy felt a flush of impatience rush through her. "I'm trying to find a way up," she answered indignantly. "Unless you have any bright ideas."

A smirk flitted across his face. "Well, since you asked nicely…"

Wendy watched in awe as Peter dropped back, then shot toward the *Fiducia* at a full sprint. He leaped toward the side of the ship and ran up the paneling, like he was sprinting along a track, until he was far enough to grab the frame and pull himself inside. He straightened and brought his hands to his hips, displaying his achievement with a cocky crow before disappearing into the ship without another word.

"Wait!" Wendy called after him. "Pan!"

"Keep it down, will ya?" Peter stuck his head out the open hatch and flashed her a roguish wink. "You've already announced your arrival to half the planet. We don't need all of Neverland knowing you're here!" He extended his hand. "Now come on!" He hoisted her to the platform then disappeared into the ship with Tinc close behind him.

Wendy hurried after, chasing his receding footsteps until she met him in the center of the main bay, standing beside a huddled figure. Tinc hovered over his shoulder, casting a faint green glow around them.

In front of them, DeLaCruz leaned over Dawes. It was hard to see in the dim lighting, but Wendy made out heavy bandages around Dawes' right arm and leg, and her face seemed paler than normal. Johns knelt beside DeLaCruz, anxiously holding the medical kit. Not far from where they stood, Michaels was propped against the wall. His eyes pressed shut, but a loud cough racked from his chest. He was alive.

"What happened?" Wendy rushed past Peter to kneel beside her medic. Ignoring the curious looks from her crew as they noticed the newcomers, Wendy studied her wounded pilot, horrified by the crimson stains Tinc's faint glow revealed.

"It's Dawes. She's lost a lot of blood," she explained with a slight edge of hysteria to her voice. Her gaze flickered to Peter cautiously before returning to address Wendy. "I had her with me, but when I tried to move her, she blacked out. I haven't been able to revive her."

Wendy's jaw tightened. "Is it safe to move her?"

DeLaCruz sniffled. "I think so. I had to tourniquet her leg. The crash shattered the Nav screen. Shredded her legs. It didn't hit the femoral artery, but it got pretty damn close. When I went in, there was blood and glass everywhere."

"Any other injuries?"

"My throat hurts like hell after that little fire stunt you pulled, but other than that," Johns started, but was cut off by Wendy's dry stare.

"Not you, Johns."

Johns let out a painful laugh that ended in a hacking cough. Wendy's lips tugged at the corners but she turned to DeLaCruz.

"Her right arm is broken. I couldn't set it, so I strapped it to her body. It's not ideal, but it will work for the time being."

"All right." Wendy gave Delacruz a tight-lipped smile. "You're doing great. Keep working," she said, then moved to check the others.

She knelt beside Michaels. His face was pale, but he fixed his focus on Tinc's glowing form, fascinated. He pulled his attention momentarily from the bot to give Wendy a weak grin as she worried over him. "Did you get my comm?"

Wendy let out a relieved laugh and shook her head. "Yes, Michaels. Your comm is safe and the two of you will be reunited soon." Bolstered by Michaels' weak joke, she scanned the rest of the room. Though her crew still seemed unsettled by Peter's presence, they were all alive. Her brow furrowed as she realized there was one scowling face not accounted for.

"Where's Boyce?"

"The idiot ran back to the mainframe looking for you." Johns scoffed. "He ran off before DeLaCruz could tell him you were fine. He's probably hoping it'll earn him a medal of honor to bring home to Daddy."

"Hoping to find my dead body, is more like," Wendy scoffed.

From the corner of the room, Peter let out a barking laugh. Wendy turned to see him studying the *Fiducia's* paneling with keen interest. Fighting a wry grin, she twisted her attention back to Michaels.

"Can you walk?"

"I think so," Michaels said. "It would help if the room would stop spinning."

Wendy snickered. "Well, let's try, anyway." She scooped Michaels' arm over her shoulder, then raised her voice to the room. "Someone help me."

Peter dropped his curious gaze and hurried over. Wendy's cheeks warmed under his intensity as he leaned to brace Michaels to stand. She cleared her throat and was about to instruct him to lift when a dark figure barreled into his back. Wendy stumbled, disoriented by the red lights dancing around the room as Tinc swarmed Boyce's head, jangling furiously while he struggled to pin Peter to the ground.

"Boyce! Stand down!"

Wendy moved to separate the men sprawled on the floor, but Michaels tipped precariously and she had to grab him before he toppled.

"Johns!"

"On it." Johns lurched forward to pull Peter and Boyce apart. He lifted them from the floor and held them apart, his muscled figure forming a barrier between the two. Wendy stepped forward, bringing Michaels with her as he strained to peer at the tiny bot, his eyes wide with admiration.

"Pan, wait outside. I need to talk to my men." She cast a murderous glare at Boyce, whose scowl deepened. Peter's furrowed brow uncurled as his gaze moved from Boyce to Wendy.

"Yeah, okay." He sized Boyce up from where Johns held him trapped against the wall while Tinc spat sparks in his face. "Tinc, stand down."

His muscles uncoiled and he marched out the hall, calling for his bot to follow.

With Peter gone, Boyce twisted himself free from Johns' grip and swatted at Tinc, who swiped his head with one last scathing dive-bomb before she hurried after her master. Boyce waited until the bot left to thunder at Wendy.

"What the hell is this?"

"I should ask you the same thing, Commander," Wendy said coolly, taking Boyce's tousled appearance. His normally slick hair was in disarray, and his lip was split in the corner, trickling blood.

"Ask me the same thing?" Boyce's chest heaved in fury. "I saw an unidentified threat and neutralized it," he hissed, before clenching his jaw shut with grinding force.

"You were out of line, Boyce."

"You don't even know who that guy is!" Boyce exploded, his eyes flashing in rage as he gestured after Peter. "He could be some foreign operative and you just let him waltz onto our ship!"

"He's not foreign, he's military," Wendy said tersely. "Brigade." She took a threatening step toward him. "And if you so much as raise your voice at me again, I'll make sure you're stuck scrubbing his shoes for the rest of your miserable career, *Commander.*"

Boyce's eyes widened in surprise, but his jaw remained firmly in place. Wendy looked around at the others.

"We found the crew, now we have to find a way home." She gestured at the ship. "This setback will require all hands on deck," she said, hearing Michaels' quiet hum of agreement as he studied the darkened *Fiducia*.

Wendy sighed and returned her attention to Boyce.

"He's here to help. Let's let him."

Boyce stiffened but gave a terse nod. Wendy tightened her grip on Michaels, shifting to center his weight. She wanted to take an inventory, but to do that, they needed light. She wondered how long it would take to make repairs. She was about to ask Michaels his opinion when hurried footsteps filled the hallways, and Peter barged in, Tinc trailing wildly behind him.

"Time to go, Cap," he said.

Wendy's brow furrowed. "What's wrong?"

Peter drew in a raspy breath. "Looks like you did catch the island's attention. We've got company."

"Company?"

"Stjarnin." Peter's face was grim. His eyes flitted from Dawes' immobile body to Wendy. "Tinc'll keep them busy for a minute, but we've gotta get out of here."

Wendy took in a deep breath, her mind whirring. "All right. DeLaCruz, how do we do this?"

"We need to move her as little as possible," the medic said. "She's stable, but if anything comes loose or she loses more blood, she'll be in a lot of trouble."

"Okay. Johns, you take her. Boyce will help. DeLaCruz, follow behind and make sure she doesn't move. I'll lead with Michaels. Got it?"

She glanced around to make sure everyone understood. Her lips drew into a tight line when she saw each of them nod in agreement. She turned to Peter, who observed them quietly, the emerald sparks cascading from his bot matching the green in his eyes.

"Get us out of here."

21

PETER

Peter led them down the corridor, surprised at the speed Wendy's team moved. In a seamless unit, they streamed to the ledge of the *Fiducia*, then buckled together to carefully lower the bandaged pilot from the ship to the shore. It required some creative maneuvering, but under Wendy's confident guidance, her soldiers made it safely down.

The pilot's body touched the ground, followed by the heavy footfalls of the others. Tinc buzzed anxiously around them, urging them forward in her static hum when a long, curved spear whizzed through the air to pierce the sand at Peter's feet.

"Mark." The Captain's sharp eye snapped to the weapon and she whipped her head around, scanning the shoreline. The Stjarnin were advancing quickly. With the weakened condition of the *Fiducia's* crew, too quickly. Wendy took inventory of her men, and her calculating stare told Peter she knew it, too.

"Johns, Boyce, get Dawes out of here, *now*," she said, passing Michaels to DeLaCruz. Hands free, she removed the sleek gun from her holster. "I'll defend the ship."

"What? No!" Johns yelled, looking at the charging group of Stjarnin. "You're gonna get yourself killed!"

"We have to protect the ship, Johns," she said, her hazel eyes flashing in the Neverland starlight. "And I have to protect you." Her lips pressed into a hard line, and before Johns could argue, she was gone, tearing through the sand toward the oncoming swarm, ignoring her crew's desperate cries.

Peter swore. The Captain was brave, he had to give her that, but there was no way she could defend the ship against the Stjarnin alone. He called for Tinc, who hovered curiously around his shoulders.

"Get them to the Boys," he said. "They'll know what to do."

With a burst of sparks, Tinc zoomed to flit around the crew. Her trail dusted their shoulders as she commanded them to follow her in nano-garble.

"Keep an eye on Tinc," he yelled back, the only instruction he had time for as he shot through the sand after Wendy. "She'll take you home!"

A faint cry followed him, but it was lost in the breeze. Peter kicked a burst of speed to catch the Captain, who had stalled about a hundred meters from the ship.

"Are my men safe?" she asked, her eyes focused on the advancing warriors. They hurried forward in a spread flank, a group of at least a dozen Stjarnin led by the Prince. They wore the same dress as Peter remembered, but this time, their bodies were decorated with dark black ink. Beautiful markings covered their skin, starting from their legs trailing to their faces, where each line converged to create a fierce mask. Armed with their curved spears and long-handled blades, they streamed forward in a frenzy as they stared at the newest intruder. The Stjarnin had always been hostile, but today they were furious.

"It's not them I'm worried about," Peter said. He pulled out his dagger and flipped it in his hand. The Prince issued a long, low cry, and the Stjarnin surged forward, erupting in a singular battle cry.

Wendy dropped to her knees and aimed, clipping one Stjarnin in the leg, sending him tumbling to the ground. With a deep, slow breath, she fired off three more shots, dropping a warrior with each hit.

The Prince bellowed and lunged at Wendy, swiping his deadly blade toward her neck. Peter jumped in front of her, parrying the Stjarnin's attack. The Prince growled and charged again, squaring off against Peter instead.

Wendy's back pressed against his as she took on the other guards surrounding them. Sand flew through the air as they matched each other's steps, defending against the alien attackers.

Suddenly, the Prince struck forward, sending his blade straight toward Peter's chest. Peter just had time to grab Wendy's arm and pull her to the ground with him so the Stjarnin's attack didn't skewer her. She rolled to her feet, and whirled around, pulling her gun from where it dropped in the sand to find a new mark.

A huge Stjarnin barreled toward her, his long hair flowing behind him as he screamed. Wendy's brow furrowed as she trained her gun at his chest and pulled the trigger. Her eyes widened when nothing happened. Frantically, she tried to discharge again, but the weapon was dead. She let out a startled cry and dove to the side as the Stjarnin swung his blade down in a violent arc. She twisted to the side as he struck again, trying to crush her.

Peter moved to help but was blocked by another wild swipe from the Prince, trapping him in place. He heard a sharp cry and turned to see the large warrior looming over Wendy, crushing her under his weight. He had drawn his blade over his head and was about to plunge it into her chest when his head jerked sideways and he fell to the ground, dead.

Peter's head jerked to where the shot came from and saw Boyce charging the field, his gun drawn. His blue eyes blazed as he looked at the Captain, who pushed herself to her feet, panicked.

"Boyce, behind you!"

Boyce whirled around, following Wendy's command to train his sights on the oncoming Stjarnin. He shot a round, but his heels sank into the sand, throwing off his aim. The bullets grazed over the Stjarnin's shoulder as it plunged its spear into his thigh. A bloody rose bloomed in his leg and he stumbled, but not without a retaliation shot. The Stjarnin's body jerked back and fell, where sticky sand clung to the blood pooling from the wound. Boyce twisted on the ground, scrabbling to look for his captain.

A loud cry rang pulled Peter's attention to where the Prince stared at his fallen warrior before his inked mask contorted in a glower and he let out a furious command to his remaining soldiers. The warriors swarmed forward and grabbed Boyce, trapping him behind their pointed spears. The Prince cast a calculating look at Peter, and swiped his blade in a warding motion before dropping back and retreating, with his soldiers and Boyce in tow. Wendy let out an angry cry as they tore across the sand, hurrying toward the jungle.

"No!" she chased after them, but her legs buckled in the foreign ground, and she pitched forward with a sharp cry.

"Cap!" Peter hurried forward to catch her before she took off again. He wrapped his arms around her shoulders, holding her back as she furiously tried to shake him off.

"Let me go!" she demanded. His breath caught as she trapped him in her smoldering gaze, her dark curls spilled down her shoulders, reminding him of an avenging queen.

"You won't be able to fight the Stjarnin alone," Peter said, his jaw tight. "We're going to need help." He sighed, glancing to the jungle.

The boys weren't going to like this.

"This way."

They took off, staying hidden in the brush. Their steps were heavy as their feet sank into ground that hadn't quite merged from sand to dirt. Wendy walked quietly beside him, her mouth drawn in a solid line as she followed his footsteps over the rough terrain—a silent warrior walking the path of defeat.

Peter's lips twitched with the ghosts of encouraging words, but affirmation was as much a stranger to him as the Captain, so he forced them away and continued their stolid path toward the treehouse. Peter's skin warmed and small beads of sweat formed over his brow as the Stars centered in the Neverland sky, warming the jungle around them. Wendy's cheeks flushed with exertion, but her pace never wavered, and soon they passed through the underbrush into a small clearing where a crooked hollow tree cast its tangled branches toward the Stars.

"Tootles! Nibs! Curly! Get out here!" Peter yelled, drawing them from the treehouse in a whirlwind of hurried questions.

"Peter! Tinc came home with a bunch of strangers!"

"Did you see their suits?"

"Who are they?"

"Why did you send them here?"

"Did you see the *size* of the dark-haired kid?"

"Are we going home?"

Peter paused and looked at Tootles, whose eyes shone with unadulterated hope. He swallowed, stalling as he tried to figure out how to answer when he wasn't even sure.

"Fall in, men," he ordered, commanding them into position before introducing them to the Captain. They waited shoulder-to-shoulder while he told Wendy their names, each by eyeing the Captain with keen interest. He didn't blame them. Wendy was easily the prettiest of her crew, and they hadn't seen a girl in a long time. He was proud they kept their jaws in place.

"Who are these people, Peter?" Curly's suspicious nature broke the silence as he gave Wendy a skeptical side-eye.

"Neverland caught them, too," Peter said, figuring he'd save the bigger details for later. "I brought them here because they need our help." He stiffened and looked at the boys, noticing the way their eyes lingered on the Captain. "This is Wendy." He gestured to the girl with a stern dip of his brow. "Captain Darling to you."

The boys nodded, solemn. Peter gave them a proud grin, then turned to Wendy. He slapped the knot on the tree, revealing a hidden door. "Come inside," he said. "We've got a lot to talk about."

Wendy gave a curt nod and followed him in, not blinking an eye when he jumped down the hatch to the sliding entrance. She stuck a perfect landing, more graceful than any of his boys and looked around, studying her surroundings. Relief flooded her face when she saw Johns at the table beside Michaels, his oversized fists wrapped tightly around an ancient tin cup.

"Darling!"

Johns jumped up, sending the chair tumbling underneath him. He didn't give it a passing glance as he barreled toward the Captain and wrapped her in a tight embrace. She let out a relieved laugh, sending a strange twist through Peter's stomach. The muscular Commander set her down and stepped back, arranging his features in a stern scowl.

"What were you thinking, running off like that?" He frowned. "You could have been killed! Did you at least get Boyce?" He grinned and looked around, then paused as confusion took him. He glanced at Wendy, surprised.

"Boyce is gone," Wendy said. Her eyes glassed over and cleared her throat before continuing with fiery resolve. "But we're going to get him back." She turned to Peter. "You said you have intel about the Stjarnin."

Peter nodded. "Yes, but first, I have a few more questions." He looked around at his men, who lined the edge of the tiny room, listening closely. "Have a seat Captain."

He kicked the empty chair out from under the table so she could sit. Wendy hesitated a moment before sinking into it. Peter gave her a minute to sip from the cup Slightly brought her. When she set it down, Peter leaned forward, his mouth drawn in a hard line.

"Start talking, Cap."

WENDY

Wendy's smile was tight. She looked at Johns, who had shifted to stand beside her. He tensed as he waited at attention. She smoothed her hand over her hair, appalled at how disheveled her bun had become. Quickly, she pinned it in place to regain some semblance of propriety.

Peter waited, his gaze trained unflinchingly on her. When she finished, Wendy dropped her hands to the table and straightened her shoulders.

"I've already introduced myself, but this is Lieutenant Elias Johns, my Reconnaissance Specialist. He also doubles as my second in command. The remainder of my crew you've seen. Marisa DeLaCruz is the medic working on my injured pilot, Arielle Dawes. I'm assuming my tech specialist, Michaels, is being tended as well. And Boyce…"

Wendy's jaw clenched as she remembered the way he'd been carried off. Johns laid a heavy hand on her shoulder. The familiar touch comforted her, and she cleared her throat, her gaze fixed on the center of the table.

"Aidan Boyce is our Liaison Officer. I intend to bring him home with us."

Peter watched her silently, waiting for her to continue. She looked around the crowded room, noticing the rudimentary build. It was simplistic, obviously a shelter that had evolved into a home.

"We were sent by the Brigade as part of the Expeditionary Fleet to rescue and recover the crew of The *Jolly Roger*. We received a transmission from Captain Hooke beseeching assistance. He informed us the ship had crashed on an alien planet that exhibited strange phenomena, specifically the aging process. Neverland." She indicated to Peter. "Clearly, you are experiencing the same effects."

"That's what the mirror keeps telling me," Peter said.

Wendy's lips pressed together in a tight smile. "It is an interesting turn of events." She glanced around the lived-in room. "But what I'm more curious about is why your men aren't with Hooke."

Peter stiffened. "I believe you were telling the bedtime story, Captain."

"There isn't much to tell. We were sent here to locate the crew of the *Jolly Roger* and return them home. For that, I need to speak with Captain Hooke."

"I'm not sure what good meeting Hooke is going to do if your ship's out of commission."

Wendy sighed. "Mission Control won't look for us unless we can get another transmission out. If they can't verify we're all right, they'll assume we've been lost in space," she explained. "That's why it took so long for us to come to you."

"Then you might as well get comfortable, because it looks like you're gonna be here a while." Peter stretched his arms above his head. "Do you want the grand tour now or later?"

"I want you to take me to Hooke." Wendy's eyes narrowed. Though Peter acted with authority, his uniform held little in the value of status. Aside from the patches that identified his position in the Fleet, his ranking was barely higher than a Lieutenant. Every one of her crew members held a higher rank than he did.

Peter didn't seem to notice.

"I hate to break it to ya, Cap"—his informality made Wendy grit her teeth—"but Hooke is *really* not the person you want to see."

He flopped into a makeshift hammock, making himself comfortable.

"Don't be absurd." Wendy bristled. "My orders were to rendezvous with Hooke. He is exactly who I want to see."

"And what *exactly* do you expect to do once you meet the elegant Captain?" Sarcasm dripped from Peter's words as he pushed himself to sit. "I told you, your tech won't work."

"The Captain managed," Wendy countered. "We'll find a way to contact the Brigade. I'm sure a soldier of his caliber is more than able to overcome a minor setback. More than a frigate mechanic, I'd venture." She looked to Peter's outdated mechanic's uniform.

Peter grimaced. "Forgive me," he muttered sarcastically. "If the *Captain* can do it, then my men must just be bumbling idiots."

Wendy's cheeks warmed, but she refused to stand down. "I'm sure your men are more than capable," she snapped, "but I'm beginning to have my doubts you can take me to the *Roger*. I suppose it will depend on whether your lack of social graces got you kicked out." Her brows raised in a challenge. "Either way doesn't matter—just let me know if I should take my crew and go now."

Her mother would be appalled by her lack of manners, but she didn't care. She was not impressed by this boy and his attitude.

"Social graces aren't everything." Peter's ears tinged pink, but his eyes sparked ferociously. "Some of the most proper people in the world are the biggest jerks. It would do you good to remember that."

Wendy froze. She'd often thought the same thing, but speaking it out loud was entirely different. Her whole life she'd been taught the importance of decorum—from when it had been militaristically drilled into her as a child, then reinforced by the ranking and structure of the Academy. The two worldviews warred in her mind until Peter interrupted her inner battle.

"And what do you plan on doing with your pilot?" he challenged. "She's in no condition to traipse around Neverland. I'd be surprised if just getting her off the ship didn't do her more damage."

Wendy's mouth opened to retort, but froze, empty. He was right. She couldn't risk Dawes any further. She had already lost one soldier, and she'd be damned if she was going to lose another. This was a rescue mission, not suicide.

Noticing her hesitation, Johns stepped forward, but Wendy pulled him back.

"No." She paused. Her small voice reflected her feelings. "He's right. We can't move her again." She gripped her cup so tight her knuckles turned white. "But we need to meet with Hooke." Her mouth set in a firm line as she leveled a steely gaze at Peter. "Those were my orders and I intend to comply. You don't have to take me, but I will find him. You will house my soldiers. Willingly would be easier, but if not, we'll assume military rule."

Johns gripped his fists and cracked his knuckles, making his muscles bulge under his shirt.

Peter's eyes flashed with indignation, but Wendy saw the wheels turning in his head. He deliberated a moment, then looked back in grim determination.

"Fine." The word was a gunshot. "We'll help you. But if I take you to Hooke, I expect your assistance in return."

Wendy nodded. She had anticipated negotiation. "What are your terms?"

"Safe passage on the return flight to London as well as immunity from any and all accusations from Hooke."

Wendy exchanged a concerned glance with Johns. He gave a quick shrug, and she turned to Peter with narrowed eyes. "*Any* accusations? What happened when you landed?"

"Nothing you'll get an honest story from Hooke about," Peter retorted. "What *is* true is that we need to get off this planet. And soon."

"You've been here a hundred years." Wendy fought to keep the disdain from her voice. "Aside from less-than-ideal living conditions, what's the sudden hurry?"

Peter's face was haunted. "There are worse things on the island than Hooke and his pirates."

"Do you mean the natives?" Wendy remembered Hooke's words. "What will they do to Boyce?"

Peter averted his eyes.

"The *Stjarnin* have never been friendly, but most interactions we've had have only been skirmishes. Until recently." His gaze flicked toward Wendy, who turned her face in shame. Her gut twisted as she thought of Boyce trapped behind enemy lines. She was drawn from her guilt when Peter's story continued.

"Not long ago, Tootles and I were apprehended. We escaped, but not before we were taken to their camp, where we acquired some very"—he swallowed—"unwanted information."

"Like what?" Wendy leaned forward attentively.

"There's a deity the natives worship," Peter said. "They call it Itzala—the Shadow. We don't know what it is or where it came from, but it's real. And powerful."

"What proof do you have?"

After a moment's deliberation, Peter slowly pulled the neck of his jumpsuit, exposing his collarbone and the blotchy black mark seared into his skin.

Wendy jumped back so quickly her chair fell over.

"What is *that?*" She scanned her memory for all the communicable diseases she'd had to study and their symptoms. She'd never seen anything like it.

"We don't know," the small boy Peter had introduced as Tootles piped up from where he stood by the door. Wendy looked at him in surprise. Though he had the face of a cherub, his eyes were aged, haunted. "It showed up after Peter's episode."

Wendy's eyes tightened. "Episode?"

"When we were captured, the Shadow tried to take over his body. To possess him. I was right next to him, and I didn't see anything except Peter fighting. I tried to help, but it was like he didn't notice anything going on outside him. Somehow, he broke free, and we ran. When we got home, Peter found his mark."

Wendy craned her neck to peer at Peter's collarbone again. Catching her stare, he pulled his jacket to cover the mark.

"It's been there ever since. No change in color or size. It doesn't hurt; it's just there."

"And this Shadow—it was hostile?"

Peter's jaw clenched. "Very."

Wendy clasped her hands together as her resolve steeled. "We have to get him back."

Peter let out a brittle laugh. "And how do you plan on doing that, Cap?"

Wendy gave him a cool glare. "We get help."

She looked at Johns, who straightened to attention.

"We'll split up," she announced. "We need to find out more about what we're up against, and I'd like to know exactly what this Shadow is. Johns and Michaels will accompany your men on an intel run while you and a crew member of your choice escort me to meet with Hooke." Wendy flexed her shoulders to release their tension. "We rendezvous tonight and move forward from there."

Peter was skeptical as he studied her, but after a tense moment, he shrugged and let out a shrill whistle. On command, the remainder of his crew hustled through the door to file in, filling the cramped room. While Peter debriefed his men, Johns leaned toward Wendy.

"You sure this is gonna work?" he asked.

Wendy thought about the mission and the complications they faced. It had been a long shot when all they had to do was retrieve Hooke's men. Now they had to mend a broken ship, a broken crew, and fight some invisible deity. She needed coffee.

"Not at all," she whispered. "Not at all."

22

PETER

It only took Peter a few minutes to give the boys their orders. Curly was instructed to stay with Wendy's medic and injured pilot to tend to the base while the rest were sent to spy on the Stjarnin. Tootles fought to stay with him, but quieted under Peter's fierce glare.

"You have to go with them, Tootles. You're the only translator we've got. I need you there."

"But Peter, why are you going alone with her?"

"While I don't think the fair Captain is going to pull any tricks, we need to be ready for anything," Peter explained in hushed tones. He glanced at Wendy. She stood next to Johns, having her own lowered conversation. No doubt strategizing, the same as he was. "Worse comes to worse, you boys are gonna need all hands on deck."

The boys saluted to show they understood. Peter smiled.

"All right boys." He raised his voice for Wendy to hear. "You know what to do. We meet back here tonight. Be ready to report."

The boys let out a loud whoop, then hurried to arm themselves. Curly retreated to the back room to retrieve a confused-looking Michaels. His head had been neatly bandaged, and he looked much steadier on his feet as he furiously worked to revive his handheld device. Peter considered telling him to give up while he was ahead, but thought better of it as Michaels walked over to join Wendy's briefing. They leaned together in a quiet huddle, until the Captain finished with a formal goodbye before Johns swept her up in a big hug.

Wendy laughed, and Peter couldn't help but notice how lovely it sounded. It lit her whole face, erasing her severity and softening her features. He watched Johns twirl her in wonder. When the Captain's feet hit the ground, she caught his gaze and flushed. He had stared too long. Embarrassed, she hurried to straighten her uniform.

"Are you ready, soldier?" She smoothed her hair to match her jacket.

"Peter," he corrected. "Just Peter."

"Yes. Well…" Wendy cleared her throat. "Peter. Are you ready?"

"Ready as I'll ever be," he answered. Tinc hummed in agreement and flitted to his shoulder. "Let's move out."

Soon, they were traipsing through the jungle in quiet determination. Tinc zoomed to scout the area ahead of them, and it was quickly becoming clear that Wendy wasn't like any girl Peter had ever met. She preferred to keep to herself rather than chattering on. He was thankful not to have to entertain endless conversation, but he'd never exactly been the strong, silent type either.

"So what's your plan for when you meet the elegant Captain?" Peter jabbed as he jumped over a fallen log. He hurried along, jumping and sliding through the underbrush without pause, testing to see whether the Captain could keep up.

"I intend to tell him the same thing I told you. From there, we'll decide how to proceed. I imagine we'll have to determine which vessel will be the easiest to repair and go from there."

Peter snorted. "Go from there. You're just gonna fix a grounded ship and fly off. No big deal."

"I'm sure it won't be easy," Wendy said, matching pace. "But Michaels is the best mechanic I know, and from what I've read, you aren't half bad yourself."

Peter turned to her, surprised. Wendy smiled.

"I knew I recognized you. You're Hooke's mechanic. The one he adopted from the streets."

Peter's shock transformed into a grimace. "Ah yes, the benevolent Captain Hooke." He rolled his eyes and stalked off, pressing through the trees, leaving Wendy to follow after him.

"You don't think so?" she challenged, catching up from behind. "You were fond of your life in the slums?"

Peter's gaze hardened. His jaw clenched in silent fury, but his eyes only tightened before he slowly turned to continue down the path.

"Hooke isn't as upstanding as everyone believes," he whispered.

Wendy's brow furrowed. "That seems rather vague," she argued, giving him a sideways glance. "And unlikely. We have no record to indicate Hooke was anything less than honorable."

"Well, Hooke is all about 'good form,'" Peter grumbled, his muscles tightened as he pushed the underbrush from the path with pent aggression.

"If you know something about the Captain, you are duty-bound to report it to the Brigade."

Peter laughed and gave her a sideways glance. "Cap, I know more about James Hooke than most people know about themselves. Trust me when I tell you, we had our reasons for leaving."

Wendy stopped, forcing Peter to turn to face her. He faltered when he saw the storm brewing in her eyes.

"Are you saying you're a defector?" She spat the word like it was contaminated. Her body tensed, and though she gave no outward signs she was ready to fight, Peter had no doubt she would pounce if he made a move.

"I guess it depends on your definition of defector." He forced bravado into his lazy tone.

"It's not a difficult concept," Wendy shot back. "Denying your captain and abandoning your post are pretty solid examples." The flush was back in her cheeks, but now it was from anger.

"Your captain?" A sly smile tugged the corners of Peter's lips. "Not the Brigade?"

"Well obviously." Wendy scoffed. "A captain is both commanding officer and representative authority for the Brigade. Any actions taken against him are, in effect, steps against the Brigade."

"And what if your captain is the one who defected?" Peter asked, enjoying the way Wendy's eyes widened in surprise. "Wouldn't disobeying a direct order from a threat to the Brigade make you, by default, a loyal soldier?"

A strangled noise escaped Wendy's throat as she choked on her words. Her mouth pursed as she struggled to form an argument. She glared at Peter, her eyes smoldering.

"Hooke wouldn't do that!" she argued, her voice pitched with genuine shock. Peter was surprised at the passion in her voice. It rose steadily with each defense she provided. "He's a decorated captain who has never displayed anything but dedication to the Fleet. The *Roger* disappeared at the peak of his career. He would have returned home hailed as a hero!"

"Right," Peter said bitterly, troubled at the way her regard for Hooke twisted his gut. "Because mission reports and history books provide detailed insights into Hooke's mind."

He stood so close they were nearly nose to nose. Wendy's breathing was heavy, matching his uneven gasps. Peter held her stare, noticing the slight flush that crept to her cheeks the longer they stood. It highlighted the delicateness of her features, revealing a softness that he doubted the hardened captain even knew she had.

Peter's mouth curved in a small smile as he dipped his cheek nearer to the Captain's. Though he meant to rattle her further, his own throat caught and his words tumbled out in a husky whisper.

"Believe whatever you want, Captain, but I'm telling you right now; James Hooke is not who he seems."

"I'll be the judge of that, thank—" Wendy's words were interrupted by a shower of orange sparks as Tinc swooped in. She hovered in front of Wendy's face and let out a stream of unintelligible garble before whirling around Peter's head in a frenzy.

"What is it, Tinc?" His lips pulled in annoyance as he angled from Wendy to attend to the bot until a haunting melody swept in on the breeze.

Surprised, Peter checked their surroundings. The first star was setting, leaving Neverland enveloped in a greenish cast. Starfall was approaching, but danger had already arrived. A long, lilting note brushed through the lonely woods and sent a shiver down his spine.

"What was that?" Wendy's tense posture mirrored his as she responded to the eerie tune.

"That's a mermaid's song." Peter's voice was grim. "We're in Mermaid Cove."

Wendy glanced at him, disbelief clear across her face. "Mermaids?"

Peter nodded, then hurried to the edge of the trees. The wooded area thinned, revealing a beautiful lagoon that glowed emerald in the haze of Never's eve. Wendy took in a sharp breath, and Peter followed her fixed gaze to the ethereal performance in front of them. He raised a finger to his lips.

"We have to pass them to reach the *Jolly Roger*," he whispered.

Unaware of their presence, the mermaids continued to preen and sing from their stage. Tinc buzzed quietly, her steady hum translated in his cochlear device, breaking the spell they seemed to weave. He glanced at Wendy. The eerie sheen cast by the Second Star set a faint glow to her face, making her appear even lovelier. The mermaids would not appreciate her beauty. His jaw clenched as he thought of what would happen if the jealous creatures saw the pretty Captain.

"Be careful," he warned. "They're not as friendly as they look."

Wendy's lips parted, as lovely as rose petals as she breathed, her gaze never wavering from the cove. "They don't look friendly at all," she said.

"Exactly."

WENDY

Wendy studied the creatures in front of her. They were eerily beautiful, made more enchanting in the green cast of the Second Star. A foreign melody swept from the middle of the lagoon where they sat, weaving shells into each other's hair, carried on the night breeze. It sent shivers through her as she listened.

Suddenly, she wanted nothing more than to share their song. She stepped toward the clearing, leaving the safety of the trees to see the creatures better. Heavy fog rolled through her thoughts, swirling over everything but an early memory of her mother singing as she plaited Wendy's hair. The ghost of a caress brushed her cheek, and she was little again, desperately craving her mother's warm embrace.

Stuck in the memory, Wendy crept closer until her movement drew the attention of the mermaids. Surprise registered on their features when they first saw her, but transformed into welcoming smiles as they reached for her, and their song dissipated into the melody of her mother's favorite lullaby.

"Pretty baby, bloom and grow,
Sleeping beauty, Mommy loves you so,
Precious girl, stay young and new,
Then the world will love you too."

A cold sensation surrounded Wendy's torso, and she looked around, the mermaids' spell momentarily broken as she realized she was standing waist deep in the lagoon. Frightened, she swiveled her neck, searching for the mermaids and saw them sitting at the edge of their rocks, eyeing her hungrily. Their song intensified as each one joined to lure her, filling the cove with the sinister tune. Peter's frantic calls echoed behind as he sloshed in after her. Realizing her mistake, Wendy jerked to retreat.

Her sudden movement startled the mermaids and their faces twisted in rage. They surged forward, howling as their bodies sparked and transformed. Their lovely hair and skin disappeared, revealing withered skeletons with ferocious teeth and claws stretching toward her. Their wicked song played on, but underneath the beautiful melody, Wendy heard their hungry growls. She backpedaled furiously, slipping on algae-covered rocks under her feet. A pair of strong arms grabbed her from behind, and she shrieked until she realized it was Peter.

"What are you doing? You're gonna get yourself killed!"

The mermaids shrieked and reared back on their fins, but now the spell was broken, Wendy realized that what she thought were flowing fish tails were more like skeletal snakes' tails, coiled and ready to strike. The closest mermaid let out an angry hiss and dove into the water, followed by her sisters, who careened through the lagoon toward Wendy and Peter. Their backpedaling put some distance between themselves and the rocks, but in the water, the mermaids were *fast*. Spinning on clumsy legs, Peter and Wendy would be caught before they escaped the water.

The mermaid leading the charge was the first to reach them. She shot out of the water, arms wide as she lunged for Wendy. Her claws swung, and Wendy twisted to the side, leaving the mermaid grabbing for air. She crashed into the water, but before Wendy could see where she had landed, one of her sisters attacked from the other side.

Wendy reacted and shot a quick round at the mermaid's shoulder, but the slick rocks made her footing unsteady. The shot hit its mark with a glancing blow, cutting an angry red slash through the mermaid's shoulder. The monster screeched and recoiled, then lunged, furiously swiping the gun. Her long hand struck Wendy's wrist, jarring her arm and knocking the weapon from her grip. It spiraled in the air until it fell into the lagoon with a sad thump and disappeared below the surface.

"Let's go, Cap!"

Peter gripped her arm and pulled her toward the bank, but as Wendy watched the creatures circle, she knew running wouldn't work. As soon as their backs were turned, they'd be dragged under and drowned.

Relentless, the mermaids raised from the water, their skeletal frames bobbing as they surrounded Wendy and Peter. They started singing again, and a sudden vision of the monsters sitting on their rocks stringing necklaces filled Wendy's mind. In front of the singing mermaids, a dark form floated on the water's surface, but Wendy couldn't make out the figure until it slowly rolled on its side, revealing her own face, paralyzed in a silent scream of fear. Her teeth were missing, and where eyes should have been were only gaping holes. Wendy's heart lurched as she looked closer at the mermaids' handiwork, and realized their delicate beads were her own stolen teeth. Her eyes had been strung into a seashell crown that rested upon the brow of the leader.

Wendy shook the image away and realized the mermaids had resurfaced while she was distracted. Nearest to her was the mermaid she had envisioned wearing her eyes, followed closely by the remaining four, flanking in pairs of two. It lunged and Wendy lashed out with a quick punch, connecting with her face. The mermaid's eyes widened in surprise as she crashed into the water, disoriented.

Wendy grimaced. She could keep the monsters at bay, but without a weapon, they would just keep coming. "Give me your blade!"

"What?" Peter continued to tug on her arm, his brow furrowed like she was speaking nonsense.

"A knife! Give me your knife!" She screamed, frustrated by the confusion covering his face. He acted like he'd never seen a woman fight before. Mercifully, understanding dawned on him and he reached into his pockets to retrieve a medium-length dagger and tossed it to her.

Wendy caught it then spun around, brandishing the blade. She slashed the mermaid in front of her then plunged the dagger into her heart. The creature fell with an earsplitting shriek, but Wendy gripped the blade, and with a sickening squelch, pulled it from the creature's chest as she vanished underwater.

As their sister sank to the depths of the lagoon, the mermaids howled and advanced on Wendy. To keep them at bay, she swung her blade as she swept a wide kick in a double attack. Her foot connected with the midsection of one, sending it sprawling across the water like a skipping stone while her blade sliced across another monster's neck, cutting it clean through. It let out a strangled cry and disappeared into the depths, never to resurface again.

The remaining mermaids hissed in a rage, but instead of striking again, they bared their teeth and slowly retreated to the rocks. This was no longer a battle they were willing to fight. Wendy scuttled out of the water, as high onto the beach as possible before her body crumpled beneath her. She stared across the lagoon at the two remaining mermaids. They were singing again, but now it was a duet, a mourning song for their lost sisters.

A twinge of guilt twisted Wendy's stomach, but as the mermaids' skeletal forms reverted to the beautiful creatures that had lured her to the water, she realized she had done what she had to. She remembered her vision of the mermaids playing with her teeth and she covered her face with her hands and shuddered.

Beside her, Peter sprawled on the sand, watching her. His sopping T-shirt clung to his strong chest, highlighting each rasping breath he took. Dark red tendrils plastered his forehead, streaming droplets down his face. Tinc buzzed worriedly, demanding attention, but his focus was on Wendy as though she was a puzzle to solve.

Wendy's cheeks warmed, and she turned from the intensity of his gaze. Her attention fell to her disheveled appearance, and she let out an embarrassed cry. Mud covered her boots and base of her pants, dotted with bits of purple seaweed, making them appear more brown than black. What wasn't muddy was wet, sopping from the lagoon. Her jacket sagged, heavy with moisture, and splattered with the mermaid's slick green blood. She discarded it on the beach, a lost cause.

Peter laughed and poked the gaping hole in the knee of her pants, sending warmth radiating through her leg.

"Pretty impressive, Cap." He winked, then propped himself in the sand, serious. "Where did you learn to fight like that?"

"The Academy, of course. We've all received standard combat training. Any member of my crew would have been able to do that."

Peter stared at her. "No," he argued, his gaze hard. "Any member of your crew would not have been able to do *that*." He sat up to inch his face closer to hers, revealing the depths of his forest green eyes. Wendy's flipping stomach stilled when a sudden buzz fluttered against her wrist and Nana's cool chime echoed through the air.

"Alert: Biceps Laceration. Seek medical attention."

Wendy twisted to check her arms, confused. Though her flesh was still numb from the freezing water, Nana was right—bright red blood trickled from a neat lateral slice across her upper arm.

"Oh shyte!" Peter said, jumping to his feet. He crouched over her, gently drawing her arm to examine the wound.

"It's fine," Wendy said, trying to pull from his grip. "It's just a scratch."

"That is not a scratch." Peter eyed her arm. "You probably need stitches."

"It doesn't even hurt," Wendy argued. To prove her point, she pushed herself to stand. The world tipped, and she found herself tumbling toward the ground before Peter's strong arms caught her and deftly lowered her to the sand.

"Uh huh." Peter's brow quirked. "Humor me anyway and sit still," he said before ripping the sleeve from his own shirt, exposing a sleek biceps. He squeezed the fabric to remove the excess water, then gingerly wrapped it around her arm.

Wendy sat still, allowing him to finish his makeshift bandage. The crease in his forehead deepened as he tightened the knot, securing the wrap in place. He lifted Wendy's arm, studying his dressing as her muscles contracted and flexed. Satisfied with his handiwork, he returned his gaze to Wendy.

A slow burn flushed up Wendy's face under the intensity of his gaze, in stark contrast to the chill that had set inside her bones. Unbidden, a shiver ran through her body, ending with a slight tremor of her jaw. Peter's brow furrowed and he pressed the back of his hand to her neck, radiating heat from his skin down her collarbone. The warm sensation lingered on her skin even after he pulled away to shrug out of his pale jacket to drape it around Wendy's shoulders. She tried to protest, but another shudder rushed through her, chattering her teeth and rendering her argument useless.

"You're freezing," Peter said, cutting off her argument. "The mermaids are built for the cold—you're likely to catch hypothermia if we don't warm you up." He pulled the jacket snug around her shoulders, then slowly rubbed his hands up and down her arms, warming her from the inside out.

Wendy's breath caught as she watched him. His focus was so sharp but his touch so gentle, just another juxtaposition of the puzzling man before her. Try as she might, she couldn't get a solid read on the mysterious mechanic—his emotions and reactions were so mercurial she always ended wondering which way was up.

Peter finished massaging her muscles, and Wendy was relieved to note she had regained feeling in her fingers. They clutched Peter's jacket to her body, holding tight to the age-softened material. He glanced up and caught her watching him, sending a sly smile creeping across his face.

"I think you'll live," he said decidedly, then laughed at the scowl his diagnosis earned from Wendy. It sounded like sandpaper, rough from disuse. It disappeared into the air as he studied her, suddenly serious.

"You were brilliant out there you know," he said, searching her face. There was an intensity in his stare that Wendy hadn't seen before, but with a quick twist of his head it was gone, replaced by a cocky grin. "Although you wouldn't have been half as impressive without my knife."

"Oh!" Wendy exclaimed, realizing her mistake. Her cheeks flamed hotter and she fumbled to retrieve Peter's blade. "Here."

Peter held up his palm. "Nah, you keep it. I'll get another." He grinned like he was going to say more, but his next words were cut short when Tinc flew between them. Her mechanical body shot off red sparks.

"Not now, Tinc." Peter brushed her away with a flip of his wrist. The bot tumbled back with a flurry of furious fireworks. She emitted a stream of angry jangles, then flew to a branch in the trees above them, watching them sullenly.

Wendy turned to Peter, eyes wide with confusion. "What was that?"

"Meh." He shrugged. "Tinc gets overprotective." He pushed himself up and extended his hand to Wendy. "She'll get over it."

"Right." Wendy eyed Tinc as she accepted Peter's hand. She could still see the nanobot's sparks showering down from the trees. Realizing she was staring, she turned her attention to Peter, who still had his hand clasped around hers. Her throat caught, and she tried to clear the sudden lump inside. With a jerky motion, Peter released his grip and ran his hands through his hair, averting his gaze.

Wendy busied herself with brushing the drying sand off her arms and legs. Her damp hair fell over her shoulders, cascading in loose waves. She smoothed it self-consciously before she realized how silly she was acting and cleared her throat.

"Thank you." She pocketed the blade in her hip sheath, pleased that it fit perfectly. "I'll return it as soon as I find a replacement."

"No worries, Cap. Consider it a gift."

Wendy bristled at the informal address, but decided not to press it. "Call me Wendy," she offered.

Peter smiled, his eyes mottled in the most striking shade of green she'd ever seen. "Wendy," he agreed.

23

PETER

Peter stared at Wendy longer than was probably appropriate, but he couldn't help it. Her hair, normally pulled tight behind her head, tumbled around her shoulders, shattering her reserved appearance. Combined with her dazzling galaxy eyes, she was breathtaking. Even if she hadn't entranced him with her fighting dance—where each movement was a new step in a finely executed performance in a battle for life or death—he would still be captivated by her.

Tinc emitted another angry buzz from her perch, telling him exactly what she thought of his attention to Wendy. He ignored her.

"If you're done playing with the mermaids, we can move on our way," he told Wendy as he removed his jacket to squeeze the excess water from the lagoon.

Wendy let out a harsh laugh. "I think I've had enough fun to last a lifetime." A haunted tone clung to the edge of her voice.

"That's how it usually happens," Peter said. "I don't understand why. They're always so welcoming," He joked and shrugged into his damp coat.

"A little *too* welcoming, perhaps." A small smile tugged Wendy's lips, chasing away the remaining evidence of her apprehension.

"Maybe." Peter tilted his head toward the edge of the beach. "C'mon. I promised I'd take you to Hooke. Since the mermaids didn't do you in, I guess I'd better stick to it."

He started down the beach. They were about halfway across when a soft crackle sounded in his ears, followed by a flurry of static and a light pressure on his shoulder.

"Nice to have you back." He laughed at Tinc's unladylike response. He had programmed her well.

Wendy watched his interaction with Tinc in awe. "She isn't like any of the other nanobots I've ever seen."

"That's because I designed her that way. Completely one-of-a-kind," Peter crowed. A shudder of pride buzzed through Tinc at Wendy's praise.

Wendy's brows rose. "*Designed* her? Weren't all military nanobots standard issue?"

"They were. I'm sure most remained that way. All except Tinc." Peter patted the bot on the head. She let out a whirring purr and her core processor glowed a lovely soft pink. "Now she's fully loaded. She has over a hundred different upgrades, complete with her own personality." Tinc interrupted Peter with a happy jangle. He paused, then laughed at the unshared joke.

"How do you understand her?" Wendy interrupted. "All I hear is static.

Does she have a voice?"

Peter pointed to his left ear. "I installed a special chip in my ear. It's my own device. It translates Tinc's processing into speech. It's a little higher pitched than I'd like, but it's how we communicate."

"That's pretty advanced for an engine mechanic." Wendy's grumble couldn't conceal her admiration.

"Just one of many things to love." He grinned. "Now let's get moving before the ladies decide they want to try for round two." He pointed his thumb over his shoulder at the mermaids. Wendy shuddered.

Together, they traipsed through the wooded area, the only sounds coming from the delicate hum under Wendy's breath. It was so soft that Peter doubted Wendy even realized she was doing it. Compared to the eerie melody of the mermaids' song, Wendy's voice was light and sweet, like a lullaby. But since he had never had one sung to him, he couldn't be sure, so instead of pointing it out, he just plodded along, enjoying the sweet tune.

They pressed on in an unspoken battle. Though Wendy had started following him, she kept unwittingly pulling in front. Peter stepped ahead a few times only to have her overtake him again, and eventually ceded the lead. They were almost to the *Jolly Roger* when the trees surrounding them rustled.

Disturbed from its slumber, a shadowed animal crawled from the bushes and crouched to pounce. Peter reached for his knife but grasped only air. He cursed, remembering he had given it to Wendy. Unable to incapacitate the animal from where he stood, he yelled for the captain.

"Wendy, watch out!"

WENDY

By the time Wendy heard Peter's warning, it was too late. Before she could react, something rammed straight into her midsection. The impact knocked her to the ground, where she was pinned under the heavy creature, gasping for breath. Wendy shuffled to reach Peter's dagger. With a quick flip of her wrist, she trained it on the creature above her. She was about to plunge it into the beast's hide when she realized she wasn't being attacked.

Though the animal had her pinned, it wriggled as it sat on her chest, emitting a low rumble from the back of its throat. Wendy shoved it off, and was surprised to see it was the size of a small cat, even though it weighed nearly fifty pounds. The creature let out another purr then buried its nose deep in her hair. Wendy shrieked and tried to pull it out, but it nestled istself on the bridge of her shoulders.

"Wendy!"

Peter rushed forward, his eyes wide as he tried to find where the animal had disappeared to. Wendy had to fight back a laugh at the concern on his face.

"I'm fine," Wendy stilled, feeling the creature's nails brush against her skin as it tried to situate itself in his new burrow. She pulled her hair off her neck so Peter could retrieve the animal. "Help me get it."

The weight lifted from her shoulders as Peter untangled the creature from her curls. Wendy loosed her hair then turned to Peter with an expectant look and extended hands. Peter gave her an incredulous stare but dumped the creature in her arms.

Wendy clutched it to her chest, gripping it tight so it couldn't wriggle free and into her hair again. The creature let out a happy purr as it watched her curiously from a triangular face that narrowed into a tiny nose. It resembled a hedgehog with its beaded eyes and rounded ears, but instead of spiky tines, it was covered in fine downy fur. Its coat was the softest thing Wendy had ever felt, and absolutely beautiful. Soot gray hairs with fine strands of white poked through underneath as it moved, shimmering in the light. Its bushy tail was twice the length of its body and wrapped around Wendy's shoulder to anchor it to her as it continued to wriggle in her arms.

"Aren't you the sweetest thing," Wendy nuzzled the creature. It grabbed her face with paws like a raccoon and rubbed its nose against her cheek. Wendy fought back a squeal of delight.

"Cap! Put that thing down." Peter eyed the animal. "You don't know where it's been!"

"Oh please. It's just a baby."

"How could you possibly know that?" Peter cried.

"Look how cute it is!"

Peter stared blankly at her. "Cute. That's your scientific evidence."

"Hey, you've got your robot, I've got her."

"Her?" Peter groaned and rubbed the bridge of his nose in disbelief. "You don't know it's a girl! You don't even know what it is!"

Wendy rubbed the bridge of the creature's nose. "You can be the seventh member of the *Fede Fiducia*," she cooed, scratching the wriggling beast between the ears. It snuggled deeper into her arms, then stretched its mouth into a giant yawn.

"Seventh member of the. . ." Peter spluttered over his words before dropping his head into his waiting hands. "In the name of all that is good." He fixed Wendy with a stern glare. "You know you can't keep it, right? What if it's venomous? What if it gets hungry?"

Wendy looked at the fluff ball in her arms. She had always wanted a pet, but had never been allowed one at the Academy. One of the "perks" of the military.

She studied the creature, trying to stay objective. It had curled into a tight ball with its tail wrapped tightly around its body, forming a mini-cocoon. Watching its peaceful breathing—a stark contrast to the ragged gasp of Peter's breath as he'd tended to her wounds—Wendy had a hard time believing it posed any sort of threat, but Peter was right. It wasn't practical to keep an alien as a pet.

"Stay here," she whispered, giving the creature one last caress before gently setting it in the bushes. Her lower lip poked out in a small pout as she sighed and turned to Peter. "All right, let's go," she said, hurrying to distance herself from the underbrush before she could reconsider.

Peter let out a bewildered laugh and hurried after her.

"You're hard to peg, Cap, you know that?"

Wendy turned to face him. He stood behind her, his head cocked. Though his tone was light, he studied her face like she was an abstract art piece.

Wendy's cheeks warmed under the intensity of his gaze. "I can't imagine why," she said. "I'm pretty uninteresting."

"I beg to differ," Peter said. He stepped toward her and lowered his voice to a hum. "You are the most vexing and endearing box of contradictions I have ever seen. You fascinate me, Wendy." His mouth quirked in an uncertain smile, emphasizing his chiseled features. Looking into his eyes, she was acutely aware of him, from the slight tremor in his voice to the ghost of his lips against her own.

A warning pulse shot through Wendy's wrist and Nana's voice cut through the quiet clearing.

"Alert: Elevated oxytocin levels impacting core functions. Accelerated heart rate and increased blood pressure resulting in above average body temperature. Recommendation: a cool comp—"

Wendy her hand over the scanband to muffle Nana's assessment, while her cheeks caught fire. Peter coughed and covered his mouth, but even with the attempt at discretion, Wendy saw the curl of his smile. Wendy clamped her hand tighter against her wrist as Nana buzzed again, vowing to dismantle the band as soon as she returned home. She looked shyly at Peter, certain her face was every shade of red imaginable, but to his credit, he simply smiled.

"Neverland hates Tech," he said with a shrug.

Wendy let out an unattractive snort. "That makes two of us." She buried her face in her hands, feeling the heat radiating from her skin. A cold compress indeed.

There was a soft tug at her hand, and Wendy peeked from behind her fingers to see Peter trying to pry away her makeshift mask. His green eyes lit mischievously as he grinned at her.

"But I don't." He winked. His hand clasped around hers as he drew it toward his body. Gently, he pressed something into her palm, then pulled away. Parts of her skin that burned from his contact now felt too cold in his absence, but she looked to see what he had given her.

Resting in the center of her palm was a small, metal pod shaped like an acorn. Formed by metallic wires and tiny gears, it shimmered chrome, morphing into hues of silver, blue, and purple in the light.

Wendy breath hitched as she studied the beautiful trinket. The little acorn was more beautiful than her mother's finest piece of jewelry. Peering closer, she pressed a smooth button on the side, revealing a tiny compartment. Her brow quirked at Peter in a question.

"For your watch," Peter said, his voice husky as he studied her reaction. "At least, until I can fix it for you," he added with a cocky grin.

Wendy laughed. "That's the second gift you've given me today," she said as her lips drew into an amused smirk. "But I don't have anything for you."

"I could think of a thing or two," he said, and swept a stray curl from her eyes. His fingertips brushed against her cheek, sending a jolt of electricity through her, leaving her hyperaware of the way his hand lingered beside her ear.

Peter tilted his head toward hers, but before he inched closer, Tinc buzzed in, shooting orange and red sparks across Wendy's vision, blinding her with their brightness. The bot jangled a stream of shrill notes as she fluttered in Peter's face, forcing him away from Wendy.

Wendy flushed, embarrassed by the emotions flooding her chest. She turned to see Peter, swatting angrily at the nanobot as she buzzed in his face.

"Cut it out, Tinc!"

He knocked the back of her processor, sending her spinning through the air in a flurry of orange sparks. There was a stream of angry jangles as she swooped around and flitted back into Peter's face to scold him with her gibberish.

"Just leave me alone, will you?" Peter pushed past her to stand beside

Wendy. "Can't you see we're busy?"

Tinc froze in midair and her body dropped precariously until she caught herself a few inches above the ground. A shower of blue sparks rained from her body before they flashed a brilliant shade of green. With a broken hum, she shot off, leaving a flurry of crackling red electricity trailing behind her like a tiny comet rocketing through the forest.

"Was that necessary?" Wendy reprimanded Peter with a cross expression.

A flash of guilt flitted over Peter's features before his boyish smirk returned.

"Ah, Tinc knows I'm kidding. She's just got a temper. She'll be back before you know it."

Wendy's lips twisted. The nanobot did seem rather temperamental. She wondered why Peter programmed such big emotions in the tiny bot.

"You should go get her." She didn't know why, but she felt responsible for the tension between the two of them.

Peter laughed. "Nah. Tinc needs to get over herself. We'll keep going, and she'll catch up."

"Are you sure?" Wendy rooted to the ground. She had been trained never to leave a man behind. Though Tinc wasn't technically a person, she had ample enough personality to qualify as more than just a hunk of machinery.

"Yeah," Peter said decisively, though he scanned the canopy. "Come on, let's keep moving."

He pushed ahead of Wendy, and continued through the jungle, walking through the underbrush. To pass the time, he played a jaunty tune on a small panpipe, but it was clear he missed Tinc's crackling hum. Though he still walked proudly through the woods, the longer the bot was gone, the more anxious he seemed.

"She's been gone a while," Wendy observed.

"Yeah." Concern laced Peter's voice, but he forced a cocky laugh. "She's just messing with us."

Wendy quirked her brow. Peter's smirk faltered under her stern gaze. He ruffled his hands through his hair and let out a heavy breath.

"All right, I'll go look for her," he said. "But only because I'm tired of waiting," he added quickly. "Wait here, I'll be back in just a few minutes." He hurried off, his tight muscles coiling and bunching to vault over the fallen branches and trees like a flying squirrel.

Wendy shook her head as she watched him leave. For all his boasting, Peter acted a little boy who had never quite grown up. She looked around the clearing and found a large rock not far from where she stood. She made herself comfortable and studied the surrounding area.

Neverland was breathtaking. Lush greenery sprouted everywhere, except it had more of a purplish tinge to it than green. The deep hues filled the land with an intoxicating ambiance that Wendy could easily lose herself in.

She leaned against the boulder and looked up at the stars. Her breath caught as realized how different the atmosphere was here than back home. The galaxy shined so bright, it almost seemed as if the heavens were moving, dancing a beautiful waltz in a court of night. And in the middle of it all were the Stars; with the first star the reigning king, deferring to his queen's breathtaking beauty.

Wendy could have stayed like that the entire night, but the crackle of electricity sounded in her ears, and she turned to find Tinc fluttering impatiently over her shoulder. The little bot buzzed, her foreign static unintelligible.

"Tinc!" Wendy said with relief. "Peter went to find you," she explained, hoping Peter hadn't programmed some voice-recognition feature in the bot to make her understand only him, though she wouldn't have put it past him.

Tinc hummed and swooped in a large circle toward a break in the trees. She hovered in the air and let out another flurry of bossy jangles.

"He went the other way." Wendy, exasperated, pointed in the direction Peter left.

A shower of orange sparks shot out from Tinc's processor, and she buzzed impatiently as she circled back around again.

"You want me to go that way?"

Tinc bobbed up and down as she jangled excitedly.

"Did Peter find you?" Wendy's brows furrowed. She was surprised Peter hadn't come back for her himself, and if she was honest, a little disappointed.

Tinc gave another slow bob.

Wendy let out a small sigh and nodded.

"Lead the way."

She hoped Peter wasn't far. She wasn't thrilled at the idea of following a nanobot she couldn't understand through the jungle of an alien planet. Tinc hummed impatiently and swooped around her to urge her forward. Wendy bit back a growl and let the bot guide her. She didn't need to add *cranky* to her list. She followed Tinc to a small clearing. The nanobot began to slow, but Peter was nowhere in sight.

"Where's Peter?" Wendy slowed her pace as she walked toward where the nanobot hovered.

Tinc zigzagged in the air, drawing Wendy forward. When Wendy reached the middle of the clearing, Tinc let out a brilliant round of crackling sparks, shooting yellow electricity into the air. Without warning, a large hand clamped down on Wendy's shoulder. A wheezing laugh sounded in her ear as she was drawn to something solid. A meaty arm clapped across her chest, locking her in the stranger's grip.

"Well aren't you a pretty one?" the man holding her growled.

A momentary flare of panic surged through Wendy, but she steeled her nerves as she assessed the situation. Hundreds of sparring hours had prepared her for this. She was at a disadvantage since she was already in a hold—usually, she wouldn't let her opponents get close enough to get hands on—but she hadn't had much of a choice this time. Based on the position of his hold, her captor was large, probably somewhere around the same build as Johns. And he was strong.

But she had beaten strong opponents before.

She stopped struggling, feigning weak. To overtake him, she needed him to let his guard down. To think she wasn't a threat.

"P-please don't hurt me," she whined, putting as much fear into her voice as she could muster.

"Be a good girl and I won't have to." The man's breath was hot in her ear. He leaned in to inhale the scent of her hair as he spoke, and Wendy had to fight down the urge to lash out too early. Though his advance was unwanted, it was a solid indicator he was feeling confident.

Good. She let out a small whimper for good measure. When a cruel, gravelly laugh escaped the man's lips, she knew it was time. Wendy threw all her weight and strength forward, flipping the unprepared man over her shoulder and sending him tumbling to the ground. Arms free, she grabbed for Peter's dagger, brandishing it at the hulking man. He sneered at her as he stepped closer, his shirtless body exposing a tangle of tattoos that rippled as he moved. His size alone gave the impression that he could snap her neck if he wanted, and his leering expression indicated he might be considering it.

"That wasn't nice, luv," he growled as he squared off against her. Wendy wasn't intimidated. This was a fight she could handle. She held her dagger firmly between herself and the man, forcing him to keep his distance.

"Neither is sneaking up on people," she countered brashly. "Or didn't your mother teach you that?"

A flash of surprise crossed the burly man's expression, but then he laughed. "Captain's gonna like this one," he said to someone over Wendy's shoulder. A wheezing cackle responded behind her.

The action caught Wendy off guard. She hadn't considered there was more than one person in the clearing, but listening carefully to the strained laughter, she realized her mistake. In her panic, she had miscalculated.

Wendy whipped around to size up her other assailant and immediately wished she hadn't. The old man watched her hungrily through a tangled web of white hair covering his cataract-laced eyes. His movements strained under heavily stooped shoulders, but there was a crazed look on his face that told Wendy he was unpredictable, which made him more dangerous than his partner.

Before she could figure out what to do, the old man swung, hitting her upside the head with a stout club hidden behind his back. Peter's dagger fell from her grip, thudding uselessly to the ground. Her vision began to fade, and as much as she struggled against it, a wave of dizziness overtook her, sending her tumbling into the outstretched arms of the giant before her.

"Peter..." His name escaped her clumsy lips as she fought to maintain consciousness.

"He's not here, luv." The man laughed cruelly. "You'll be for the Captain now."

Beside him, another round of wheezing laughter escaped the other man. He leered at her with cold eyes and a distorted smile. The terrifying image was erased by a blanket of black covering her vision. Through the haze, the man holding her issued one final command.

"Grab the bot too. Now we've got the girl, Captain's got one more job for it."

The last thing she heard was a string of angry buzzes followed by a manic cackle of laughter.

PETER

Peter scoured the jungle searching for Tinc. It wasn't strange that she had left in a huff—she had run off on him a dozen times. But she always came back a few minutes later, after her cylinders cooled. But he had doubled all the way back to Mermaid Cove with no sight of her. That was different.

"Tinc!" he yelled again, earning bitter scowls from the mermaids. He was too far for their song to reach him, so they satisfied themselves with hissing at him before slipping back underwater.

"TINC!"

Nothing. Breathing a heavy sigh, Peter turned to head back to Wendy. He had been gone much longer than he'd intended, and he didn't need her wrath directed at him, too.

He crashed through the jungle, hurrying to the clearing. He called for Tinc a few more times with no response. She'd probably gone back to the treehouse to pout. He'd find a way to make it up to her later.

"Sorry I was gone so long, Cap. I—"

Peter froze as he pushed through the trees to a now abandoned clearing.

"Wendy?"

He looked around, wondering if maybe he had gotten turned around. That would have been even more surprising. Peter was a natural navigator and perfectly remembered the lay of the land after one trip through. And he had traveled all over Neverland. He had the whole place memorized.

"Cap? Where'd you go?"

He forced a light laugh in case she was trying to play a trick on him, but he realized how stupid that was. That was something *he* would do, not Wendy. Confused, he was about to call out again when he noticed a set of light footprints crushed into the grassy trail. They went farther into the jungle, toward the *Jolly Roger*.

Irritation washed over Peter. Though he'd taken longer than expected, he'd thought Wendy had more common sense than to go traipsing through an alien planet alone. After experiencing the mermaids, she should have realized that.

He let out an impatient growl. The stupid fuzzy thing she found in the bushes must have lulled her into a false sense of security. He trudged after the footprints, grumbling about girls and their fascination with cute things. His grousing cut short, however, when Wendy's trail abruptly disappeared.

He froze as he realized he was looking at clear evidence of a struggle. Crushed foliage surrounded the space, bordering an arena displaying Wendy's tracks joined by two additional sets of footprints in a scuffle. Not far from the tracks, he found a ratty old handkerchief with the Brigade's emblem stitched into the corner.

"Hooke."

In a breath, Peter was charging through the jungle back toward the treehouse. He felt a pang of déjà vu as he barged past Mermaid Cove and the angry sirens hissed before scattering underwater, but he wasn't on the beach long enough to care.

He hurried on, weaving around low and fallen branches until he made it back to the treehouse and flung himself down the hatch into the living room, where the rest of the boys waited. Johns and Michaels were there too, joined by another soldier—tall and broad-shouldered, with golden hair and arrogant blue eyes that held a newly haunted edge. Pink skin puckered under a set of expertly applied butterfly stitches. They had recovered Boyce.

Peter didn't have time to donate to the newest house addition as he scanned the room, Tinc's empty perch confirming his worst fears.

"Where's Tinc?" he demanded.

Confusion laced the boys' features as they slowly registered that Peter was alone. Johns' face transformed in a rage, but before Peter could react,

Boyce surged forward and slammed him into the wall, bringing his deep line cut into focus. No matter how neatly DeLaCruz had bandaged his face, it would always be marred by the Stjarnin's scar.

"Tinc?" The Commander's eyes sparked furiously as he pressed down on Peter's collar, squeezing the fabric tight against his trachea. "Nobody cares about your electric gremlin," he snarled. "Where's *Wendy*?"

Peter coughed as the air whooshed from his chest. "We have to go," he wheezed, "Hooke's got her."

"Got her?" Boyce crushed Peter further against the wall but stopped when Johns stepped forward. Johns pulled the Commander's shoulder, releasing the tension against Peter's neck enough for him to breathe, but his eyes were hard as he stared at Peter.

"What does that mean?" he asked, his voice low. "You were supposed to meet with the Captain, then return. It was part of the plan."

"We didn't get that far." Peter coughed. "We got separated. Tinc flew off, and Wendy told me to go after her. When I went back, she was gone."

"Why would Hooke take her hostage when she was going willingly?" Boyce demanded, his lips drew a tight line as he gradually increased the pressure against Peter's windpipe.

Peter's vision began to blur. "It's what I *tried* to tell you," he gasped. His cheeks burned, and he was sure he was changing colors faster than the Neverland starset. Behind them, the angry shouts of his boys vaulted over Boyce's taut shoulders as they cried for him to release Peter. "Hooke isn't the hero he's been made out to be."

Johns and Boyce exchanged a quick glance before the Commander slowly let go of Peter's collar, allowing his feet to slide to the ground.

"Explain," Boyce growled, his voice laced with cold fury.

Peter met the eyes of the men surrounding him as they waited for his answer. Stern faces from Wendy's men mingled confused looks from his own crew. A sharp turn of his gut told him to say nothing, but then a flash of Wendy smiling up at him through mermaid-soaked hair played in his memory. Still breathing heavily, Peter cursed and straightened to address his men.

"Before the *Roger* blinked, I found out Hooke had gone rogue. I hacked his transmissions and uncovered that he already had a plan to go chasing immortality. It was dangerous and crazy, so I sabotaged the ship."

"And that's how you crashed." Boyce seethed.

Peter nodded.

"It wasn't supposed to happen that way. It was a freak accident. Bad timing. I fritzed the *Roger* as we were passing Neverland. We were navigating the Uncharted Sector, and Hooke hadn't disclosed the planet's location. Hell, I don't even know if it had registered on his navs."

Peter ran his hand through his hair as a fresh wave of guilt racked his body. He had never admitted his part in the *Roger*'s demise to anyone—not even Tinc. His stomach flipped, and he made the mistake of looking down at Tootles, whose face filled with such hurt and betrayal that for the first time, Peter wondered if he had made the wrong decision. He swallowed the lump in his throat and continued.

"Hooke realized what I did and tried to stop me, but it was too late. The *Roger* was grounded. I assembled the boys, and we left. We've been on our own ever since."

The silence in the room was stifling. To Peter's surprise, the Twins broke the quiet.

"I believe you," one said, while his brother backed him with a silent nod. "We remember what it was like on the *Roger*. If we'd stayed, who knows what woulda happened to us?"

"Is it anything like what will happen to Wendy?" Johns interrupted, his voice hard. He stood before the group, pain evident on his features.

Peter straightened his shoulders. "No," he said, feeling resolve steel his chest. "Because we are going to save her." He spoke determinedly, watching as each man silently enlisted in their new mission.

"We'd better do it quick," Michaels interrupted, pulling his gaze from a still blank comm. He glanced at Boyce.

Peter's brow furrowed. He looked at Tootles, who nodded before clearing his throat. "We have some bad news too."

"What kind of bad news?" Peter's voice was sharp.

Tootles swallowed, then stepped forward. Even standing tall, he was still a good foot shorter than all the other boys, but that didn't stop him from meeting every eye, his jaw set as he addressed the room.

"The Stjarnin are preparing for war."

"What?" Peter yelled. "*Why?*"

Tootles' lips twisted in a nervous frown. He turned to Boyce, whose face was ashen, save for the angry red gash trailing from the edge of his brow to the base of his jaw.

"The Stjarnin have a missing person of their own." He felt silent, his gaze empty as he wrung his hands around the raw red rings of skin circling his wrists. After a quick exhale, he straightened his posture to complete his report. "The Prince's bride, Tiger Lily, was kidnapped as well." He let his words sink in. "And since we don't have her, that means she's with Hooke too."

24

THE CREW IS CARRIED OFF

WENDY

Wendy woke on a down-feather bed with an elaborately carved wooden canopy. It was so lovely it took her groggy mind a minute to remember how she had gotten there. As soon as she did, she snapped up, alert. She scanned her surroundings, assessing her situation. Her jacket and boots had been removed, leaving her dressed only in her black tank and torn leather pants. Upon further inspection, she found Peter's jacket draped on the edge of the bed, her boots sitting neatly below.

Wendy rubbed her head. She had been captured by two men and was now being held prisoner...here? The room's finery looked as though it fit would better in her mother's parlor than the scenario her mind was painting.

Quietly, she dropped from the bed and crept to the center of the room. It was beautiful, filled with fine art pieces and a built-in bookshelf that housed the most gorgeous sets of literature she had ever seen. An ornate mahogany desk rested against the opposite wall with a massive matching chair covered in plush red velvet.

A carved, elaborate shelf hung above the desk, covered in small trinkets. There was a silver bowl, so tiny it looked more like a thimble. Wendy picked it up, and slid it onto her finger. Though clearly old, it was polished to such a shine that its intricate carvings were still clearly legible—even if they were in a foreign writing.

She peered closer but froze when the sharp sound of boots approached the door, accompanied by happy humming. Startled, she pocketed the trinket and reached for her dagger, swearing when she realized it wasn't there. She swept the room for a weapon, until her gaze landed on a small, sword shaped letter opener. It wasn't ideal, but it could be useful. She scurried up the platform and shrugged into the bed, concealing the tiny blade under the burgundy comforter. She was nearly situated when she realized that Peter's mechanics jacket was still resting on the edge of the bed. Quickly, she lunged for it and tucked it under the covers beside her. Better to see where she was before revealing allies.

Wendy clutched the letter opener against her body and pretended to sleep, peeking through a tiny sliver in her eyelids. The door creaked open, letting in the chipper hum that had been masked by the heavy frame. A tall, slender man with a pointed nose and wire rimmed bifocals strolled briskly through the door. He carried in a tray loaded with biscuits and a strange pink fruit. The smell of coffee wafted from a small pitcher in the center and Wendy had to force herself not to throw herself at it.

Using the tray, the man prepared a lovely place setting before strolling to her side. Wendy pinched her eyes shut to keep up her ruse.

"Time to wake up now, miss." He rocked Wendy's shoulder, both his touch and his voice much gentler than the men who had ambushed her. "The Captain will be in to meet with you soon. He sends breakfast with his best regards."

Wendy pretended to stir, feigning disoriented. As she pressed her hand to her temple, a sharp pain reminded her of the beating she'd taken. She groaned, adding sincerity to her act.

"Where am I?"

The lithe man stared down at her. His sandy hair was slicked neatly underneath an antique Brigade hat that perfectly matched the vintage uniform Wendy recognized from her studies.

"You're on board the *Jolly Roger*—the best expeditionary ship there ever was." He beamed. "You are here as an official guest of Captain James Hooke."

He tipped his head in a polite bow, indicating to the place he had set. The motion caught the light streaming through the window, reflecting metallic gold orbs. Wendy started and the man tilted his head curiously, emitting a faint whir from the bend in his neck.

"Who are you?"

"Well miss, that's very thoughtful," the man said as a rosy flush crept up his neck. "I am the *Jolly Roger*'s Synthetic Maintenance Engineering Emissary—the Captain's First Hand, but you may call me 'Smee.'" He gave a small laugh and a deeper bow, and Wendy felt a wry smile tug her lips as she watched his adapted mannerisms.

"Nice to meet you, Smee." She glanced around the ornate room. "How did I get here?"

Smee's smile faltered as embarrassment laced his features. He dropped his golden gaze.

"I'm dreadfully sorry about the mix-up." A dark look crossed his eyes. "Some of the men seem to have forgotten themselves."

Wendy's brow furrowed. It seemed a weak excuse, but perhaps the Captain would have a better explanation.

"Will I be able to speak with the Captain?"

Smee brightened and motioned to the place setting on the table. "Of course. He requested you enjoy your meal until he is able to join you."

Wendy followed his hand. The coffee roast had slowly wafted throughout the room, filling it with the rich, bitter scent. She dared to hope.

"Is that *real* coffee?"

Smee nodded. "Indeed. From the Captain's reserves. Quite a treat." His angular features twisted into an impressed look. He chuckled as Wendy craned her neck to get a better look at the plate. "It would be easier if you had a seat, miss."

Wendy cleared her throat, embarrassed. "Yes, well. Since the Captain was so kind." She flashed her most diplomatic smile. "Especially since you went through all the work to set it up."

A tiny hum buzzed from the robot's chest as his synthesized skin slowly manufactured a pink tinge around his cheeks. "Yes, miss. I do appreciate the thought."

"Please, call me Wendy," she offered. "Captain Wendy Darling of the

Fede Fiducia."

"Another Captain!" Smee delighted. His hand clasped hers, wrapping her in his cool grip. The synthetic skin felt clammy against her palm. "What a pleasant surprise!"

His neck twisted then froze as his gears buzzed, caught in the stiff pose before he rapped his knuckles against his head to release the catch. He turned to Wendy with a sheepish look.

"Excuse me, Captain. The atmosphere does not quite agree with my joints." He flexed his wrist with a series of clicks. He swooped his arms in an elaborate gesture. "Have a seat, please, while I go and fetch the"—Smee paused to let out another amused chuckle— "*other* Captain."

Wendy rose from the bed, leaving the blade she'd pocketed nestled safely under the blankets with Peter's jacket. She had made it to Hooke. There was no need for weapons or—knowing of the tension between the Lost Boys and Hooke—to show her full hand. She straightened her tank and smoothed her hair before taking her boots to follow Smee to her prepared seat. She allowed him to pull out her chair as he chattered pleasantly before pouring her coffee and dropping a cube of sugar into the steaming mug.

"The captain will be so delighted to meet your acquaintance. Absolutely delighted."

"Thank you, Mr. Smee. Please send in the Captain. I am ready to speak to him." She smiled warmly, sending another manufactured pink tinge creeping across the first mate's cheeks.

"Yes Captain." Smee scurried through the door, picking up his song where he had left off.

Wendy forced herself to waiting until the door closed to tuck in to the meal. The biscuits were nothing special, but the coffee almost made getting bashed upside the head worth it. She would need to address that with H—

Wendy froze as a small thrill raced up her spine. She was about to meet Captain Hooke. Her mind catalogued his many accomplishments while his memorized photo flashed through her thoughts. In just a few moments, she would be staring into his eyes for real…

A soft knock at the door sent Wendy out of her skin. She cursed as her hand bumped the tray, toppling her fork to the floor with a loud clang. She retrieved it just in time to meet the Captain's entrance with a rushed salute.

Hooke didn't return the Fleet's greeting. Instead, he flashed a brilliant smile and crossed the room to clasp her hand in his. His cool mechanical prosthetic whirred quietly as it delicately gripped her fingers. With a flourish much more graceful than Smee's, he brushed her knuckles with a trace of a kiss.

"Captain Darling, I presume?"

Wendy's brow dipped as she studied the man before her. His long, dark hair was streaked with silver and lines etched his skin, giving what might have been a strong, smooth face a tired texture. His build resembled the Captain's—tall and broad—but his shoulders dipped with age. Only his eyes were the same, the intense blue of the sea after a storm.

"Captain Hooke?"

The man before her chuckled, flashing a smile that momentarily transformed him into the man from her file. "Pleased, I'm sure."

"But…" She paused, remembering the Captain's transmission. "The transmission we received…" she trailed off as her mind tried to make sense of what her eyes were attempting to convince her. Her eyes darted to his mechanical hand, which whirred and flexed as the Captain followed her gaze.

Hooke's smile dipped before he fixed it in place with a small sigh. "Taken a lifetime ago, I'm afraid. It has been so long, I fear the Fleet would not recognize me. We've used the same recording since we first landed."

Wendy faltered for a moment, then forced the shock from her face.

"Of course." She untangled her hand from his grip. "I'm pleased to tell you, Captain, your transmission was successful. It is an honor to make your acquaintance, sir."

Hooke nodded and motioned for her to sit.

"The pleasure is all mine, my dear. It's been quite some time since my men have seen another soul on this planet besides the natives. Let alone one so stunning."

Wendy's cheeks warmed. Though this Hooke was not the dashing Captain she'd daydreamed about, he was still an honored Fleet leader. She smoothed her hair before setting her soldiers' posture. "You're too kind, Captain—"

"James." Hooke interrupted with a flip of his wrist. "Call me James. Please."

"Yes. Well, thank you so much for your hospitality Ca—James. Although I must admit, based on how I boarded the *Jolly Roger*, I was rather concerned for my well-being."

Hooke's face darkened like a passing storm.

"I do apologize for that. My men have been rather on edge as of late. Things on Neverland are not as peaceful as they once were." There was a heavy thud as his metal prosthetic rapped against the table. "I assure you the situation has been handled. Please accept my humblest apology."

"Of course." Wendy nodded, studying fine lines etched from his knuckles to his wrists—wrinkled skin and rusted metal. "That is why it is important for us to leave posthaste. As soon as our repairs are finalized—"

"Repairs?" Hooke's face narrowed in a shrewd expression before his features twisted in a dejected grimace. "You hit turbulence outside the atmosphere. You're grounded, too."

"There have been some complications," Wendy admitted, before quickly adding, "but my crew is highly skilled and already working on a solution."

"You don't think my crew did the same?" Hooke asked. Though his smile fixed in place, there was an edge to his voice that didn't match his charm. "Or that they were in any way less skilled?"

"Of course not." Wendy searched for the best words to explain. "It's just that, our tech has evolved exponentially in the last hundred years. We—"

"One hundred years?" Hooke's heavy hand thumped against the small table, knocking the Smee's neatly laid out place setting askew. "You mean to tell me that we've been stranded on this blasted island for *one hundred* years?"

Wendy nodded solemnly. "Yes, Captain. Our ship launched 16 May 2393. We performed a half-blind Hypershot based on the coordinates we gleaned from your transmission. We made the jump, but our ship was damaged and we had to perform an emergency landing."

"So you're as caught as we are," Hooke clipped. "This is no more a rescue than a glorified tea party."

Wendy bristled. While she understood the Captain's frustration, it was not the reaction she had expected from the celebrated hero.

"As I said before, my men are currently analyzing our status. I am confident that with Peter's help—"

"*Pan?*" Hooke's metal fist swung, this time sending a teacup soaring. "Pan is a murderer and a mutineer! I will NOT have him on my ship!" He slammed the table with his palms and forced himself to his feet to glower at her.

Wendy steeled her shoulders as she waited for Hooke's tirade to end. When his rage waned, she slowly stood to meet his gaze. It was a trick they taught in the Academy—never give your opponent the upper hand. Even body placement provided powerful advantages in perception; and with Hooke towering over her, he was definitely in a higher position. She needed to assert herself for the information she was about to disclose.

"I understand that there is some conflict between you and Pan," Wendy acknowledged, her voice even. "However, I have been tasked with retrieving your crew by any means necessary. Trusting Pan may be a risk, but in the interest of not being here *another* one hundred years, it is a risk I am willing to take."

Hooke's eyes sparked, but after a tense moment, he gave a terse nod and lowered into his seat, then gestured for her to sit across from him. Wendy held her position, forcing him to wait before she slowly dropped to her chair. Once she was situated, he quirked a tight smile from across the table.

"I apologize for my outburst, Captain. However you must understand my concerns." His metal hand clutched at top button of his elaborate jacket, pulling at the squared clasp.

"Of course," Wendy spoke calmly, but her body pressed forward as her curiosity got the better of her. "What happened?"

"The transmission I sent contains most of the information I know," Hooke admitted, "but I have reason to believe my ship was tampered with." Hooke paused to let his words sink in, then gave her a pointed look. "I believe that Pan is responsible."

Wendy's jaw dropped. "What evidence do you have to support your claim?"

"As I'm sure he told you, he was the *Roger*'s lead mechanic. He knew my ship inside and out. I'm ashamed to say he probably knew more about her than I did. He has a particular gift for tech, you see."

"If he was so skilled, then why would he let something happen to the ship? Perhaps it was just an oversight?"

Hooke knotted his brows and lowered his voice to a conspiratorial whisper. "Peter is many things, but careless is not one of them—especially where tech is concerned. He is a brilliant mechanic. There's not one thing that could have happened on this ship he couldn't have maintained, which is why I brought him on board." A hurt look flashed across his eyes and Wendy had to fight not to lay a comforting hand across his. "I guess you could say I'm the one who trapped us here."

Wendy's brain reeled. If what he was saying was true, then Peter had duped her. She studied Hooke's face. It was the same face she had stared at for years, touched with the traces of a life long-lived. He was a hero decorated by the Fleet, and lauded by millions; a fellow leader. If she couldn't trust another appointed Captain, who could she trust? Peter?

The vexing mechanic's green eyes flashed through her mind. Unbidden, she dipped her hand into her pocket to clasp around the trinket.

"I'd say the blame lies with whatever caused the crash," Wendy stated firmly. "The truth will come to light in London, once all passengers have made it home."

"Indeed." Hooke nodded with a tired sigh. "I suppose the next logical question is, how exactly do we go about doing so? I'm assuming at the very least, your vessel will need minimal repairs. Clearly, mine requires attention as well."

"Yes. Our ship will need attention. Unfortunately, we have not been able to complete a full diagnosis, as there was a hostile situation with the Stjarnin shortly after landing. My mechanic is working to see what he can salvage. I would also like him to check the *Roger*, if you would allow it."

"Of course!" Hooke smiled. "I'm thankful to hear your encounter left you unscathed. Many of my men have not been so lucky. The Stjarnin are a savage people, much like early humanity. Even their faith is primal. They worship of a deity passed down from stories and drawings."

"The Shadow?" Wendy guessed the name Peter had given her.

Hooke's lips curled into a wry smile. "Shadow. That *would* be an appropriate name for it. The Stjarnin's representations are always rather dark. Whatever it may be, they believe in its power."

"Did the Stjarnin tell you this? Have you made further contact?" Wendy asked.

"My men have as little contact as possible," Hooke clipped. "We have done what we needed to survive—peace negotiation was not one of those things."

"So, how do you know about the Shadow?"

Hooke walked to his desk. He looked at the charts scattered across the top while toying absently with the buttons drawn up his chest.

"I have been searching for a very long time," he breathed.

Wendy jumped as the door burst open and a new crew member hurried in, filling the room with the smell of oily sweat.

Hooke turned from his maps, annoyed. "What is it, Mullins?"

"The tech is almost prepped, Captain. Took some time to crack the code, but with the bot onsite, she was a lot easier to troubleshoot," he reported eagerly. "And Cecco says the other captive—"

Hooke cleared his throat. Mullins paused, confused, and his eyes widened when he saw Wendy.

"I mean, uh, the other *Captain*, is waiting for you below deck…" He trailed off nervously under Hooke's stormy gaze.

The Captain blinked, his face a blank slate before he smiled and moved to a large urn beside his desk. He grabbed a handle protruding from its lip to reveal an elegant blade. He looked lovingly at it as he stepped toward her.

"May I get you some more coffee, Captain?"

Wendy's voice faltered as she rose from her seat. "I'm fine, thank you." Alarms crashed against her ears and she cursed herself for letting her guard down. "I've already been out longer than expected. I must return to my men and inform them of our new plan."

"I hardly think we've put a plan in place." Hooke stepped closer to her. "There are still several rather large issues that need to be discussed." The blade crackled to life, covering the sharpened conductor in a coat of electricity. Wendy's eyes widened at the ancient szikra. They had been discontinued shortly after Hooke's disappearance in favor of more cutting edge technology. But as the dangerous blade hissed, Wendy realized what a formidable weapon it truly was.

"And they will be," Wendy said, backing toward the door. "But first I must reconvene with my crew. They are my responsibility, as I'm sure you are aware."

Mullins closed in behind her, trapping her between the advancing captain.

"I'm afraid that just isn't possible." Hooke's face twisted sympathetically, but his eyes were cold. "There are still matters that must be tended to."

Wendy looked around the room and she realized what a fool she had been. Though the walls were draped in finery, she was in nothing more than a gilded prison cell. Her only way out was through the door behind the Captain.

"My men are waiting for me."

Her voice faltered as the door opened and the burly man who had captured her lurched into the room and leered while he awaited the Captain's orders.

"That *is* an unfortunate setback," Hooke agreed. He turned to the man. "Cecco, fetch the bot. Perhaps she can make herself useful one last time."

Defiance surged through Wendy. "What have you done with Tinc?"

Hooke laughed and tsked at her. "I haven't done anything with Pan's precious companion—yet. But I must say, it's touching that you are so concerned about her well-being when she didn't give a damn about yours."

The door opened and Cecco returned with Smee in tow, pushing a small cart with a large metal cage on top. Between the slats, Tinc's tiny frame bashed against the walls, showering red and orange sparks with each frenzied hit.

Wendy's confusion turned to fury as Hooke whipped his head back in a bout of laughter. She balled her fists. "I don't know what you're talking about."

"Clearly." A wry smile crept across Hooke's lips. "How do you think my men found you, Captain?"

Tinc let out a sad jangle from inside the cage and Hooke's smile deepened, furthering the wrinkled crease surrounding the corners of his lips.

"The bot you are so gallantly defending betrayed you. Seems she didn't appreciate the attention you were garnering from her master. Who knew a robot could get *so* possessive?"

"Why are you doing this?" Wendy surged toward Hooke, but the Captain raised his blade to her chest and the szikra's crackling electricity stopped her cold.

"Come now, Captain. I would hate for this to get messy." He motioned to Smee. "Bring me the bot."

Smee hesitated, casting a sorrowful look in Wendy's direction.

"*Now*, Smee."

The First Mate shuddered, then with a quiet hum, hurried to follow orders, his shoulders tense as he struggled to hold the flailing bot. Beside him, Cecco sneered then wrenched Tinc from the first mate's unsteady grip. A shower of sparks shot from Tinc's processor, earning a startled yelp from the massive pirate as they singed his skin.

Hooke watched Tinc's frantic struggle, his expression cold before he slowly pulled open his desk to retrieve a tiny black microchip. He raised the tech triumphantly then turned to Wendy and his lips twisted in a cruel grin.

"It's a special piece I commissioned after our unfortunate landing," he boasted. "It took Mullins quite some time to develop. I was beginning to wonder if I'd ever get the opportunity to use it. What a happy coincidence that fate wanted to rid Pan of his insect as much as I."

Wendy's head felt heavy. "Are you saying… is that—"

"A virus," Hooke finished. "And a rather nasty one at that. Its ghost program will override the bot's core processor. Everything will remain intact, but all the software will be recoded so it responds only to me. Simply put, it will effectively turn Pan's precious companion into an untraceable double agent."

Hooke signaled for the men and Cecco slammed the struggling bot against the tabletop. There was a sickening crunch followed by a weak buzz as Hooke ripped off Tinc's back panel to insert the chip. His features twisted with glee as he withdrew his hand, waiting for the program to execute.

Tinc froze then went limp. Wendy watched in horror as the little bot stirred, then sat upright. Her core whirred softly and she rose in the air, hovering above the desk as she watched Hooke expectantly.

"Nanobot," Hooke commanded. "Report to Pan. Bring him and the others to me."

"No!" Wendy cried, but it didn't matter. Tinc bobbed obediently before she shot off, disappearing to find Peter. Wendy let out a frustrated yell and turned to Hooke.

"It doesn't make any sense! If Peter is truly responsible for your marooning, let the Fleet take care of it! Don't put other people's lives at risk!"

Hooke chuckled cruelly. "Your idealism is touching, Captain. But Pan's punishment is only half of it." His face darkened as his wrinkles deepened into a scowl. A manic glaze overtook the steel in his eyes as his good hand absently rubbed his center button, his gaze turned inward. "We have *plans* for Peter. Plans for all of you."

Hooke traced the tiny button at his chest a moment longer, lost in a trance. Then with a quick shake of his head and turned to Smee.

"Bring out the other prisoner," he ordered. "It's time to show the good Captain what we *really* know about the Shadow."

25

PETER

Peter didn't remember much between the revelation of Tiger Lily's abduction to his mad dash through the jungle. Everything blurred together, ending with his careening across Neverland toward the *Jolly Roger*, with his crew in tow. Running alongside them, Wendy's crew hustled, with haunted expressions. They had all insisted on coming—even the medic had wanted to join, but Johns had insisted she stay with the fallen pilot.

"We'll bring her back," he'd promised, though his jaunty grin couldn't hide the worry in his eyes. Peter was sure his looked the same.

"I should kick your ass for not telling us everything you knew sooner," Johns hissed, drawing Peter from his reverie. The Commander focused on the rough terrain as he ran, but Peter felt the rage radiating from him. "If anything happens to her, I'll kill you."

"If anything happens to her, I might beat you to it."

Peter put on another burst of speed. He didn't know what Hooke was up to, but nothing about it could have been good. James had begun slipping into madness long before the *Roger* crashed, following fairy tales and searching for immortality. He could only imagine what a hundred years of being marooned on an alien planet had done to his plans.

Peter's gut clenched, and he pushed on, ignoring the burning in his side. He moved so quickly that when he leapt over a rotten log, he almost collided with Tinc.

"Tinc!" Relief flooded through him as the bot flitted erratically above him. "Where have you been?"

Blue sparks shot from the bot's middle. She let out a quiet tinkle and drooped so low she was barely hovering above the ground.

Peter scooped her up, her apology humming through his ear. "Aw, Tinc, it's okay. Besides, if you hadn't gone, Hooke might've got you too."

Tinc's wings shuddered, but she allowed Peter to scoop her up before fluttering wearily into the air. Peter gave her a worried look. "Are you sure you're okay?"

The bot bobbed a wobbly confirmation, then zipped toward the *Roger*. Peter watched her until she let out an irritated jangle, then whooped and hurried after her. With Tinc leading the way, they resumed their pace, ignoring everything as they ran—even the mermaids didn't have time to sulk at them from their lagoon. A burn raced down Peter's side as he pushed on, determined to get to Wendy. He led the others at a breakneck pace, crashing through the jungle, until it slowly shifted into the dark sand surrounding Pirate Cove.

They were nearly there.

"We're not far out, the *Roger* is just past that—" Peter's directions were cut off by a sudden lurching swing from Tinc. The bot, who had been flitting alongside him, suddenly swooped left, nearly colliding with his jaw.

Peter skidded to a stop, watching in confusion as Tinc rose into the air, then dove at his head again, forcing him to dodge out of the way.

"Cut it out, Tinc! Now isn't the time!" Peter fixed the bot with a cross look, but the pinched expression didn't hold long. Tinc hefted her tiny body into the air and dropped in another narrow miss, singeing his shoulder with a loose burst of sparks.

"Shyte, Tinc!" Peter cried out. He glowered at the bot until suddenly, her body began convulsing and shaking erratically in the air. "Tinc, what's wrong?"

Tinc let out a cross buzz and struck again, this time nearly zooming into Boyce after Peter ducked out of the way.

Boyce swatted the air, catching Tinc's tail end and sending her stumbling through the sky with a furious jangle before she ratcheted herself above the canopy line, ready to attack.

"What the hell is going on, Pan?" Boyce seethed. "Can't you control that thing?"

"I don't know," Peter admitted, casting another wary glance at Tinc. "She's never done this before." His explanation was cut off by another sharp dive from above. Tinc swooped so closely to Peter's head he could hear the hushed hum of her processor as she passed.

"Well, we need to stop her before she kills someone!" Johns yelled from where he hovered protectively over Tootles.

Peter's jaw set. He traced Tinc's bobbing trajectory, noting the chaotic pattern. A faint hissing sound emanated from her body as her processor began to overheat, showering them with bright red sparks. Peter edged away from the clearing, his focus on the bot. Her body turned slowly after him, keeping her mark.

Peter backed up, moving slowly until his fingertips brushed the rough bark of a Nevertree.

"Tinc, this needs to stop," he commanded.

Another cascade of red fell from Tinc's body before her body jerked up, then shot down straight for Peter. His eyes widened at her brazen attack, but he held position until Tinc was close enough for him to make out her mechanic features, then he tumbled to the ground. There was a loud crunch as Tinc's momentum hurtled her into the Nevertree, shaking loose some of the soft purple leaves.

Tinc slid down the side of the tree with a strangled buzz before landing in a heap on the floor.

"*Tinc!*" Peter rushed forward to scoop her up, ignoring the searing heat radiating from her overheated core. Her wings shivered, sending a shot of electricity through Peter's hands. Peter studied her worriedly, aware only of the curious audience that had gathered around him when Michaels pushed through the crowd and pressed in closer.

"She's sick," the tech said, extending his hand. "It looks like she's caught a virus."

Peter placed Tinc in his open palm. Michaels' glasses glinted in the light as he carefully scanned Tinc's tiny body.

"Or..." Michaels interrupted his diagnosis to gently pop Tinc's back panel and sift through her hardware. After a short pause, he revealed a tiny black chip. "She's been tampered with. I'm guessing this is responsible."

"I didn't install that." Peter grabbed the foreign device and showed it to his bot. "What happened, Tinc?"

Tinc let out a shuddery whir, and Peter hissed in a breath.

"What?" Peter looked at the chip and back to the bot. His throat caught and he glanced around at the others who were watching him expectantly. Boyce turned to him with an impatient grimace.

"What happened?"

"I—" Peter tried to explain, but no sound came out. Tinc's confession was still burning in his cochlear device, echoing her treachery, but still, he didn't want to believe it. Tinc had betrayed them. She was the reason Wendy was with Hooke. Boyce's eyes narrowed and Peter's back stiffened. Mad as he was, Tinc was his nanobot. *His* responsibility.

"It doesn't matter," he said, his voice dead as he gave Tinc an empty glance. "She's defective. She's not coming with us."

There was another sharp crackle as Tinc tried to push herself out of Michael's palm. She hovered in the air for a moment, before slumping against the tech's thumb, exhausted. She looked up at Peter and let out an agitated hum.

"No Tinc. You're not," he said. He turned from Tinc's broken body to hide how hard his next words would hit. "Go home. I don't need you."

A strangled hum escaped Tinc's processor, but Peter held fast, his fists clenched at his sides as he took a slow step away from her, followed by another, then another until he was coursing through the jungle, fleeing her traitorous confession.

Hurried footsteps sounded beside him, and he didn't have to look to know Johns and Boyce had joined his frenzied pace. The trees began to thin and the hulking form of the *Jolly Roger* appeared, as if waiting for their arrival. Peter allowed one last thought to the broken bot on the jungle floor before he pushed the memory from his mind, ready to fight.

"We're coming, Wendy."

WENDY

"Captain, I really must protest." Smee's golden eyes blinked rapidly. His gaze flicked to the door, as if he could see something beyond the heavy metal. "Treating the princess this way is bad form. She is a lady."

"Lady?" Hooke's szikra singed the air as he whirled to face the synthetic soldier. "That thing is no more a lady than I'm the Admiral of the Expeditionary Fleet!" He leveled the conductor to train the beam at Smee's chest. "Do your job, Smee, before I disassemble you for parts!"

Smee cast a helpless look at Wendy. She averted her eyes, feeling the sting of tears when he scuttled, ashamed, out the door. Mullins snickered and followed behind, his scruffy beard and tattered clothes making him look every bit the part of a dastardly space pirate.

That's what they are, she realized. *Peter was right all along.* The thought burned white hot as she whirled to face Hooke.

"We came to save you!" Wendy's voice cracked. "I believed in you…"

"But I didn't need saving."

Hooke laughed cruelly and pushed her to the main hall, forcing her along the corridor while she struggled to break free. Wendy almost escaped with a heavy lurch forward, but Hooke's withered grip was surprisingly strong as his resting szikra pressed against the fleshy part of her hip.

"I wouldn't try that again, if I were you," he hissed.

Wendy spat in his face, earning a furious growl from the Captain. She expected to feel the bite of the szikra, but the world only rocked as Hooke whipped her like a rag doll.

"Bad form, Captain," he growled, the brightness in his eyes contrasted starkly with the age spots dotting his cheeks. "Now behave or I'll make *you* the spectacle."

Wendy resisted as best she could, but with the szikra's electric threat urging her forward, Hooke herded her to a large, open bay where the other pirates waited impatiently. They watched with hungry eyes as Hooke pushed her forward and fell in line, forming an ominous circle around a small dais filled with a mysterious dark liquid. Directly behind it, Smee hunched over a metal chair, latching the clasps to thick leather straps that bound a girl to the seat.

At least, Wendy thought it was a girl. A loose shift covered her body from chest to thigh, tight enough only to reveal the basic outline of her shape, which was more slight and angular than the warriors Wendy had encountered on the beach. The Stjarnin watched Wendy from ebony eyes that made up most of her face, resting above slits that must have formed her nose and mouth. Though she didn't speak, her eyes shone bright against her beautiful emerald skin as she observed the Captain's movements. She faced him with such a sense of propriety that Wendy felt she could give the Admiral herself a run for her money.

"And how is our princess today?" Hooke's voice took on a theatrical tone as if he were putting on a show. The alien didn't respond. Instead, she pointedly ignored him. Hooke's brow furrowed at her upstaging.

"Never you mind, Captain." Smee hurried forward anxiously. "Miss Tiger Lily just isn't feeling well. She hasn't been eating—"

"I don't care whether she's been eating or not!" The Captain roared. "She's a prisoner. Royalty among savages means nothing!" He clenched his hands as his temper spiked, gripping Wendy's arm. She let out a small yelp as the mechanical vise crushed her muscles and he turned, surprised, as if he had forgotten she was there. A smile broke out across his face, and he dragged her to where Tiger Lily sat.

"Captain, let me introduce you to my esteemed guest, Princess Tiger Lily." He paused, letting his introduction echo through the metal room. "Or is it future princess, as you are merely the prince's betrothed?"

Though Tiger Lily's face was still angled away, the dejected slump of her shoulders betrayed her. Hooke let out a mirthful laugh before he turned to Wendy.

"The princess arrived not long before you, my dear. How interesting that we had no visitors for years, apparently, only to be graced by two such esteemed ladies at once." He ran his finger along Wendy's jaw, and she shrank away from his touch. The pirates in the audience laughed at her discomfort.

"I happened along the princess much by accident, in one of our recent excursions along the coast. You see, not long after my transmission went out, I stumbled upon an interesting discovery." He turned to Tiger Lily. "Or rather, it was forced on me. You see, our sweet princess's dear subjects were always *so* hostile, as my transmission clearly explained. It was the source of great contention, and the loss of several of my soldiers—"

"Pirates, you mean," Wendy interrupted, her eyes blazing.

"Perish the thought, my dear." Hooke smirked. "But if it makes it easier on you, then by all means, *pirates* we shall be." He continued as if Wendy's outburst was no more irritating than a fly buzzing around his nose. "It wasn't until our last interaction with the Stjarnin that I finally realized the motives behind their anger. And when I did, I must admit I felt rather foolish for not putting it together sooner."

At this, Hooke pulled another trinket from his pocket. It was a long chain with an amulet on the end, made of some sort of precious stone. The working was crude, but the stone was breathtaking, greener than any emerald Wendy had seen. A faint glow emanated from the heart of the stone, making it look like a tiny replica of a familiar star.

"The Second Star..." Wendy's gasp earned a startled glance from Tiger Lily. The princess' eyes fell on the necklace and her angular shoulders drooped closer to the ground.

Hooke's smirk deepened.

"Yes. The Second Star. What I've been pursuing all these years. Turns out, they were followers of the Star long before me. As was their Shadow, or, as I believe they call it, *Itzala.*"

Tiger Lily's neck whipped around so fast Wendy was surprised it didn't break. Her empty eyes widened in horror, sending Hooke into a round of raucous laughter. His reaction spurred the first sign of life Wendy had seen from Tiger Lily as the princess struggled against the bindings to launch herself at him. Unbothered, the Captain continued his malicious laugh, spurring the pirates in his audience to echo the action. The room filled with evil cackles, sending shivers down Wendy's spine.

"How delightful to know I'm right." Hooke leered at Tiger Lily's struggling form. "And how unfortunate for you, my dear, that it's just a matter of poor timing." The Captain's lips drew into a mock pout. "You see, I wanted to leave for a *very* long time. I was furious you know, thinking I had finally found immortality, but at too high a cost. Eternity in exchange for a lifetime on a godforsaken planet."

Hooke glanced at Wendy, who stared coldly back. A wicked smile crept across his face as he turned toward the dais.

"But I was very wrong."

Hooke's voice whispered in hushed reverence as he brushed his mechanical hand along the rim of the dais and the dark liquid inside shuddered and began to throb.

"Itzala has shown me the way to true immortality. Now, I have another directive." Hooke watched the churning liquid and rubbed absently at his sternum, his eyes filled with a haunted light. "We must follow the Star."

Hooke withdrew a tattered piece of parchment from his coat pocket. The page was so brittle and torn that small pieces flaked off the corners as Hooke unrolled it, but that didn't stop him from gazing at the paper like it was a priceless artifact. He gave her a wry smile.

"This is one of the many pieces of memorabilia I've claimed in my quest. Possibly the most important piece."

Wendy's brows knotted as she studied the foreign markings.

"It's a spell," he told her delightedly. "An old and powerful revival spell."

Wendy's stomach lurched as her eyes darted across the paper. Though the inscription was in another language, the pictures accompanying it were easy enough to interpret. *Binding, summoning, sacrifice.*

Her gaze whipped to Tiger Lily, bound to the chair, and she realized what Hooke was going to do. She was about to object when a small explosion echoed down the hall, sending the pirates into a frenzy.

"Smee! Find out what's going on!" Hooke demanded. "Take Cecco and Starkey and report to me immediately! We're doing this today!" He lowered his voice so only Wendy could hear his next words. "I've waited far too long for this."

The wild look in his eyes set Wendy's nerves on edge, but she was more excited than afraid. Hooke knew full-well what the commotion was, and so did she.

Peter was coming.

PETER

The outside of the *Jolly Roger* was quiet as the Lost Boys approached. The small group huddled behind a raised dune that separated the jungle from the shoreline. It resembled the beach where the *Fiducia* crashed except the land that disappeared into the ocean was rocky and jagged instead of smooth sand.

"I don't like it," Curly whispered. "We could be walking into an ambush."

"I don't think so," Tootles piped in. "We've been watching their movements for the last few days and they normally go out twice a day. Once in the morning and once before Starfall. The Star set a while ago, I'll bet they're in for the night."

Peter looked at the skyline. The Second Star hovered in place, casting the land in green. Tootles was right—Starset had happened a while ago. The First Star was slowly making its way to eclipse as it completed its orbit. It was almost directly in front of the Second, dulling its glow and making the green no more than a dim cast. Nevernight. The pirates would have long gone inside. Even Hooke knew better than to keep his men out after the Second Star hid its face.

Johns looked incredulously at Tootles. "So what do we do?"

"We need to bust in..." Peter trailed off as he scanned the *Roger*. She was banged up, but still sturdy. Breaking in wouldn't be as simple as picking a lock. He scrubbed his hair as he thought until an idea struck. "Nibs! How many Nibblers you got?"

Nibs sprang forward, reaching deep into his pockets. "Enough to do the job." He grinned and dumped a handful of tiny spheres shaped like miniature coconut shells into Peter's outstretched hands. "Give me five minutes and the door's good as gone."

He grabbed the pile and bounded towards the hatch of the *Roger*. Peter shook his head.

"Slightly, go with him. Make sure he doesn't kill himself."

Slightly saluted and hurried after Nibs, hissing at him to be quiet so they didn't blow their cover. The others watched with bated breath until Johns broke the silence.

"So, we break down the door, then what?" he demanded, his gaze hard. "Do you have a layout of the rig so we know where we're going?"

Peter nodded.

"Chances are, they'll keep Wendy in Hooke's quarters. They're easy enough to get to. Problem is, they're starboard, so we'll have to make it all the way across the *Roger*. She's split into multiple compartments, and there's no telling where the pirates will be. We should expect a fight."

Johns and Michaels exchanged a worried glance. "This Captain isn't jumpy, is he?" Michaels asked, his face darkening as he studied the *Roger*.

Peter's eyes narrowed. "Jumpy?"

Johns' jaw tightened to match the rest of his tensed frame. "If he gets spooked, will he hurt Wendy?"

"Not likely," Peter said, earning an exhale of relief from Wendy's crew. "Hooke is all about good form. He fights dirty, but one thing you can count on is him keeping honorable appearances. The problem will be getting to him."

Boyce's mouth set in a firm line. "Oh, we'll get to him."

Just then, Slightly and Nibs careened around the bush, ducking under their hands.

"Cover!" Nibs' yell gave the others enough time to react before his explosion burst the eerie calm. Scraping metal rocketed through the clearing as the door burst off its hinges. The smoke hadn't even cleared before Peter was hurtling to the door with Boyce on his heels, motioning wildly for the others to follow.

They barreled through the crumpled door straight into a rush of pirates. The bay was chaos as Peter's men squared against Hooke's in a tangle of limbs, but it was easy to see that though they fought well, the Boys were severely outnumbered.

Only Johns seemed to give the pirates pause as he stood in the middle of the bay, surrounded by a handful of Hooke's men. He lashed out, knocking them back as they pressed in a singular attack. His giant fists caught two pirates, incapacitating them, but while he swung at a third, one of Hooke's larger men—an Ammunitions Tech named Starkey—cracked a chair across the Commander's chest. Johns responded with a bone-crushing bear hug before dropping him in a broken pile on the floor and stepping to his next victim.

Nervous looks covered the pirates' faces and a wry grin danced across Peter's lips. He turned his attention to the portly navigation specialist in front of him, and with a quick jerk of his hands, wrenched the man's arm back until he heard a splintering pop. The man screamed and dropped, but before Peter could move on, a heavy fist crashed into the side of his head.

Disoriented, he stumbled back to see Cook's massive girth towering over him. The pirate lurched forward, a wicked butcher blade in his meaty hand. Peter reached for his dagger, and swore when he remembered it wasn't there. Cook stepped closer, edging Peter into the corner of the *Roger's* bay. The cool metal brushed against his fingertips, but this time, there would be no dodging. Cook's piggy eyes narrowed in a miserable grin as he raised his knife high in the air.

"Got you now, Pan," he wheezed through his exertion. "Too bad the

Captain isn't here to see it." He let out a hissing laugh and drove the blade down. Peter jerked back, but before the knife's stinging bite hit his skin, Cook let out an agonized shriek as Boyce slammed into his legs and shattered his knees. In a smooth motion, Boyce flipped the pirate over and smashed his wrist against the *Roger's* floor until Cook released the dagger with a shrill howl. Peter moved to help, but Boyce turned to him from where he knelt atop the writhing pirate.

"Go!" Boyce struck Cook's skull, knocking the man unconscious. His eyes blazed as he turned to Peter. "We can handle the pirates. You get Wendy!"

Peter met the Commander's gaze with a solemn nod, then hurried from the room. The shrill sounds of battle drowned out his thoughts as he careened down the hallway. He just needed to get to Hooke's quarters, then he could—

Peter skidded on his heels as he turned the corner into the *Roger's* main bay. He scanned the room in shock and realized he had been wrong. Hooke wasn't in his room.

He was waiting for him right here.

26

HOOKE OR ME THIS TIME

WENDY

Hooke's malicious laughter echoed through the room as Peter slowed in shock. Wendy's eyes met his across the bay, and she gave a meaningful shake of her head, silently warning him from the dais in the center of the room. Peter stood in place, hands clenched as Hooke's gleeful laugh continued.

"So nice of you to join us, Pan." Hooke grinned, projecting arrogance as his mechanical hand tightened its hold on Wendy. "I was just showing the good Captain my greatest discovery, which I might never have found had it not been for you."

Peter's eyes flashed and Hooke's smirk deepened.

"Immortality is so droll without power to accompany it." Hooke's whisper sent the hairs on Wendy's arms standing on edge. "And soon, I will have that power. Once my summoning manifests the dark god's true form, I will be rewarded. Itzala is generous to those who serve him."

He raised the scroll and began reciting the inscription. His voice was mesmerizing as he read, hissing and sliding the words together to make sounds Wendy had never heard before. Her attention pulled away only when Tiger Lily thrashed against her restraints and screamed in the same language.

The contents of the dais began to swirl, stirring the murky liquid into a dark pitch. As it churned, darkness seemed to rise from the altar's bowl, covering everything it touched. Wendy struggled against Hooke, but he was entranced. Everything about him had turned to stone except his lips as they uttered the unholy words. She was trapped.

The spell transfixed Peter. He stared at the liquid seeping from the dais with horror. He had lost what little color his skin held, and his shock of red hair made him seem even paler. But he was the only one who could help now.

"Peter!"

Wendy screamed, hoping to break him from his reverie. From what she had seen in the inscription, the only way to stop the summoning was to take away the sacrifice—the princess trapped in front of the dais. She looked in horror as its contents continued to rise and spill over the edges, blanketing the floor as it crept toward Tiger Lily.

"Help her!"

Peter stood rooted where he was, his eyes huge as he watched the darkness. Wendy didn't know where the liquid kept coming from but as she watched, it morphed from a liquid to a gas, taking a larger form as it clouded around the room. She could almost imagine the tendrils turning into arms and reaching out to grab the terrified princess. At that moment, she realized what Hooke had meant when he was talking about the Shadow. It was the darkness, and it was evil.

She thrashed against the paralyzed captain, trying to break free, but it was no use. She might as well have been wrapped in metal. Even Hooke's skin felt cool against her body as his voice continued its haunted monotone.

"Peter!" she called again, desperate to wake him. "Get her out of there! It's the only way to stop him!"

She gazed at the Shadow. It hadn't reached Tiger Lily, but it was creeping closer, and the way it thickened told Wendy it was getting stronger. Her arms ached where she slammed against Hooke, and her throat was raw from screaming, but she tried once more, channeling all her strength and desperation into her final cry.

"Peeeeeetteeerrr!"

PETER

Wendy's terrified scream ricocheted around the haunted space in Peter's mind, snapping him from his paralysis. He swiveled his neck to look at her and saw her thrashing against Hooke. The Captain held her against him like a vise, his figure stone still as he continued his unearthly chant. A foreign cry drew his attention to where Tiger Lily sat, fighting to free herself while the Shadow snaked its way up her legs. He had to move.

He launched himself across the room, skirting the dais to slide behind the metal chair before furiously working to release her bindings. As he did, the Shadow steadily gained ground, crawling up to her torso. The farther it climbed, the more solid its billowing form became. Peter fumbled with the straps, the panic in his chest making him clumsy, but soon he had one strap free. Just one more to go...

The room fell quiet as Hooke's chanting stopped. The Captain froze. Peter turned to face the Shadow and saw it had almost enveloped Tiger Lily's entire body. The cloud had become a thick fog, and Peter could feel its rage. With his last burst of speed, he unclasped the final latch and buried his hands into the Dark Cloud that surrounded the Stjarnin. Blind, he wrapped his arms around her and pulled, sending her tumbling from the Shadow's clutches.

A furious screech echoed through the room as Tiger Lily sprawled on top of Peter. He pressed her behind him to free her from the Shadow's reach as it roiled in the air. Deprived of its sacrifice, it rose higher and higher, spinning until it formed a hovering whirlwind. Peter ducked and covered his head, ignoring the way the wind whipped his ears as he searched the room. Not far from where he lay, Smee huddled in the corner, his golden eyes an eerie beacon in the darkened room.

"What has Hooke done, Smee?" Peter yelled, straining to raise his voice above the howling Shadow.

Smee's features twisted in a conflicted grimace. He looked from Peter to the Captain, who stood over the dais, feeding the Shadow. Hooke's eyes blazed electric blue while tendrils from the Shadow swirled around his body, its billowing body leeching from his feeble form as it searched for its promised soul.

"Smee, that's not your Captain!"

The synth gave one last look at the haggard Captain and with a jerky dive, pulled the princess to her feet and looked at Peter, awaiting his orders.

"Take her to the Boys!" Peter screamed over the Shadow's fury. "Get them out of here!"

Smee tipped his head in silent agreement and wrapped his arm around the princess to hurry her from the room. Peter watched with relief as the door slammed behind them, then turned to find Wendy. She stood next to Hooke, sagging in relief. But as she glanced at Peter, her body wracked with a huge convulsion and she screamed, arcing her back into Hooke's tightened grip. Peter's heart lurched at the agonized sound that escaped her throat, ending with an exhausted shudder as she slumped against the Captain's frozen body, her hair cascading around her shoulders in disheveled waves.

Peter's vision flashed red and he surged forward, imaging the ways he would make Hooke pay when an icy wave of fear pulsed through his body, emanating from the stain on his chest.

"Not so fast, Pan."

27
WENDY

Everyone froze as the menacing voice resounded across the hall. Wendy cringed as the words slithered in her ears, reminding her of the crawling pain that had just ravaged her body. It was so unnatural—so *evil*—there was no way such power could have been possible. But as she craned her aching neck toward the sound of the voice, her worst fears were confirmed. Though Hooke's mouth formed the words, the sound that escaped did not belong to him. It was a high-pitched hiss that sounded like nails cutting against a chalkboard. Hooke's eyes were vacant as the Shadow continued, using him as a life-sized puppet.

"Peter Pan…"

The Shadow's terrifying shrill trailed off as it burst into a round of nightmarish laughter.

"I remember you…"

Hooke's face twisted into a broken smile, as if the Shadow was trying to force the expression, but didn't quite know how.

"Such dark thoughts… Such hate… You would have been a much better choice for my summoning…"

Wendy turned to Peter. He stood stock still as he watched the Captain's movements, transfixed. His face was ashen and his withered arms shook so much that she could see his fingertips trembling from where she stood.

"I thought all my efforts had been for naught when you pulled the princess from my grasp," the Shadow called, filling the room with its distorted hiss. *"But now it seems an even better option has come along. Surrender, Peter…"*

"And why would I do that?" Peter's voice sounded cocky, but Wendy heard the vulnerability behind it. The Shadow must have too. Hooke's neck craned to look down where Wendy was trapped against his chest. She forced back a cry as she looked into his face. His once beautiful eyes were possessed, replaced by the tars of hell. His aged smile fractured further as he gazed at her, sending freezing chills through her body.

"Because if you don't, I'll take her soul instead…"

Panic raced through Wendy as her eyes flicked to where Peter stood his face pale. Peter knew that pain. She'd seen the mark—a permanent reminder of the Shadow's cruel power. She thought of all that he had endured and what he was risking by coming back for her. She wanted to tell him to leave—to take the boys and run as far as they could, but before she could move, the Shadow's golem raised her so her feet were no longer on the floor and her cheek rested flush against his. He let out another unnatural hiss and the vibrations in his throat pulsed against her skin, sending her flesh crawling.

"Though she's purer than I would like, a soul is a soul all the same."

Peter let out an arrogant snort. "Take her," he said, his emerald eyes hardening as he looked at Wendy with a cool sneer. "She's just a girl."

Hooke's brows shot in surprise, but he thrust back his head, splitting into another round of heinous laughter. Peter's jaw tensed, but he stood firm.

"An excellent bluff, Pan," the Shadow hissed. *"But you forget, I've been inside your mind. The way you look at this girl is the way you wished someone would look at you all those years. In fact, she may be the only good thing about you…"*

Peter blanched. His gaze seared into Wendy's. Her chest ached at his helpless expression.

"Peter, just go!"

Hooke's laughter was cold on her neck. *"She is brave,"* he murmured. *"I can see why you like her…"*

"Peter, *RUN!*" Wendy yelled, but as Peter's mossy green eyes met hers, she knew that wouldn't happen. An imperceptible shift took over his stance, and his shoulders squared as he stood taller. His devilish smirk quirked the edges of his lips as he glared back at Hooke.

"Don't worry, Wendy." His green eyes blazed. "I've played this game. I beat this thing once, and I'll do it again." He glared at the malevolent cloud. "This time it'll stick."

Peter rushed Hooke, tackling him around the middle. He slammed into the Captain's body, sending it rocking, but the Shadow behind it held it firm. His eyes widened when he realized his attack failed, but he continued, beating against Hooke, trying to sever the connection between the two of them.

"Peter, it's *inside* him!" Wendy yelled. "You have to—" Her words were cut short by a powerful gust of wind that flung her across the room and into the wall of the Main Bay. Her vision erupted into a spiral of angry orange and red hues before she crumpled to the ground.

"Quiet, stupid girl!" the Shadow seethed.

Wendy's head exploded. Everything in the room reduced to blobs of color as her body was swathed in anguish. A shrill keening broke through the rolling waves of pain, and Wendy realized with a distant part of her brain that it was coming from her.

She was screaming.

Wendy plummeted through the air in a terrifying weightlessness that was a million times worse than the floating among the mermaids until she heard a dull thud followed by a sickening crack.

"No!" Peter's voice cut into the darkness, like a beacon, parting the thick fog encircling her mind enough for her to blink her heavy eyelids open to the scene before her. Through her haze vision, she made out the bay of the *Jolly Roger* filled with shifting figures.

The Shadow looked the same, a pitch-black mass towering over a small gray body underneath its writhing tendrils. The Shadow struck, knocking the body sideways, sending it tumbling into the wall. Wendy winced as the ship clanged in protest. The figure tumbled to the ground but pushed itself up with a cocky laugh that she recognized.

She shook her head to clear the muddied thick surrounding her. The pain had finally seeped from her bones, leaving only the memories of the Shadow's grip as its attention shifted to its newest victim.

Wendy blinked again clearing the last of the fog from her mind in time to catch Peter's gaze as he watched her worriedly. A relieved smile broke over his face, but his distraction cost him. From the corner of her eye, Wendy saw the Shadow's attack. Before Wendy could cry out, a billowing arm struck at Peter like a snake, aimed directly at his heart. Peter's eyes widened as he realized his mistake, but before the Shadow's mark rang true a tiny white blur shot across the room and knocked Peter out of its path, surrounding him in a halo of yellow sparks.

Wendy let out a strangled breath of relief as she watched Peter push himself off the ground to fix a beaming smile at Tinc.

"You came back!" His voice flooded with relief as a stream of furious buzzes crackled back at him. His melodic laughter ricocheted through Wendy's heart, settling her clamoring nerves.

"Of course you're forgiven. Just get Wendy out of here!" He pointed to where she lay crumpled on the floor. Tinc bobbed then jetted toward Wendy as another wave of dizziness threatened to overtake her.

Wendy forced her heavy neck up, weakly fighting the oncoming blackness. She struggled to focus, and her eyes widened in horror as the Shadow let out a keening howl and pulled back into a roiling cloud before piling into Hooke, fully claiming the Captain. The *Roger* shook under the force of the Shadow's power until suddenly Hooke arced back and screamed before rising unsteadily to his feet to face Peter, with nothing but pools of black filling his once-beautiful eyes.

Using Hooke's body, the Shadow raised his sword and swung at Peter. The spry mechanic ducked and bounced out of the way. The Shadow pressed on, slicing again and again as Peter danced back, the two of them performing a complicated waltz.

Peter crowed with glee as Hooke's attacks continued to miss. He became more brazen and darted toward the Captain to provoke him. It was exactly what the Shadow was waiting for. While Peter focused on Hooke's attacks, the Shadow inched behind him, forming a long tentacle that shot from the back of Hooke's body like a whip.

Tinc hovered uncertainly over Wendy's head, torn between following orders and helping her master. Her body shuddered, mirroring Wendy's movements, save the frightened purple sparks that shot from her processor each time the Shadow attacked.

"Tinc—help him!" Wendy cried.

Tinc flittered to Wendy's face and let out a quiet buzz before zooming into the fray. Peter had fought off the Shadow, but it continued to surge forward, billowing in a massive cloud over Hooke as it manipulated him like a tireless puppet. The Captain surged forward, sword in hand, while the Shadow's whips struck endlessly. Peter dodged a quick strike but was caught off guard as the Shadow launched a second whip straight at his throat.

It was about to wrap around Peter's neck when Tinc barreled into the darkness, dissolving the whip with a stream of frantic sparks. A furious howl filled the room, but the Shadow spun, determined not to be interrupted again. It launched itself at Tinc, swirled around her in a thick haze as it raged until it turned into a spiraling orb encasing the nanobot.

Suddenly, it parted and Tinc collapsed to the ground with a flurry of ash trailing after her. She hit the ground with a weak thump, mangled beyond repair. Wendy heard Peter's strangled cry as the golden sparks from the nanobot's core processor muted and faded to gray, but the Shadow wasn't finished. It clouded into a heavy haze and flowed toward Wendy.

She tried to push herself up, but her body was too heavy. She could only watch as the Shadow crept closer. Terror gripped her, but she refused to cry out—she wouldn't let Peter get taken. She tensed, preparing her mind the way Commandant Martinez had taught her what felt like lifetimes ago. She didn't know what to expect from this opponent, but she wasn't going down without a fight.

The Shadow was almost on her. Wendy felt its cold seep into her bones as it arched like a snake, ready to strike. She clenched her jaw, she was ready.

It was the strike from the side that caught her off guard. It flung sideways in a blur of dizziness and pain. When the world stopped spinning, she turned and saw Peter's eyes burning into hers as he lay sprawled on the ground where she had been.

"Peter, no!" Her brain dumbly pieced together what was happening. "You can't—you need to go—" Her voice broke as the warmth of his gaze burned into her heart. "You'll die…" The threat of tears overtook her words as she gulped to fight them back.

Peter watched her with a small smile playing on his lips, his eyes sparkling into hers.

"To die will be an awfully big adventure," he whispered, his voice warm as melted caramel.

He gave her a quick wink, then jumped to his feet.

"You want me?" he asked the Shadow defiantly. "You got me!" He let out one last proud crow, then launched himself at Hooke, laughing the entire time.

Peter's brazen attack caught the Shadow off guard for the first time. It shrank back in surprise, but its momentary lapse soon disappeared. It struck with a newly materialized tentacle. Peter twisted as he fell to hit the ground running, but the Shadow was ready. Another arm pummeled him in the back, sending him sprawling.

By this time, the Shadow had also reinstated its employ of Hooke's body and the Captain advanced on Peter, towering over him like a bear. Peter's eyes widened at Hooke's withered appearance, which deteriorated more with every step. The dark wrinkles that had etched themselves into his skin began to dry and crack until tiny flecks whipped into the storming air surrounding them, leaving the Captain a decaying shell. But more frightening was the Shadow's coils drifting above his body, forming a seething cloud that threatened to overtake the entire room. Hooke's snarl deepened exposing a hollowed cheek as the shrill pitch of the Shadow's hiss broke through the thick hanging cloud.

"You escaped me last time, Pan. You will not be so lucky again."

Small tendrils snaked out and latched onto Peter, burrowing under his skin as he thrashed helplessly against them. He screamed as his body convulsed, sending his back arcing in a bridge before he slumped in a heap, panting heavily.

With a burst of strength, Wendy pushed herself off the ground, feeling her leg give out underneath her when she put pressure on it. She shrieked as she fell, clutching at her knee. Warm liquid seeped between her fingers. Her vision blurred as she looked down and saw her bone protruding below her knee, shattered in an unnatural angle.

Another heart-wrenching scream from Peter cleared the stars from Wendy's vision and forced her attention to her fallen comrade. He hunched over his knees and elbows so his head rested against his clenched fists.

"Hold on, Peter…" She gasped as another wave of pain rocked out from her leg through her entire body. "I'm coming," she said, dragging herself across the floor to where Peter cowered in pain.

"Give yourself to me."

The Shadow hissed as he approached Peter. It was closing in, but Wendy was closer. She forced the pain from her mind as Peter continued to contort in disjointed positions.

"Don't give in," she called. "I'm still here."

The Shadow began to laugh as it watched her struggle. *"It's no use my darling,"* it menaced. *"He's mine now."*

"No, he's *MINE!*"

Wendy launched herself to cover the space between her and Peter. She landed on top of him, pinning him to the ground. Her body shook with the impact of his convulsions. She fought back a shriek as the jolts struck her damaged nerves, but she held firm, clasping his head to her chest.

"I'm here, Peter! Don't leave!" Tears streamed down her cheeks as she sobbed, clutching at him desperately. "Damn it, stay with me!"

Cold air covered Wendy as darkness enveloped her skin. She clenched her eyes shut as she cradled Peter, praying he heard her.

"Don't give up yet," she whimpered. "Don't give up."

PETER

Pain. There was so much pain.

That was the only thing Peter could think as the Shadow pressed in on him, seeping into his bones. It was amazing how his body could feel frozen yet blaze in searing agony at the same time. It screamed at him, furious he would let this happen a second time. Except this wasn't the second time. This was something completely new. This was nothing like what he had experienced with the Stjarnin. Then, the Shadow had only been in his mind, sending imaginary spasms through him. This was real, tangible, absolute anguish, caused by the Shadow as it forced its way into his body.

"Surrender."

The Shadow whispered in the hollowed-out recesses of Peter's mind.

"You won't last much longer…"

Peter struggled against the invader. He had fought it off once. He could do it again…

His vision grayed as another round of pain shot through his body. He wanted to die. It had to be better than what he was experiencing now. He turned in on himself as the Shadow pressed in his mind, leaving cold imprints of its deepest desires. Staining Peter's consciousness with everything his body was currently experiencing tenfold—pain, fear, darkness, death.

He couldn't let the Shadow win.

With every ounce of willpower he had, Peter conjured the happiest thoughts he could muster. Flying, running through the wilds of Neverland—

but those weren't enough. The darkness kept pressing in.

A frightened voice burst through the haze in his mind. Even in the darkness, it was beautiful. Rich and soothing in a way he hadn't felt in a very long time.

"Peter. Peter, I'm here. I'm still with you, but you have to wake up!"

Wendy.

Sudden flashes of beauty burst through the darkness. Wendy's lovely face filled his mind. Her captivating eyes and rose petal smile. But it was more than that. Her *essence* seared through the dark. Honor, dignity, courage, determination. All the things that made her burst through like a lightning bolt, cutting through the dark in a streak of brilliant light, showing him the way home.

Sensing something was off, the Shadow edged in on its prey.

"Don't fight," it coaxed. *"I can give you everything you desire…"*

A vision of Wendy in a beautiful dress misted in, beckoning for him to join her, to run away from everything together.

"…or I can make you relive your worst nightmares for an eternity."

Peter gritted his teeth as another wave rolled through his body. Wendy disappeared and suddenly he was a small boy on the corner of the street calling for his mother. She'd left him there two days ago, and he was getting hungry. The winter rains had started, and his clothes were soaked to the bone. He thought he would never be warm again—

Another gray cloud washed over his vision and Peter rolled over, his teeth chattering as beads of sweat popped out above his brow line.

"You're stronger than this!"

Wendy's plea shook him free. He wasn't searching for his mother. He had given that up long ago. It was just a nightmare the Shadow was using to twist his mind. And Wendy would never run off with him. She wouldn't leave her men, just like she wouldn't leave him. She would fight to the death—or until the Shadow consumed her.

An ache entirely different than the Shadow's searing presence stabbed his heart. The thought of Wendy's brightness falling to this evil was something he couldn't bear. He clung to every good thought he had, strengthening them with underlying images of her. Wendy's kindness, her faith, her spirit, her love...

"NO!"

A weight lifted from his shoulders as the Shadow rolled back. It was only a momentary stumble before it rushed at Peter, swirling to break in, but before it could hit him it stopped, blocked by an invisible force field. The Shadow screamed as its onyx tendrils lightened and dissipated into vapor. It pushed harder, sending more smoke unfurling to take him over.

Peter didn't notice. He was waging a war inside, clutching at happy thoughts and projecting them outward to stave off the dark. His body ached with every pounding throb of his head, but he held firm, clutching to Wendy to save his soul.

Furious at his defiance, surged over him, but this time, as it washed against Peter, the thick, dark form was riddled with light and blasted into no more than a murky fog.

Bellowing in rage, the Shadow recoiled like a wave on the surf. It pulled away with an angry hiss, flooding the *Roger* with its fury. The hull shook and trembled under a huge peal of thunder as the Shadow surrounded the abandoned body of James Hooke. It coiled around, lifting the Captain into the air with a vengeance. Peter's gut twisted as the Captain's icy blue eyes widened in a brief moment of clarity and he brought a withered hand to his fragmented face. For the first time since he had entered his trance, Hooke screamed, a sound of terror and agony Peter had never heard from the Captain before.

"Pan—*Peter*—help me!" Hooke bellowed. Peter stirred, reaching for his old friend, but it was too late. The Shadow swept over Hooke, wrapping him in swirling tentacles as it rushed out the bay and through the *Roger* like a receding storm.

Peter watched in shock as the Shadow's billowing cloud retreated, howling in rage. The echoes of a thought washed through his mind, fading the farther the Shadow fled.

"I'll see you again, Pan…"

The room stilled, leaving Peter like a hollowed-out shell. His knees trembled under the weight of his body, and he collapsed, smashing his face against the floor.

"Peter!" Wendy's cry evaporated as the room swirled around him. Her voice sounded thousands of miles away, but something wrapped him in its embrace. Warmth trickled into his body, filling the gaping holes the Shadow had left inside him.

"Peter, can you hear me?" He turned toward the sound, surprised to see Wendy's face beside his, worry etched on every line. "Say something!"

Peter look at the beautiful girl cradling him in her arms. Silent tears streamed down her face, and landed on his, sending a few cascading drops down his own cheeks. Each one felt like a tiny kiss of heat against his freezing skin.

"Wendy," he rasped. "You saved me."

He tried to caress her cheek, but his arm wouldn't cooperate. Wendy saw the failed movement and brought her hand to clasp over his instead.

"Saved you?" she asked, a nervous smile crept across her lips. She was watching him like he was a ghost. She brushed the tears pooling in her eyes and forced a smile to her lips. "But I'm *just a girl*."

Peter stared up at her, noting how the golden flecks in her eyes shone more beautifully than the most dazzling galaxy and softly shook his head. His head spun as the world teetered, but he pressed his hand to cup her cheek, refusing to miss this moment.

"Oh Wendy," he murmured, bringing his face closer to hers. "Don't you know? One girl is worth more than twenty boys."

His fingertips trailed down her porcelain cheek as the warmth of her smile burn into his memory and his vision faded to black.

WENDY

Wendy was still hunched over Peter's body when Johns burst into the Main Bay, Boyce in tow. The Commander skidded over, eyes wide with panic.

"Darling? Are you all right?" Johns grabbed her shoulders, searching her face while Boyce frantically patted her down. His hands deftly ran over her in a quick status check, until he reached her leg, and recoiled, his blue eyes wide in horror.

"Jesus, Darling! What happened to you?"

Wendy didn't answer. She stared at the boy in her arms, waiting for him to stir.

"Peter's hurt." Her voice was distant. "The Shadow tried to take him…"

"The Shadow?" Boyce paled as he scanned the destroyed room. "Here?"

Wendy nodded. "Hooke summoned it." She gestured to the empty dais, but her haunted expression stayed on Peter. "He tried to use the princess as a sacrifice. Peter stopped him."

"Stopped him?" Johns forced Wendy to look at him. "What are you talking about, Darling?"

Wendy let out a haunted shriek, furious that no one was listening to her.

"Help him!" Her arms trembled as she drew Peter nearer, feeling tears well in her eyes again. Johns' voice softened as he leaned forward.

"It's okay, Wendy. We'll take care of him, but you have to let go."

"But he's not—" Wendy brushed Peter's coarse hair through her fingertips. His skin was so pale, so *cold…*

"We've got him," Johns promised. "But we need you too."

Wendy's lips quivered, but she unlocked her grip. Johns gently scooted her over then leaned forward to check Peter's pulse. His face etched with worry until a small lift of Peter's chest split his lips into a wide grin.

"He's alive, Cap." Johns let out a relieved breath. "It's gonna be okay."

He's alive…

Life fluttered tenuously through her veins. She moved to hug the Commander but her injured leg buckled and she yelped in pain. Johns motioned for Boyce to take Peter and rushed to her side. He wrapped his arms around her to keep her still and she let out a frustrated grunt.

"Johns! Let go of me! That's an order!"

The return of Wendy's spark seemed to set Johns at ease. "Hold on, Darling." He chuckled at her feeble protest. "You know I think you're superwoman, but you really gotta slow down. At least until DeLaCruz checks you out."

"I'm fine!" she insisted. "It looks worse than it is." She tried to stand to prove her point. Multicolored spots covered her vision as the pain searing from her leg shot to her head, sending the world into a tailspin.

"Sure you are, Darling." Johns chuckled but gently transferred her into Boyce's arms so he could retrieve Peter. Wendy watched fiercely as the Commander carefully scooped up the mechanic's body and solemnly walked him out.

Satisfied, Wendy allowed Boyce to steady her body against his chest. She leaned against him to steady the earth, and felt him brush her tangled hair back as he leaned forward to whisper in her ear, "Don't worry Captain, we'll get you home."

Wendy wanted to respond, but finally safe, she realized how exhausted she was. She forced her eyes open to look at him.

"DeLaCruz checks Peter first," she ordered before her head tumbled back against his chest.

"As you wish, Captain."

28

THE RETURN HOME

WENDY

Wendy woke up feeling like she'd slept through a nightmare. When she saw she was in a makeshift bed with heavy tree roots dangling from the roof of a hole in the ground, she realized she hadn't dreamt it—she had survived it. She stirred under sheets tucked so tight they practically strapped her to the bed and was just wriggling free when Johns barged in with a small tray holding a glass of water and a dehydrated sandwich.

"She's aliiiiiive!"

Johns flounced on the bed beside her. Wendy winced and jerked her leg, feeling how weighed down it was with heavy bandaging. DeLaCruz had been busy. Johns jumped off the bed and vaulted back, worrying over her from across the room.

"Oh God, Cap! Are you okay?"

Wendy laughed at his mortified expression. "I'm fine, Johns. Get back over here," she commanded. "I'm gonna need your muscles."

"I don't know, Darling…" Johns hesitated. "DeLaCruz said you aren't allowed out of bed until it's time to launch."

"Launch?" Wendy's brow quirked. She wondered how long she'd been out. "What launch?"

Johns' grin widened. "Michaels did it," he explained, crackling with energy. "It took a few days, but he got a full diagnostic on the *Fiducia*. She was pretty beat up—he restored her with tech from the *Roger*."

"A few days?" Wendy's head felt thick.

"You've been out for a while, Cap. But DeLaCruz is as skilled as she is fine." Johns waggled his eyebrows then ducked away as Wendy smacked at his arm. She groaned.

"Okay, so the ship's been restored." She paused as she tried to sort through the current events. "But how did you get to the *Fiducia*? What about the Stjarnin?"

"They were a lot more cooperative after Tootles and Boyce returned their Princess," he explained with a smirk. "Seemed the prince was quite distraught over the loss of his bride. Bringing her home built quite the bridge."

Wendy's head spun. "But what about the Shadow—Itzala—whatever they call it?"

Johns' expression darkened. "Boyce told us about that, too. A long time ago, the Stjarnin worshipped the Shadow." He shuddered. "Eventually they realized it was bad news, but it was too late—it destroyed their planet and fled, searching for another world to consume. They followed it and trapped it in Neverland, holding it prisoner to make up for their mistake."

"But they were sacrificing people," Wendy argued. "Hooke told us as much." A pang of regret surged through her conscience at the thought of Hooke, but she pushed it away—he'd made his decision.

"Yeah, well, I guess part of the way they kept the Shadow grounded was by keeping it full." He looked a bit bewildered too, even though he was the one explaining. "Tootles tried to explain, but it doesn't really make sense. Basically, they were only sacrificing people to keep it from getting hungry. They were afraid if it did, it might make a break for it." He scratched the back of his head. "I guess when they got the chance to feed it something other than their brothers and sisters, they kinda jumped on it."

Wendy's mouth pressed into a hard line. Johns was right—it *was* confusing. But as she watched Johns sitting there, happily munching her sandwich, she understood. She wouldn't have wanted to sacrifice her brothers either.

"Johns, we need to get out of here."

"We know, Darling, that's what we're working on—"

"No," she interrupted, her voice stern. "That monster is still out there. I saw it take Hooke. It was beaten, but it was still alive."

She shuddered, remembering the cold voice that had hissed through her thoughts as it had escaped.

"And it's angry. It's not going to stay hidden again."

Johns nodded.

"We're pulling things together as fast as we can. Had some trouble at first, trying to figure out what to do with all of the pirates. Luckily that kid

Curly's gotta pretty good head on his shoulders. Helped Boyce rig a holding cell to keep them out of the way so we could focus on rebuilding the *Fiducia*. It's been a rush job, but we've rallied. Been difficult with both of our CO's out of commission though." He nudged her arm. "Michaels is gonna be glad to see you. We haven't been able to pull him away from a piece of tech for more than five minutes at a time without your mothering."

Wendy rolled her eyes, then paused. "Wait. *Both* commanding officers? Peter's not up yet?"

Johns shifted uncomfortably beside her, his eyes fixed on the blankets. "He's been out for as long as you have." He cleared his throat. "DeLaCruz doesn't know if he'll ever wake up."

"WHAT?" Wendy flung the blankets away from her. "Why didn't you say that first?" She raged. "I told you—I *told* you, Johns, take care of him first. That was a *direct order*. Why are you here with me?"

She pushed herself out of bed and swung her legs over the ledge. They pulled down, heavier than she realized and she glanced at the bandaging, then jerked back in surprise. Her right leg was swollen under heavy wrapping and encased in a bulky metal contraption that ran from her knee to her ankle. Wendy looked at the brace, studying the pins and screws that molded it together to cast her leg.

"Michaels made it," Johns explained, carefully watching her reaction. "DeLaCruz bandaged you as best as she could, but she had to do some pretty heavy…reconstruction."

"Reconstruction?" Panic laced Wendy's voice. "What the hell does that mean?"

Johns bit his lip, then took in a deep breath before the answer whooshed from his lips. "Most of the leg is yours. There's just a few parts inside that are—"

"Parts?" Wendy exploded. "My leg is made of *parts?*"

"Only the best ones," Johns shrugged helplessly. "Michaels and DeLaCruz made sure of that—even the botpirate helped."

Wendy let out a deep exhale as she sorted through her jumbled thoughts, then pushed them away, remembering why she had gotten up in the first place. She twisted to Johns, her eyes narrowed.

"We'll come back to this later," she promised. "First, I want to hear why Peter was not seen to." Wendy fixed him with a furious stare before returning her attention to her mismatched legs. She hesitated just a moment then lowered her feet to the ground and stood. Her knee strained under the weight, but the metal reinforcements circling her leg kept it from buckling.

"Whoa!" Johns caught her before she fell. "We did see to him. She wasn't happy about it, but it was the first thing DeLaCruz did. But he went through a lot of—what's the word Rissa uses?" His brow furrowed in concentration. "*Trauma.* The report she gave when we brought him back was *bad.* She said it was a miracle he wasn't already dead."

"Take me to him," Wendy demanded, leveling a steely gaze at her First Mate.

"But DeLaCruz said—"

"Take. Me. To. Him." She leveled her fiercest glare and Johns backed down. His lips turned down in obvious discomfort but he nodded.

Wendy hobbled down the hallway, half supported by Johns and half by her good leg as she adjusted to the heavy brace. She kept trying to go faster, but Johns kept a slow, steady pace, and her reliance on him forced her to crawl along with him. By the time they made it to Peter's room, she was almost bursting with excitement.

The room was empty except for Peter's bed and a small box resting on the table beside it. Peter lay, unflinching in his sleep. Wendy tottered over to him, thankful for Johns' support. Her legs went weak when she saw how pale Peter's cheeks were.

She lowered herself to the bed and brushed his flaming hair, her eyes glued to Peter's peaceful expression.

"You're dismissed, Johns."

"But Cap—"

"You're *dismissed*, Elias."

Johns shuffled awkwardly, then left the room, clicking the door shut behind him. Wendy stayed in place, her hands wrapped around Peter's, sending her warmth into them as she willed him to wake up.

29
WENDY

After she woke, Wendy lost all track of time. Per Johns, it had been six days since they had been pulled from the *Roger*, but to Wendy, it seemed like an eternity. For the first three days, she refused to leave Peter's side. Johns and Michaels took turns bringing in meals and a few cups of coffee from the stash they pilfered from the *Roger*. Almost everything went to waste—except the coffee.

Sometime in the endless waiting period, Dawes came to visit. Wendy hugged her, thankful she was all right. Dawes didn't move too quickly, but she still laughed at Wendy's reactions.

"I'm fine Captain, really." She laughed when Wendy squeezed her to her for the fourth time. "But I feel like I missed something. You weren't a hugger before we crashed. Are you sure *you're* okay?"

Wendy blushed, but Dawes was right—she had missed something. She had missed a lifetime.

Peter had visitors too. Wendy would move to a small chair Tootles set at the edge of the bed so the boys could check on their captain. They sat in a group, telling jokes and tattling on each other. They missed him, too.

Tootles took the brunt of Peter's absence. Even though he was the youngest, the small boy soon had the others reporting to him. His talks with Peter were more serious, with the angel-faced soldier reporting their tense alliance with the Stjarnin, the updates on ship repairs, and in a particularly emotional talk, Slightly's death.

"He f-fought t-t-to the e-end," Tootles said, his stutter more pronounced in his sorrow. Tears filled his eyes as he stood beside Peter. "We c-couldn't ha-ave done it w-without him." He sniffled and let out a small laugh. "B-bet those pirates were sorry they ever messed with him..." His voice trailed off as he studied his feet. "Y-you would've b-been proud of him, Peter."

He excused himself when Wendy saw the first tear fall down his cheek.

Even Smee visited a few times, bringing coffee and flowers to thank her for keeping him. After his heroic rescue of Tiger Lily, Wendy couldn't bear the thought of turning him away. Johns had made it clear that he didn't trust him, but Wendy had developed a soft spot for the kind-hearted synth. It took several arguments and more than a few orders, but the message was relayed to the Boys.

Apart from Wendy, DeLaCruz was Peter's most frequent visitor, monitoring for signs of improvement, but nothing seemed to be happening.

"Try talking to him," DeLaCruz suggested when she saw Wendy hovering over his bed. "Sometimes knowing someone's waiting for them helps."

Wendy studied his features, wondering what to say. She had started so many conversations, only to be left standing silent, trying to find the right words for so long that she memorized every angle and imperfection of his face; starting from the reddish stubble along his chin to the small scar resting at the corner of his right eye. She wondered how he'd gotten it.

Wendy massaged her knee, trying to chase away the stiffness that collected around the metallic joints. She couldn't sit for a long time without building up pressure from the pins inside her bones. Though the swelling had started to go down, her knee was still double the size of the one on her left leg. Part of her wondered if it would ever fully heal. Frustrated, she pulled her hands from her legs and shoved them in her pockets, and was surprised when her fingers bumped into a cool piece of metal.

Confused, Wendy drew it out to see the tiny thimble she had taken from Hooke. She stared at the intricate etchings dotting the outside, trying to make out the pattern. She raised it up where a sliver of Starlight streamed in from the makeshift window. The light caught the thimble, sending rays bouncing off the cylindrical shape. Wendy let out a soft cry as she looked at the ground and saw a constellation on the ground, with two large orbs centered in the middle, with the largest hovering just beneath its brother.

The Second Star.

"It's a map," she whispered, tracing the shadowcast constellation to where Neverland's marker rested patiently under the stars. She twisted the thimble in her fingers, wondering if Hooke knew what he was getting himself into when he'd first started chasing the Star.

Thoughts of the Shadow sent a ghost of a shiver through her body and she turned to Peter, who laid perfectly still on his bed. He looked so peaceful, which was a relief compared to the way he had appeared the last time she'd seen him awake. His eyes had been so haunted; she wondered if they would look the same when he woke up. She hoped not—the mischievous sparks of gold nestled inside the green had no room for darkness.

Wendy sighed. Even though no one said anything, she could tell the crew was getting antsy. Peter still hadn't woken, but Michaels had rebuilt the *Fiducia's* stabilizer.

"We're going to be ready to leave in a few days, Darling," Johns told her in his daily report. "I know you're worried, but we could really use you out here. We're setting up as best we can, but there's some things only the Captain can take care of."

Wendy nodded. She'd known this day was coming. Honestly, she already felt guilty about not helping already, but every time she tried to leave, something pulled her back to Peter's side. Eventually, she just stopped trying. "All right," she said. "I'll be out in a bit. Give me a couple minutes."

Johns nodded, but his eyes said he didn't believe her. Her heart squeezed. What kind of Captain was she if her crew couldn't trust her? She forced a smile and pushed him out.

"Really," she promised. "We'll chart coordinates today. Pull Dawes and Tootles—we have to plot our course."

"You're the boss," he said before quietly excusing himself. With Johns gone, the suffocating stillness settled in. She sighed.

"You're missing all the action." Her lips twisted into a wry smirk. "It's because you don't want the responsibility, isn't it?" She cleared her throat of the sudden lump that lodged inside. "Well, your loss," she said. "We're going to bust outta this place, back into the sky…"

She forced a laugh, but Peter had the same blank expression he'd worn every day. A surge of tears brimmed in her eyes, and she quickly brushed them away. They wouldn't do anyone any good. Instead, she leaned forward and brushed a kiss across Peter's cheek.

"Wake up," she whispered.

In the hallway, Wendy leaned against the door to catch her breath. She had never felt this way before, and she didn't understand it. She had no idea how a person she hadn't even known a few weeks ago could now be so important to her. But there were other people important to her too, and they were counting on her.

Resolved, she stepped from the room, closing the door gently behind her. Her heart beat erratically and she took in a deep breath before Nana could scold her again. She exhaled, then moved forward. She had to meet her crew.

She limped to the kitchen, surprised to see Boyce sitting stiffly at the table. He straightened when he saw her, flashing an arrogant smile.

"Nice to see you, Captain," he said, leaning back in his seat. "I was wondering when you were going to grace us with your presence."

"I always follow through, Boyce."

"That's why you're the Captain." He quirked his brow.

Wendy nodded. "Do your best not to forget it." Her lips curled in a small smile, and Boyce chuckled.

A tenuous peace had been established between her and Boyce since he had helped Peter from the *Roger*. Though they were far from being comrades, Wendy now found that she could look at the Commander without wanting to throw things at his head. She sat in the adjacent chair and straightened her leg, flexing the pins in her knee.

Boyce trailed the movement and a dark look flashed across his face as he studied the heavy metal casing around Wendy's knee. His jaw clenched, but he met her gaze with a smile. "Never could, Darling. Even if I wanted to." His blue eyes shined into hers. "Your delinquent Commander would never let that happen."

Wendy grinned.

"What's our current status?"

Boyce shifted to address her. "We've been working to mobilize," he reported, his shoulders at full attention. "The two crews have pulled together and have made quick work of it. Your tech specialist is a machine." He paused as he considered his words. "Literally. I think he may have made the final transition into a robot."

Boyce flinched, and glanced at Wendy's knee. She let out a soft snort at the panic lacing his face and waved for him to finish. Boyce let out an embarrassed cough, then continued.

"He hasn't eaten or slept in days. But it's paid off," he admitted, impressed. "The ship should be ready in a day or so."

Wendy raised her brows. That was impressive.

"And the crew?"

"Everyone's fine," he paused. "We've just been trying to figure out the best way to proceed…"

"Proceed?"

Boyce let out a heavy sigh and angled his body closer to hers. He looked as if he was the last person on earth who wanted to answer her question.

"We need to decide what to do with Peter—"

"What to do with Peter?" Wendy's sharp exclamation made Boyce wince. "There's nothing to figure out, Commander."

Boyce scrubbed his hands over his brows, then dropped them to the table. He stared at his fists as he deliberated how to proceed. Finally, he took a small breath, and met her gaze, his eyes hard.

"Darling, he's as good as dead." Boyce's words were firm but gentle. "DeLaCruz has all but confirmed it." He knelt in front of her to wrap her hands in his, swallowing them in his grip. "He's not coming back."

Angry tears pooled in Wendy's eyes and she found it hard to breathe. "That's not true." She pursed her lips as she looked at the worried crease in Boyce's forehead. "You don't know what you're talking about."

Boyce searched her eyes and let out an exasperated sigh. "I know what a dead man looks like."

Wendy jumped up, knocking the chair askew. Her cheeks blazed as she glared at Boyce, who looked up at her from the floor.

"You are dangerously close to being out of line, Commander," Wendy warned. Her temper blazed, stoked by the angry tears tracing hot paths down her cheeks. Boyce's lips parted as he studied her, a strange look of pain covering his normally cold features. Wendy opened her mouth to speak, but a strangled cry escaped her throat before her words could break through. She gasped an uneven breath and suddenly she was wrapped in Boyce's tight embrace, his muscular arms crushing her against his trembling body.

She stayed pressed against his chest until her ragged breathing stilled and she pulled away, looking uncertainly at the Commander who had so long been her enemy. He stared down at her, his blond hair glinting in the dim kitchen light. His lips pulled in the trace of a smile, then he leaned in, brushing them against hers with trembling ferocity.

His lips were soft against hers, gentle in a way that she had never associated with the disdainful Commander. His hand cupped the small of her back, and Wendy allowed him to draw her closer, until she felt the erratic beating of his heart thrum against her own. Her fingers clutched the soft fabric of his Commanders jacket and she felt the taut bunching of his muscles as he pulled her nearer to him. She had never realized before just how strong Adrian was, but with his arms now wrapped around her, it was impossible to deny. She angled her chin, opening her lips to his as she pressed her hand to his cheek with a small shudder. Her fingertips traced his jawline, rubbing the smooth flesh he kept so neatly shaved.

A flash burst through Wendy's mind. Bewitching green eyes and messy red hair. Lightning shot through her body and she jerked away, her eyes were wide as she stared at Boyce, who watched her with quiet uncertainty. Her mind reeling, she backpedaled from the room, seeing hurt pool in Boyce's eyes.

"I can't do this," she whispered, and without another word, she was gone.

Wendy dashed through the door, ignoring Boyce's calls. Blood rushed to her ears, filling them with a strange whooshing noise. The underground was stifling. She had to get out.

She burst out of the treehouse with a huge gasp, feeling fresh air rush through her lungs. Her head spun, but she wasn't sure if it was claustrophobia or realizing how Boyce really felt about her. She didn't care.

Without realizing where she was going, she ran as far as she could until her manufactured knee finally gave out, and she dropped in the sand to kneel in front of the *Fiducia*. Johns was right—Michaels had been busy. She could see where he had parted pieces from the *Roger* to fit into her broken hull. She pressed her hand the cool metal, and pulled herself to her feet, leaning against the ship to use its metallic skeleton to steady her trembling legs. A million thoughts streamed through her mind, assaulting her with every passing, and she dipped her head to steel herself from their relentless attacks. The journey to Neverland had changed her so much, leaving her irreparably altered. She wondered if she would ever feel whole again.

A racking sob escaped her throat, but before she could crumble under the weight of her despair, a cry carried over the sand to where she stood. She followed the noise and saw a lanky man running toward her.

"Captain!"

Smee yelled, flailing his arms. Wendy watched guiltily as his heavy metal legs sank into the dirt with every step. She hoped the sand didn't damage his joints. Finally, he reached the *Fiducia*, his cheeks tinged pink by his appearance simulator to feign exertion. Wendy looked into his metallic eyes, their golden sheen wide in the eerie starlight.

"You're needed at the camp, Captain." His gears creaked as he straightened his uniform. "Pan is awake!"

PETER

Peter awoke feeling like he had been hit by an escape pod.

"What the heck happened, Tinc?"

When no sassy response came, he pushed himself up on sore arms and peeked open his eyes, confused. He was in his room, but Tinc wasn't in her bed.

"Tinc?"

He stood slowly, stiff everywhere. He groaned and stretched, feeling his muscles tighten then release. Without Tinc's constant buzzing, the room was eerily quiet. As he listened, he realized he didn't hear anything outside either. Odd, since one of the boys was almost always up to something. Maybe they had taken Tinc and gone somewhere.

He shuffled out the door and almost collided straight into the medic from Wendy's crew. She grabbed him by the shoulders and let out a small squeak. "*Gracias a Dios!*"

Peter's eyes narrowed, then squinted shut when she shined a small flashlight into them.

"Hey! What gives?" He swatted her hand away, but she busied herself feeling his pulse.

"How are you feeling?" she asked breathlessly as she continued her assessment. "Vitals, good." She pressed her ear to his chest. "Heartbeat, strong…"

Peter jumped back. He stuck out his arms to fend her off. She stayed in place but continued to stare at him like he was a miracle of science. "Seriously! What's going on here?"

It was the medic's turn to look confused. "You've been in a coma for almost two weeks."

Peter's jaw dropped.

"We figured you were good as dead."

"Well, I'm not," Peter snapped. He looked around, feeling incredibly lost. "Where are my men? Someone tell me what's going on!" He froze as the memories of the attack washed over him. "Where's Wendy?" he demanded, surging forward to push past the medic. "Take me to her now!"

DeLaCruz copied Peter's earlier action, using her hands to keep him at bay. "Captain Darling is fine, sir. She's at the ship. I'll send for her, but you can't just be out of bed like this."

"I've been laying in that bed for long enough. There's no way in the 'verse you're putting me back!" Peter's voice rose louder with each word. "Get me Wendy!" he demanded as another figure rounded the corner to the hall. Peter's eyes widened, and he swooped DeLaCruz behind him. "Stay back!" he warned her. He reached for his dagger and was dismayed to find it missing. "What are *you* doing here?"

Smee's golden eyes blinked as he studied Peter incredulously. "Pan, you're awake… The captain has extended her invitation to stay—"

"Liar!" Peter lunged forward, but DeLaCruz grabbed his shoulders to hold him back.

Smee staggered back on stiff joints, colliding into Tootles as he rushed toward Peter. The little boy bounced off the synth's metal body but caught himself and hurried forward.

"It's okay, Peter. Smee's one of us now." He withered under Peter's furious glare. "Well, sorta. Wendy told us we had to keep him, so we did," he finished, shuffling his feet.

Peter looked from Tootles to Smee, then to the others who gathered around the commotion. They all watched him more nervously than the pirate. He dropped his arms as his chest deflated, and a bout of dizziness spun his brain. He brought his hand to his temple and closed his eyes to steady himself. The medic led him slowly toward the kitchen. He slumped in the chair as he tried to find his bearings.

"Bring me Wendy."

Smee tipped his head in a small salute as Tootles motioned for him to go, then scurried out the door. Peter scrubbed his chin with his hands. "I'm out for a couple weeks and you bring home a pirate," he said wryly. "Anything else you need to tell me? Where's Tinc?"

He twisted to face his First Mate. Tootles wrung his hands together then silently walked to Peter's room. He returned with a small box from his bedside table. He clutched the box in his arms as he looked at Peter, sorrow etched into his baby face.

"Don't freak out..."

WENDY

Wendy burst into the treehouse to find Peter staring at a small box filled with broken metal pieces. He didn't say anything as he picked up individual parts one by one, only to drop them into the container with a sad thump.

"Do you need a minute?"

Peter flashed a grin that didn't quite reach his eyes. "No." He let out a heavy breath. "Just trying to run inventory to see what I'm going to need to fix her."

"You can do that?" Wendy inched closer to look at the parts. They looked like a machine that had been blown to smithereens, which, she realized, was exactly what they were.

"I built her once. I can build her again." He scooted the box from his line of sight. "I might even give her a better personality this time."

Wendy shifted uncomfortably. She had never particularly cared for the bot, but Peter did. She didn't know what to say, so she changed the subject. "How are you feeling?"

"Like I had the shyte beat out of me."

Wendy snorted.

"That's a fair assessment." She took a step closer, noticing the way his stare lingered on the metal cage around her knee before shifting its intensity to her face. Wendy swallowed, wondering why she suddenly felt so self-conscious. She had been practically sitting on his lap for the past week, but now that he was awake, and his perfectly darkness-free eyes were looking into hers—

A smug grin from Peter reminded her she was staring and she averted her eyes, blushing furiously. "You had us really worried, you know," she finished lamely.

"Us?" he asked with a cocky tilt of his head.

"Well, you know, Tootles and the boys." She smoothed her hair, embarrassed. "They didn't want to do anything without your approval."

"They do that." His smile widened, lighting the mischievous spark in his eyes. "*You* didn't miss me, Cap?"

Wendy focused on the floor. "I... well, I—"

Peter chuckled and crossed the room. He reached out to cup her cheek.

"I missed you," he whispered, sending shivers down her spine.

She froze, acutely aware of how closely his body pressed against hers. She was about to respond when Dawes hurried through the door.

"Captain, I—oh! Sorry!" She let out an embarrassed giggle as she spun around, covering her eyes. "I didn't mean to interrupt. I can come back."

"No." Wendy sprang away and tried to force her brain to behave. "That's quite all right. What is it, Dawes?"

Arielle peeked through her hand, then straightened for her report. "I spoke with Michaels, ma'am. He said once he's done testing his final calibrations, we'll be ready to chart our course."

Wendy heard the words without understanding them. The ghost of Peter's body still pressed against hers, along with the warmth of his gaze and—*cut it out, Darling.*

"Excellent, Dawes... Excellent." She fumbled as she scolded herself.

Dawes stared at her as if she had grown an extra head. "Captain, do you know what that means?"

Peter snickered, watching her cheeks blaze and she kicked herself for not keeping a better bluff. She pursed her lips as she inclined her head to gesture for Dawes to elaborate. *Stupid mechanic.*

"Captain," Dawes murmured, "it means we can go home."

30
PETER

We can go home…

The words resonated in Peter's ears. *Home.* He didn't even know what the word meant. As much as he made it sound like he had been trapped in the Neverland Sector, it was the only home he'd ever truly known. He turned to Wendy and saw the relief on her face. She had a job to do, and she was almost done. She beamed at him, and he smiled back to cover his uncertainty.

"How long until everything is prepped for flight?" Wendy straightened her shoulders as she addressed the pilot. "What's our status?"

"The ship's been packed and loaded. All we need is your sign-off, and for everyone to board."

"Excellent. Round up the crew," Wendy instructed, then turned to Peter. "My team will show your men where their launch positions will be."

Peter nodded. "Of course, Captain." He wanted to scoop her in his arms and tell her how much she meant to him, but the moment had passed. Wendy was all business again.

"Thank you," she murmured. "We'll meet on board in an hour." She spoke loudly enough for Dawes to register the command, then excused herself to familiarize herself with her new vessel.

Peter watched her go, hating the slight limp that marred her purposeful stride. It was clear that she was self-conscious about the injury, although it only reinforced how incredibly strong she was. He remembered the way she had stared down the Shadow like an avenging goddess, her chin raised defiantly against its all-powerful evil. His heart thumped uncomfortably and Peter glanced around, unaware that he was staring until the pretty pilot beside him nudged his elbow.

"So. You and the Captain, huh?" She grinned ear to ear. "I wondered what was different about her." Her eyes twinkled as she left to follow her directive. "Nice," she called back, bringing a wry smile to Peter's lips.

"Nice," he whispered, feeling a surge of excitement at the affirmation. "Nice." He let out a gleeful crow, then hurried out, much more excited at the possibility of finding a new home.

Within the hour, the *Fiducia* was prepped and ready. Wendy had given a rousing speech and everyone was bristling with excitement at the prospect of returning home. The crew was all strapped in, save Wendy and Dawes, who were commandeering from the refurbished Navigations deck.

Peter's fingers twitched as he waited for the initiation sequence to start. He always got jittery before a flight. Something about the ship sitting dead in the water made him restless. He'd be happy once they were in the air.

A soft feedback whine sounded over the intercom before Wendy's husky voice cracked through.

"Initiating countdown sequence."

This was it. His stomach flip-flopped as the *Fiducia* moaned as its mended systems began to wake.

"*Ten...nine...eight...*"

Back to London. It seemed so surreal. He wondered how well he would adjust. He'd worry about it later, he decided. First, they needed to get off the island.

"*...seven...six...five...*"

A mental scan of all the compartments ran through his brain. He saw the work Michaels had done. It was impeccable. There shouldn't be any issues.

"*...four...three...two...one.*"

Peter waited for the thrust of the ship to crush him against the seat, but—nothing. Instead, the *Fiducia's* lights dimmed and flickered, then the power went out.

"Stay here," he commanded, then turned to Michaels. "Everyone except you. Come on." He waited for Michaels to unclasp his restraints then they hurried down to the maintenance bay. By the time Wendy made it down, the two of them were already busy troubleshooting the tech.

"What happened?"

"Not sure," Peter answered as he continued scanning the machinery. He was in the engine, and the heat from the metal warmed his nose. It was hotter than it should have been.

His brow dipped as he let out a heavy groan. He had found the problem. He had installed it. Finicky and stubborn inside the *Roger*, the part had given him trouble when it was new. He was sure a hundred years buried in the shores of Neverland hadn't done it any favors.

He rubbed his fingers over the piece, feeling the rust flake under his touch. It was as good as busted. It would stick and short out any startup the engine attempted. His mind whirred as he tried to come up with a solution.

There had to be some way he could override the engine compartment. If he could just...

Peter crowed as he realized what he needed to do. A manual override! He just had to... He paused as the reality of the situation set in. He looked from the engine to the Captain. She was beautiful, watching him with a mixture of worry and hope.

She wasn't going to like this.

"Wendy." Peter kept his voice calm as he looked into her deep blue eyes. Her brow creased, betraying the hint of a frown line on her forehead. Peter smiled and traced the tiny imperfection. "Wendy, you need to go."

The crease deepened as her brow furrowed further. "I know. That's what we're trying to do."

The corners of Peter's lips curved upward. "No. *You* need to go..." He trailed off to let the words sink in. It took a moment, but understanding dawned on the Captain and her confused expression turned furious.

"What are you talking about? We're all leaving together. We're one crew now, and we're going to stay that way." Her voice took on a panicked edge, as if she were trying to convince him.

"I can override the start sequence, but to do that, I need to jump the booster. We can use the reserve batteries from the *Roger*, but someone has to be there to light it off. Once you initiate the launch, I won't have time to get back on board."

Wendy shook her head, refusing to listen. He clasped his hands around her shoulders.

"Wendy. Listen to me. You can get out, but I have to stay here."

Wendy's lip quivered as her eyes searched his. Peter could almost see her brain working to solve the new problem, but he knew she wouldn't. There had been a time when he'd known the *Roger* like the back of his hand. It was a good ship, but it was old, and it was tired.

"But we can't leave you here." Her voice broke, and she ducked her head.

"Just come back for me." He pitched his voice so only she could hear. "I'll be waiting."

Tears pooled in Wendy's eyes and she shook her head again, more violently this time. "No! We can't just leave!" She whirled to face Michaels, who watched silently from the side. "Michaels, figure out another way to fix it!"

"He won't be able to Wendy, trust me," Peter said. "He knows it, and so do you. You also know you have a crew of ten other people trusting you to get them out of here. You can't just throw their lives away."

"Then *I'll* stay—" Wendy argued, then stumbled over her words. Peter laughed.

"Your crew needs their Captain more than they need some grubby mechanic." His fingertips brushed her silken skin as he tucked a loose strand of hair behind her ear. "Besides, I know the *Roger* like the back of my hand—

no one gets her like me." In his peripheral, he saw Michaels raise his finger to interject, and cut him off before he could speak. "You wouldn't be able to do it either, Wizard, so don't even offer." Peter gripped Wendy's hands in his. "It's something I can do—that only I can do." He brushed a kiss against her knuckles. "Let me help you."

Wendy turned away. He felt the tension in her body as she fought against the outcome, but it was a lost cause. She raised her head to address Michaels. "Go tell Dawes the plan, then report back. Tell her I'll be up shortly."

Michaels gave an awkward salute, then hurried to find the pilot, leaving Peter and Wendy alone. As soon as he was gone, Wendy threw her arms around Peter, clutching him to her.

"I don't want to say goodbye," she murmured.

Peter tilted her chin, forcing her to look at him.

"I don't ever say goodbye, Wendy." He wiped a stray tear from her cheek. "Goodbye means going away, and going away means forgetting."

"I won't forget," Wendy promised. "We're coming back for you."

"You'd better." He smiled. He pulled the chain around her neck to reveal the acorn he'd given her hanging delicately at the end. "You kept it."

Wendy straightened her shoulders. "You gave it to me." She reached into her pocket and retrieved the shadowcaster. The thimble that could lead him home. She tucked it in his hand. "It's only fair I gave you something in return."

Peter clasped it in his hands, but a mischievous smile danced on his lips.

"And here I was holding out for a kiss," he said, loving the way her face bloomed the color of a summer rose. She opened her mouth to retort, but before she could, he scooped her into his arms and crashed his lips into hers, pressing her against the paneling of the *Fiducia*.

Wendy stiffened as she let out a surprised cry, but just as Peter was about to pull away, embarrassed, she melted and threw her arms around his neck, clutching onto him like he was the only thing that could keep her afloat. Heat seared his lips as he felt her mouth crush against his, searching, hoping.

Trembling, he raised his hand to brush her soft curls behind her ear, relishing the way they wrapped around his fingers, tangling him in her essence. Wendy responded to the caress, and pulled him closer, crushing herself between his quivering body and the Fiducia's solid frame. His skin caught fire wherever they touched, intensifying with every exhilarating second.

Wendy shifted on her feet, and Peter gripped her waist to slip his knee between her legs and slide her up the side of the *Fiducia*, removing the weight from her injured knee. Wendy sank into his support and wrapped her legs around his hips, bumping her metallic brace against his torso. He drew back, worried that he had hurt her, but Wendy clutched his shirt collar and pulled him back toward her, deepening the kiss. Peter let out a soft groan and leaned closer, kissing her until ran out of breath and pulled back, heady with her intoxication.

He took in a ragged breath to steady the dizzying world around him. His forehead dipped against Wendy's until he could only see the galaxies shining in her eyes, green and gold, with the faintest flecks of purple.

She was mesmerizing.

He looked at her in amazement, realizing how dim Neverland would be without her. A lump formed in his throat as he stared at the beautiful girl before him and fought against every part of him that wanted beg for her to stay.

An awkward cough drew Peter's attention to the doorway, where Michaels watched them sheepishly. Gently, Peter lowered Wendy to the ground and she unclasped her arms from around his neck, leaving a cold space where her flesh had been. Crystal tears pools in the corners of her eyes, and he tipped his forehead to hers to keep the sight from breaking his heart.

Peter tucked his hand behind her ear, feeling her silky hair cascade over his fingertips. He had to hurry. If he didn't say goodbye soon, he'd lose his resolve. He placed his free hand on her hip, drawing her as close as he dared.

"You know that place between sleep and awake, that place where you still remember dreaming? That's where I'll always love you," he whispered. "That's where I'll be waiting."

He painted one final, tender kiss on her lips and breathed his final goodbye before he turned to the tech behind him.

"I'm leaving you with my ship and my Captain. Take good care of them," he said, then bounded down the hall and out the hatch of the *Fiducia*. He had to get the ship started. He had to keep Wendy safe.

"She'll fly." Peter promised himself as he crawled up the wing the *Roger*. "All it takes is faith and trust." He removed the external access panel from the *Roger* and pulled the pix.E from his pocket. He'd always thought they worked magic, even if they did get a bit dirty. He wiped the charcoal powder accumulating around the edges as the machine worked. "And a little bit of pix.E dust."

Peter held up his sooty finger and clipped the pix.E in place, fumbling around dozens of useless wires as he searched for the right cable. He wished Tinc was there to help—she was always better at locating the parts. He fumbled with them a few more moments until the familiar roar of the rear turbines grumbled awake. Soon the engine would rev to life. Timing was integral to his mission. He had to wait until the engine turned over, but if he held too long and the auxiliary turbine caught, they'd all be stranded.

He listened carefully, waiting for the parts to speak, then he heard it. The almost imperceptible *click* that signaled it was time. He sparked it to life and jumped back, praying it took.

As soon as the *Fiducia* started drifting along the shore, he knew he'd done it. He crowed with delight and ran back, clearing the launch site. He strained to locate the Navigation room. Though he couldn't see inside, he knew Wendy was in there, and that she saw him.

He blew her a kiss as the *Roger* shot into the sky.

31
WENDY

Wendy didn't relax until they hit antigrav. Letting out a sigh of relief, she leaned back in her seat and massaged her knee as she scanned her refurbished Navigation deck with interest. Signs of damage and repair dotted the ship's walls, making it clear to see where the sleek *Fiducia* married the harvested pieces of the *Jolly Roger*.

So much had happened in such a little amount of time that Wendy was still trying to make sense of it all. She didn't know what kind of magic Michaels had worked to enable the ship to break through Neverland's gravitational field, but she would find out later. Right now, she just knew she owed him big. For that, and for not telling the others about the kiss.

Her cheeks warmed as she remembered the way it felt to have Peter's arms wrapped around her. She touched her fingers to her lips, noting how cold they felt without Peter's warmth.

There was a low cough behind her, and she turned to face Boyce. They hadn't spoken since their kiss in the treehouse, and though he stood at attention, his eyes flashed brighter than normal when she met his gaze.

"I have finalized my report on the Stjarnin." He handed her a tiny chip. "I trust it is up to your standards for presentation to the Admiral."

Wendy accepted the tiny chip from his hand. When her skin touched his open palm, Boyce's hand clasped around hers. Wendy looked up, startled. Boyce's stoic gaze remained firmly in place, but his blue eyes pierced hers with a silent question.

Wendy cleared her throat and stepped back, distancing herself from the handsome officer.

"Thank you, Boyce." She clasped her hands safely behind her back, but still felt the warmth radiating from the commander's surprising touch. "I will review it at my earliest convenience."

Boyce held her gaze a moment longer, then gave a polite nod before excusing himself from the room. The door slid shut behind him and Wendy returned to her seat, sagging into the familiar chair. A small beep from the Nav panel interrupted her thoughts, and she stiffened her shoulders, forcing the thought from her mind. She had bigger things to attend to.

"How are we doing, Dawes?" she asked the pilot beside her.

A small smile played on the edges of Dawes' lips as she eyed Wendy from the corner of her eye, but the pilot merely nodded.

"Looking good Captain. We'll follow the Second Star to the right straight on 'til morning."

"Excellent." Wendy angled her face to hide the heat rushing to her cheeks and initiated her comm. She held her breath, waiting for a signal. The device shuddered, then blipped to life, running the Fleet's greeting across the display. Wendy's lips pressed in a tight smile as she brought the handheld to her face. She needed to save this message.

<<< *Captain's Report, March 30, 2394. Reporting Personnel, Wendy Moira Angela Darling, Captain of the* Fede Fiducia >>>

She paused after her introduction and shot a shaky look at Dawes. The date on the screen showed they had been on Neverland for almost one whole Earth year. What would the Fleet do when they received her transmission? Dawes tossed her flaming hair over her shoulder and gave her a reassuring nod. Wendy took in another deep breath and continued.

"This is Captain Wendy Darling of the Fede Fiducia. My crew was sent on a rescue mission to recover the missing personnel from the Expeditionary Vessel the Jolly Roger, *presumed lost in the Neverland Sector.*

"We were successful."

Wendy stopped to catch her breath, then recapped the events of their journey through Neverland. She explained everything, the crash, Boyce, the Stjarnin, Hooke. Her download was clear and methodical, with no irregularities until she reached her experience with the Shadow. Here, her voice caught as she remembered all too well the cold presence that would forever haunt her dreams.

"The Shadow was forced back, but not without losses of our own. Captain James Hooke has been missing since the Shadow's disappearance, and his whereabouts are unknown. I believe he has been taken as a host for the creature in its weakened state, and now that it is aware of our presence, it will soon try to

escape. *It is of utmost importance that we do not allow this. If it breaks free, the universe will not survive."*

Wendy paused to let her words sink in. She wasn't sure what the Admiral was going to do with this information, but she trusted the wisdom of the Fleet. She hoped the transmission reached them in time.

"We have charted our course to return to the Brigade. Our calculations put our arrival approximately four months from our current location. Upon arrival, I respectfully request to have another ship prepped to return to Neverland. We have a soldier awaiting our return."

Her mind filled with a pair of summer forest eyes and a mischievous grin. She had a soldier waiting for her. She stiffened her shoulders as she prepared to make her conditions clear to her superiors at the fleet.

"I will accompany the Crew as an advisor and provide my full and total support to any outgoing mission. But I have a promise to keep. The Brigade's support in this would be appreciated, but is not required. Peter sacrificed his life to save ours; it would be an egregious oversight to abandon him to the Neverland Sector."

Wendy clenched her jaw, biting back any uncertainty she felt at making demands of her superiors. It wasn't going to change her actions. She smoothed her hair, then prepared her sign-off. She had communicated all she needed to. She was about to end the transmission when she added in an afterthought.

"Give my regards to my parents. Keep an eye on to the heavens. We'll appear behind the Second Star."

The transmission faded to black as Wendy pressed the disconnect button. She stared at the blank screen until Dawes nervously broke the silence.

"Are you all right Captain?"

Wendy nodded. She was fine, but she had another mission to complete. She leaned against the Captain's chair, sinking into the plush velvet as she pictured her lost boy on the island, waiting for her. She clutched the acorn around her neck, remembering the kiss they shared on their last minutes on Neverland and the words he whispered in her ear.

He would be there when she returned. He had promised. His phantom breath tickled her ears as she repeated his words, feeling their truth and power.

"To live will be an awfully big adventure."

EPILOGUE

PETER

"Did you get that screw fixed, Tinc?" Peter asked as he dropped into the Captain's chair.

Tinc jangled happily in his ear, letting him know the final touches had been made on her end too. Peter stepped back, admiring his build. It was a long shot, but after a week of moping, he had started his modifications to the *Jolly Roger*'s escape hatch. Using pieces cobbled from the ghost of the *Roger* and what parts he'd harvested from the *Fiducia*, Peter had managed to mend the exterior of the newly dubbed *Fiducia II*.

"She's not pretty, but what matters is how she flies," Peter announced, looking at the makeshift pod. It wasn't shiny, but Peter was determined to get it off the ground. "We're gonna find her," he whispered. He looked to the sky, imaging a pair of galaxy eyes. He reached in one final stretch, then jumped into the Captain's seat.

"What do you think, Seven?"

Seven snuffed and lazily glanced at Peter. Her tail thumped against the ground and she purred before she settled into bed. It had taken him forever to find the mutt, but she had settled right into the family. Peter smiled and shook his head. This was what he had been reduced to, and he was pleasantly surprised to be okay with it.

He wiped his oily hand on his jumpsuit, pushing open the fabric and exposing his collarbone. His eyes fell on a faint patch of purple skin, the remainder of the Shadow's mark.

After his encounter with the Shadow, the dark mark left on him began to fade. Peter wasn't sure what had happened, but ever since the Shadow had disappeared with the Captain in its clutches, the stain covering his shoulder had slowly turned from inky black to now resembling nothing but an old bruise. Peter's lips pressed into a hard line, and he turned his attention back to the *Fiducia*, slapping the boat fondly.

"I've got a good feeling, Tinc," he said. "We're gonna make it."

Tinc buzzed nervously, and he tapped her on the head.

"I put you back together, didn't I? And you're way more advanced than this hunk of metal."

Tinc sparked bright green and she flitted to land on his shoulder.

"Faith and Trust," Peter whispered. He closed his eyes and imagined Wendy. She told him she would wait for him, but he wasn't going to keep her. He looked at the *Fiducia II*, noting the modifications that needed to be made and the sleepless nights it would take to finish them.

It was worth it. Peter smiled as he remembered the Captain's tousled hair and hesitant smile the day they had sat on Mermaid Cove. On an ageless planet, she was the only thing that made time work again. He wasn't going to miss anymore. He looked up at the Star, praying he could follow it home.

"I'm coming, Wendy."

ACKNOWLEDGEMENTS

First, I want to thank God for blessing me with the opportunity and ability to share my stories with the world. Without your gracious gifts, I would truly be lost.

Next, I want to thank my family. For my husband, Steven, thank you for the countless hours encouraging, listening to, and putting up with this crazy story. You've changed my life in so many ways, I can't wait to see what happens next.

To my children, thank you for being patient with mommy and for pulling me back into reality when I needed it. I love you all so much.

For my parents, thank you for always believing in me and encouraging me to follow my dreams. I hope I've made you proud.

For the rest of my family, thank you for being the best support group a girl could ever ask for. I wouldn't be who I am today if it wasn't for each and every one of you, and neither would my stories. Thank you.

For my friends, specifically those who encouraged and supported me on my writing adventure. Brittany, thank you for being my expert in all things Peter. This story wouldn't have gotten off the ground without you. Jessica, I am so blessed to have met you. Thanks for always being there to talk me down from all the writer feels. And the GIFs. Especially thank you for the GIFs. Katie, thank you for always being there to listen and offer advice in anything and everything. You are going to do amazing things, girl. I'm so grateful to be along for the ride. And for my betas, Mooky, Dave, Jess, Diana, Elissa, thank you for loving Peter even when he wasn't at his best and for sticking with him until the end.

For my friends at Bleeding Ink, Jon and Sherry: Thank you so much for believing in my work and accepting me into the family. You have truly brought Peter to life, and I can't wait to see what we accomplish. Holly, thank you for taking my messy manuscript and turning it into a real book. Peter wouldn't be the same if it wasn't for you.

And of course, Mr. Barrie. Thank you for your amazing story and for sharing Neverland with us all those years ago. Without your inspiration, Second Star would have never come to be. Thank you for the magic.

And last but definitely not least, I want to thank YOU, my reader. Without you, there would be no reason to take Peter's story and put it to paper. Neverland may be a piece of my heart, but it was written for you.

Thank you.

ABOUT THE AUTHOR

 Teacher by day, award-winning author by night, J.M. Sullivan is a fairy tale fanatic who loves taking classic stories and turning them on their head. She has a passion for the writing community and loves empowering and encouraging other authors on social media with #AuthorConfession.

When she's not buried in her laptop, you can find her watching scary movies with her husband, playing with her kids, or serving homage to her cats. Although known to dabble in adulting, J.M. is a big kid at heart who still believes in true love, magic, and most of all, the power of coffee.

If you would like to connect with J.M., you can find her on Twitter or Instagram at @_JM_Sullivan, on Facebook at jmsullivanbooks, or join the fun at #AuthorConfession—she'd love to hear from you.